Improper Mage

Taylor Westwood

Taylor Westwood

Contents

Chapter One

Liana Monroe sat upon a cushioned wooden stool in front of an open window in her sister's room reading a thick and heavy tome. Sunlight drifted through the sparkling glass highlighting the frayed leather bindings which were older than any relative she recalled having owned the book. Thick pages were worn from use, but the words were no less easy to read because of it. A gentle breeze lifted the curls from her neck, cooling her on this warm, summer afternoon, and bringing with it the fresh citrus scent of the magnolia tree rustling beyond.

Her lady's maid, Phillipa, pulled at the curling ribbons she tied into Liana's hair last night, letting the glowing chestnut strands dangle free. Liana gave no notice of the common routine only to tuck a piece of hair out of her face to keep reading while the room behind her bristled with activity and mindless chatter. Liana's sisters, Charlotte, and Hannah, sat on their own chairs facing the vanity while their maids spun their sun-kissed honey colored hair into beautiful braids.

"I do hope I catch the eye of Master Ranville. He is such a handsome and powerful man," Charlotte gushed while adding rouge to her cheeks. "His manor house is so grand. It would make a lovely home. And it is in such a good location near the center of the city."

"Yes, dear. Master Ranville would be an excellent suitor indeed," Lady Mary Monroe agreed with her eldest daughter, that constant simpering smile tilting the corner of her lips. That smile rarely fell, not even in the privacy of their own home. "This year's suitor season is guaranteed to be much better than last year and the year prior. I hear many more men are participating. So many in fact that the king is hosting this season. Gods willing, all three of my girls will be able to find a suitor this season," she said with a hopeful smile.

The sisters were all close in age, just one year apart from each other. Charlotte, as the eldest daughter, came out to society first. Her debut occurred two years ago, but she didn't catch much male attention, at least, attention that didn't have wealth to back it up. If you were to ask Lady Monroe or Charlotte though, they would tell you of the severely lacking presence of suitable men in attendance.

Last year it was Liana's turn to present herself to society, and just as Charlotte's had been a boring affair, so too had Liana's. This year, it was Hannah's turn and Lady Monroe was eager to get all her girls engaged and settled into respectable marriages. That was her responsibility as a mother to daughters in high society, to ensure she made proper matches for her daughters that would secure their extravagant lifestyles.

"I have my eyes on Lord Dietrich. He is so dreamy," Hannah swooned, her cheeks already naturally blushed and having no need of the rouge.

"Lord Dietrich would make a fine match, Hannah," Lady Monroe responded as she supervised the girl's preparations, her own hair and gown already primped and donned. "Your father knows him well as they both serve on Master Ranville's council. Perhaps he can put in a good word for you, my dear."

Their father, Lord Monroe, was a member of the mage council, just as his father had been before him. He served the leader of the mage, Master Ranville. So aptly named because he was one of three Master Mage in their prestigious country. It took a lot of talent and even more education to become a Master, which made the title highly respected. The Masters were able to perform magic that commonfolk couldn't even dream of, let alone perform.

It was Liana's dream to become the first female Master in all of Triaedian. She yearned to learn all that the males kept to themselves. She had the mind for it, and she thought possibly the skill for it as well. It was the education and propriety she did not have, nor would she ever. Females were not allowed to become Masters. They were to run the household and produce heirs, much to Liana's dismay.

"What about you, Liana? Who have you set your eyes upon?" Lady Monroe questioned. The girl did not hear her mother as she set the heavy tome in her lap and held her hands aloft toward the magnolia tree outside the window. As she began to quietly recite the spell, she held her hands together with the palms facing up to form a bowl.

Liana always was more interested in magic and books than gossip and dresses. Her mind sought knowledge not riches or marriage. So unlike the other high society females, everyone sought to remind her of that whenever they got the chance. Liana did her best to ignore their petty insults and focused on the things that mattered most to her, mainly her magic.

Not that she could readily practice magic without hiding most of it. The male mages might as well have outlawed females from using any magic for all the control they lorded over the females. Liana wouldn't stand for it though. She studied the magic she was born with. She cultivated it into a power equal to any man. One day, she might even reveal that fact to the world should she ever gain the courage.

"Liana!" her mother called; her tone full of scolding. She stomped over to her daughter and yanked the dirty book away. The spell died on Liana's lips and her hands fell into her lap with disappointment. "Gods above! I've told you time and time again to stop with the spells, Liana. You are a woman now. You have learned all the spells you need to keep a proper home and that is all. Now, let Phillipa get you dressed. We must leave soon."

Lady Monroe left with the book. Liana sighed but kept her mouth shut as she stood for Phillipa to dress her. She stepped into the undergarments held aloft for her and stared at the wall while her maid pulled the strings of the corset unbearably tight. When her mother returned, she no longer held the book in her possession, no doubt hidden away somewhere in Lord Monroe's study. Liana looked away from her mother as she fussed over her other daughters. A private smile tugged at her lips despite her mother's scolding. It would be so easy for her to find the spell book again just as it had been the first time.

"I do hope Ms. Lightwood does not catch Master Ranville's eye. She has been vying for him as well," Charlotte complained. "She is not as pretty as me, and her magic is not strong, nor will any children she bears. I would be a far better match for the Master."

"That you would, dear," Lady Monroe agreed.

"What of the other women coming from the country? What competition do they pose?"

Lady Monroe huffed. "None at all, my dear. The women from the country rarely match with one of our city men. They would marry any poor soul that looked their way if it meant moving out of the country. City living is much preferred, you know. They will take the eligible scholars and tradesmen. It will be our Lords and Ladies that will match together, perhaps even a Master," she said in a conspiratorial giggle, the sisters joining in. Liana rolled her eyes at the wall wishing she had her book back.

"Hurry, daughters. We must leave if we are to make it to the castle on time for the ball," Lady Monroe urged, which set the maids to work faster. "I must go check on your brothers."

As soon as their mother was out the door, Charlotte set in on Liana. "You must act normal tonight, dear sister," Charlotte warned. "If I am to marry the Master, I cannot have you tarnishing my reputation."

"I would never dream of sabotaging you, Charlotte," Liana responded blandly.

"When I do marry the Master, and you must wait for a suitor, think of how your behavior affects Hannah's chances," Charlotte carried on as if Liana had not spoken at all. "If society deems you an unfit match it will spoil Hannah's chances. You represent our family and anything you do is a reflection on us. We can't have everyone thinking mother did not raise us to be proper women in high society."

"Yes, sister," Liana replied, not bothering to listen. She had heard it all before.

"Good. Let us leave then. We must arrive at the perfect time."

Liana slipped into her new silver slippers which matched the silver dress then followed her sisters out the door. Phillipa purposefully trailed behind the others, lingering in the room to fold Liana's dressing robe. She'd seen what the girl had done earlier with that spell. She'd seen what Lady Monroe tried to prevent. There was no stopping her ward though. Liana was a force of nature with that magic, and she could perform any spell, create any potion or salve, without so much as a strain on her power.

Phillipa glanced back at the tree outside the window. Her face pinched in both resolve and amazement. Her charge was the most skilled mage she'd ever met. Such a pity the girl was a female and society would waste her talents.

Leaving the beautifully blooming magnolia tree that had barely two flowers on it this morning, Phillipa followed after the Monroe females.

Chapter Two

A long line of carriages waited along the drive to Sancta Valles Castle, named for the capital city it resided in, which stood imposingly at the point of the valley their city was protected by. Constructed of gray stone and pointed spires atop each of the many towers, the castle had been created from the image of power as Liana's books explained. Grand and sturdy, the castle stood for many centuries as a symbol of solidarity among the species of Triaedian.

When Triaedian first became a kingdom, the first king had all three species work together to build it. After fighting together to destroy the old regime, they worked together to build a new kingdom, a land of peace and equality among the three species. At least, that's how the history books relayed the tale. Liana thought Triaedian could use a reminder about how integrated they were all supposed to be because throughout her life, the species still seemed rather independent of one another.

Nestled upon the mountains, the castle loomed above the city below, an ever-present shadow lording over its people. There were twelve spires in total. Seven spires stood upon each corner of the lower portion of the castle while four others stood atop the towers at the corners of the main castle which rose above the rest. And rising higher from the center, one mighty spire pierced like a dagger into the clouds.

Liana admired it from afar for many years. This would be the first time she ever stepped foot inside and she couldn't wait. It was the only thing the young woman looked forward to this year for the upcoming courting season. Gods knew she wasn't looking forward to the men or the incessant chatter. Most of all, she was not excited about the gossip that would last for a year until the next cycle of courting arrived.

There would be endless talk of who matched with whom, and more importantly, who didn't match with anyone. Chatter about gowns and jewels would be less prevalent but still noted at least once during a conversation. If someone didn't wear appropriate attire or wore something from last season, then all rules were null because that would be the most horrendous thing one could do during courting season.

Liana hated it all and hated that she had to waste this late-afternoon summer day. It would have been fair weather to enjoy in the garden, but they were stuck inside the stuffy carriage while waiting for those before them to exit onto the castle's steps. Even with the windows open, the carriage quickly became unbearable. Liana eyed her mother and sisters as they fanned themselves vigorously. Her father and three brothers were in the carriage behind them, far too many of them to all fit inside one. Not caring about how improper it might be, Liana whispered a spell for a gentle breeze to pass through the windows. Everyone sighed and stopped fanning for a moment. Liana kept it going, her family none the wiser, partly because they had no idea such a spell existed. Also, partly because they were so untrained in their magic that they couldn't feel the telltale shift of magic in the air that a spell had been woven.

As they finally came to the stairs, a servant opened the carriage door. Lady Monroe exited first then the girls followed. They waited for their father and brothers before ascending the stairs. Torches lit their way up the stone steps even though the day was still bright. The sun would be setting soon however, and their evening would begin.

Liana gaped at the castle. From afar, she could not have appreciated the fine carvings in the stone of each archway. Nor could she appreciate how overpowering and small it made her feel. It was a structure of beauty and she wished she could ignore the ball in exchange for the freedom to explore this magnificent structure. The secrets such a place must hold. Secrets and tales a plenty she imagined.

They followed the line of lords, ladies, and other nobles to the ballroom. Along the way, they passed through the grand entrance which towered above to the third-floor balcony. Stone staircases ran along either wall, framing the hall that led toward the ballroom. Walking along a dark red carpet, Liana nearly tripped twice because her eyes were so focused on admiring the castle's details. They moved too quickly though for her to see much.

As they entered upon a terrace with a staircase to either side leading down to the main floor, their mother made the girls take a dramatic pause. As they looked over the balcony to the grand room below, it gave everyone a chance to glance up at them and see the next women available for claiming. So, there they stood like cattle up for bidding. The three Monroe daughters, purebred and raised to society perfection. They would go for top dollar in this city.

Everyone took a good eyeful. The men appraised for a suitable wife, one that would gain him the most. Liana knew there were always two questions men asked themselves when choosing a wife. First on the list to consider was how much a woman's dowry was worth and how influential her family name was. The greater her fortune and more clout he could gain with their marriage the better. Second to consider was her beauty. Not that it mattered entirely because the male would likely seek the comfort of another female after the marriage had been consummated and an heir secured.

And all the while, the women inspected for flaws and something to gossip about. Beauty mattered far more to the other females than the males ever cared for. Liana couldn't stand any of it, could hardly stand thinking about it.

Standing shoulder to shoulder, Charlotte stood first on the left. She kept her shoulders back and chin high with her hair in beautiful braids twined around her head like a crown while the rest fell in tight curls down her slender back. Charlotte's navy gown complemented her creamy complexion and overflowing bosom, not that one could get a good look before being caught by all the jewels adorning her body. One look and someone was at serious risk of being blinded.

To her right stood Liana. Whereas Charlotte and Hannah looked much like their mother with soft, womanly features, Liana took after her father with sharp cheekbones and tall stature. Darker chestnut hair contrasted with theirs while her skin tanned a few shades darker. That could also have a lot to do with the fact that Liana spent much of her time outdoors while her sisters remained cooped up inside. Liana's dress gleamed a pretty silver that reflected in her emerald eyes while her jewels were much less likely to seriously harm. They were sparkly and eye-catching yet not overdone. Understated elegance is how Phillipa described them.

Petite Hannah radiated with innocent beauty in her wine-colored gown. It would have been too bold a color for Liana but for the shorter girl, it gave her the exact right amount of boldness to not get lost in the crowd but not garner unwanted attention. All of her curly hair was piled atop her head in a youthful updo to show off her slender neck and the iridescent pearls collared around it.

Lady Monroe took her husband's arm before descending the stairs. Their eldest child, Wesley, took Charlotte's arm. Liana was paired with her younger brother, Carlisle. Hannah with the youngest Monroe, William who was merely eight years old but still full of Monroe decorum.

Liana kept her eyes ahead, refusing to meet any of the many eyes tracking their movements. She thought it was all in her head, but even the slightest bit of attention made her uncomfortable. She hated these balls so much because her only purpose here was to grab the attention of others.

There were so many already in the ballroom and not just mage. Everyone of importance in the kingdom attended. Vampires, shifters, and mage alike. Everyone was here for one purpose - to arrange a marriage - either for themselves or for their daughters.

Instead of focusing on them, she turned her attention to the room. It matched the imposing nature of the outside of the castle with massive stone columns lining either side of the longest walls to support the arched ceiling. Opposite the stairs, the far wall contained the dais and the king's throne. There were two columns along the wall, framing an alcove where his throne sat. From this far, Liana could not discern the details of the throne only that the cushion was made of a purple fabric, the frame glinting with gold.

The family was served immediately by a servant with a tray full of champagne flutes once they'd descended the stairs. Someone also brought glasses of juice for the two youngest Monroe boys. Soon after they were served from trays of Hors d'oeuvres. Liana grabbed quite a few much to her mother's disgrace. The girl scarfed them down before they were inundated by the many suitors and introductions of families.

An unbearable hour of smiling and curtsying later, the clinking of glasses had everyone quieting. The crowd turned toward the front of the ballroom where the dais and throne were. A man stood there now, a man that had Liana staring while everyone else curtsied or bowed.

Rooted to the spot, Liana beheld the reclusive king. Much gossip circulated about the vampire king. Most of which revolved around his handsomeness and how he had not married during his twenty-year reign. He still had eighty years left of his allotted one hundred, but he also needed a wife and heir within that time which everyone had an opinion on.

The Ashwood line held the throne since Triaedian's creation and Damien Ashwood would not be the first monarch to break the line of succession without an heir if the status-grabbing ladies of high society had any say in the matter. They spent too much of their time gabbing on about his sex-life or lack thereof considering he made no show of keeping a lady or harem of ladies.

Liana presumed the man liked his privacy on such matters. She certainly would have if she were a male. As for her, if she even thought of having a male companion, she'd be tarnished and ruin the family name. Lady Monroe would probably kill Liana herself rather than suffer the shame of such a promiscuous daughter.

Staring up at him as he stood upon his throne, the first thing she noticed about him was the power and confidence he displayed. Tall with proud shoulders and a stoic face that might as well have been chiseled from stone, he exuded intelligence and cunning. The only thing the gossip mongers probably had right was his handsomeness. With deep, olive toned skin and midnight dark hair, his matching heavy brow remained stoic, intensifying the mysterious air about him. When blue eyes so light they were nearly white landed on her own, she froze. Acutely aware that she was the only one not posed in deference, Liana's heart pounded. The king stared at her with those intense eyes until she finally forced her eyes off his and fell into a curtsy.

Palms sweating, chest rising and falling too quickly, she waited for the order of guards to take her for the unintentional slight. While the people of Triaedian gossiped freely about their king, they were sure to never speak ill of him because he was as merciless as he was mysterious. All Ashwood monarchs were ruthless leaders. They had to be. They ruled over three different races and had to keep them united. It took a strong will and hardened heart to keep everyone happy under vampiric rule.

"Welcome, my people. Please rise," the king greeted, his voice deep and loud, carrying easily throughout the crowded room. Liana breathed in deeply, relieved he didn't humiliate her in front of the entire ballroom. Everyone stood once more, staring raptly up at their king. "We begin another season of matching tonight, and it is my honor to host such a prosperous event. I wish you all well on your courtships and hope that you have a wonderful evening. May the gods bless us all."

As one, the room intoned, "May the gods bless us." Then clapping and cheers followed the king's short proclamation. Her heart still needed a moment to calm which came in the form of Lady Monroe dragging her into a conversation that didn't involve her at all. Charlotte and Hannah snared the attention of two handsome gentlemen, brothers by the looks of it.

Liana kept a polite, interested look upon her face even as her mind flashed those stunning blue eyes before her own. She was mortified that the king caught her staring. Mortified that he may think her daft, or worse, vying for his attention. Unlike most of the women there, she did not want his attention at all, especially not in such a manner. If anyone else had seen her, which the guards most certainly did, she would never hear the end of it from her mother.

Not hearing a word that was said, she found her eyes straying back toward the king. He sat upon his golden throne staring out over his people from his elevated perch. He leaned onto his left arm, a goblet in his right hand while his shoulders slouched slightly to give him an air of nonchalance despite the intimidating gaze he leveled upon the crowd. He watched the ball as if this were his entertainment for the evening, that glinting gold crown upon his head decreeing he could do as he pleased, and they could only hope to please him.

Before she could get caught staring, she turned away from the king and focused her attention on the two scholars speaking with Charlotte and Hannah. Lord and Lady Monroe stood nearby as chaperones while the male Monroe children were free to roam about unaccompanied. Liana listened to the conversation reluctantly despite not being a part of it. Charlotte and Hannah gave great performances as they feigned interest in the low-ranking men. A dance was promised for each man then they departed to search for more available ladies.

"Master Ranville," Lord Monroe called as the man passed nearby. "Come, have a chat." Proud that he finally caught the biggest fish in this ocean of eligible men, Lord Monroe puffed up his chest.

"Lord Monroe," the Master greeted with a nod. He took Lady Monroe's hand in his and placed a kiss upon her knuckles. "Lady Monroe, such a delight to see you again. Your husband really must invite me over more often for your famous sweet biscuits."

Lady Monroe blushed and giggled. "Oh, Master Ranville, you flatter me too much and of course, you are always welcome." Liana's eyes strained to stay in place as she fought the urge to roll them. Those sweet biscuits were a product of their skilled chef. Her mother simply requested them. Somehow though, such an insignificant crumb of information circulated the gossip mills touting Lady Monroe as a sweet biscuit aficionado and creator.

"Ranville, you remember my daughters, Lady Charlotte Monroe, our eldest daughter." Master Ranville took Charlotte's hand and kissed her knuckles while looking into her eyes with a glint of mischief. Charlotte smiled and looked away demurely playing her part perfectly.

"Lady Hannah Monroe, our youngest daughter," Lady Monroe introduced, and Master Ranville offered her a kiss on the hand as well. And so it went for Liana as well. "And Lady Liana Monroe, our middle daughter." Liana curtsied keeping her knees slightly bent as she stood considering she stood nearly the same height as Master Ranville and men didn't like to be overshadowed or stand on equal footing with a female. Not that they were equal in any way, the males made sure of that, but appearances were everything.

As the family got to talking with the Master, Liana was once again forgotten as she stooped and tried to blend in.

"It has been too long since I have seen you all considering I see your father nearly every day. We should dine together more often, I would much rather look upon your pretty faces than his," Master Ranville teased.

Charlotte smiled politely with a giggle while her father guffawed, patting the man's shoulder. "Right you are, Master. We spend too much time sequestered in the Council building. You are always welcome at our home."

"Much appreciated. I shall look forward to more visits," he responded with a respectful nod.

"Lord Dietrich," Lord Monroe interjected as he snagged the man while he walked by, interrupting the conversation to nab another big player. "So glad you made it tonight. You remember my dear Hannah that I was telling you about. Allow me to introduce everyone," the Lord said, going through the introductions for the thirtieth time that night.

Each sister spoke with her dream suitor while the parents split chaperoning duty. Liana stood on the outskirts of it all, not bothering to pay attention anymore which gave her ample time to sneak glances at the king. It was purely out of curiosity, she told herself. She loved mysteries and the king most certainly personified mystery. He hadn't moved from his perch, although he now held a glass of wine instead of the silver goblet he held earlier. She wondered if he would join the festivities this evening, or if he would seek a wife during this courting season. Gods only knew what he was waiting for in finding a wife. The vampire had already been king for twenty years. He needed a queen and an heir.

Liana considered that a moment. To be so burdened already by the responsibility of ruling a kingdom then to be forced to choose a bride for the solitary goal of creating an heir. That must be why he had not chosen anyone yet. An act of rebellion on his part to not bow completely to the crown.

A derisive snort escaped her at the outlandish imaginings she conjured. His responsibilities were no different from any female in this room - their only purpose in this life to produce heirs for whichever male chose them. She did not pity the king for his burden because that's what they all faced. Only difference being he bore his in the lap of luxury. As a male though, and the king, he had a say in the matter whereas the ladies were forced to bow down to the desires of men.

Liana hadn't realized she'd been staring until she focused on him again, her thoughts receding as she noticed the king staring directly at her. He lifted a questioning brow, not taking his eyes off her. She blushed all the way down to her toes and turned away quickly. Downing the rest of her drink, she searched for another. Chasing a servant behind a pillar, she nabbed a glass and hid from those piercing eyes.

Gods, she was so embarrassed. It was one thing that he caught her staring twice now, he probably thought her another desperate female vying for his attention, but he caught her laughing at him. She would surely be punished by the end of the evening, or at least completely ostracized from high society. Perhaps he didn't think she was laughing at him but simply laughing, she told herself while taking a deep breath. There was no way he could know what she thought and laughed at, that was just her imagination dramatizing everything as usual. Sucking down her glass, she snuck out from behind the pillar to rejoin her family, her eyes set forward and not straying to the dais even an inch.

Her family hadn't even noticed her absence as she rejoined them, their conversations uninterrupted. When the music started, everyone fled to the outskirts of the ballroom, the courting couples taking up partners in the middle. Liana found herself being ushered out of the way by her parents as they found a bench to sit on. Sighing in relief as her feet had a chance to rest, Liana watched the dancers begin.

"Stay here, Liana. Now that your sisters are taken care of, we must find you a suitable match." Lady Monroe turned to her husband as they whispered amongst themselves although Liana could hear it all. "Who do you think? Perhaps Keeper Olivier? He is older and widowed, but he has heirs already. He's a very passive man as well. I believe he would allow for Liana's… peculiarities," Lady Monroe said after a bit of hesitation. Peculiarities had always been her mother's way of nicely saying Liana was odd. That she preferred reading to gossiping. That studying magic was her passion and not pretty dresses.

"Don't be harsh, Mary. All of my daughters deserve a respectable choice. Did she not say who she favored?" At least her father stood up for her most of the time.

"Your daughter favors no one. She would rather die a spinster than be married," Lady Monroe huffed. She always referred to Liana as 'his daughter' whenever she was upset at Liana or annoyed with her behavior. Lady Monroe thought her daughter cursed with the mind of a man with all her lofty ideas and sought to complain about it every moment she could.

"Mary, honestly. There is no need to be so dramatic. If she is not picky, then it shall be easy to find her a husband," he reasoned. She huffed in response before they walked off together to find someone for their daughter.

Liana sighed and grabbed more food from a passing servant. There would be no formal dinner tonight and her stomach growled angrily for any form of sustenance. Content to sit in silence, she took another drink while digging into the delicious morsels. She cast a longing look toward the dancers, noting how beautiful and elegant the dances were and how the orchestra played the music to perfection. Although she hated most societal norms, dancing was one of her favorite things. Such a pity she never had a partner though, except for her father of course. He always danced when she asked.

A smile pulled at her lips as she recalled the moments when he reluctantly obliged. Usually late at night after everyone else had retired for the evening, she would sneak downstairs to his study and convince him to join her in the small ballroom of their manor home. She chose the dance each time and spelled the instruments to play by themselves. Lord Monroe had been a good father to her. He indulged her far too much in Lady Monroe's opinion, but Liana loved him all the more for it.

"It's no wonder she has no suitors." Liana overheard a woman beside her speaking. "Look at how much she is eating and drinking."

Another woman scoffed. "She's always been the odd sister. Always with her nose in a book or digging around in the dirt. You know, I saw her just two days ago in the city square kneeled at the fountain with her hands digging through the flower beds."

The other woman gasped, neither of them realizing how loud they were speaking. Or perhaps they did. Used to people talking about her, Liana considered that they were so loud to ensure she overheard. Ladies behaved as such quite frequently around her. A passive aggressive move that Liana rarely gave any thought to. It was impossible to block all of it out, despite her effort to do so.

"What was she doing?"

"Not a clue. By the time she was done though, her hands and dress were filthy. Covered in dirt, she then had the audacity to go into the bakery and buy some bread."

The other woman gasped again. "There must have been dirt everywhere!"

Liana planted a new batch of tulips around the fountain that day. There was nothing so scandalous about it. She noticed that the old batch did not recover after the winter and replaced them since no one else seemed so inclined.

"Luckily she didn't touch anything," the woman huffed. Liana recognized their voices as Mrs. Sanders and Mrs. Henson. Their husbands were scholars and professors at the university. They were barely classified as high society folks and made up for that fact by knowing everything about everyone and spreading it through the ranks whether it was true or not.

"I don't understand how her sisters are so well behaved. They are the true embodiment of what a proper lady should be in society and then there is her."

They clucked disapprovingly. "Something very off about her. I feel sorry for her mother."

Liana had enough of their gossip. Taking her drink, she walked calmly away, not giving them the satisfaction of riling her up. She was far from calm though. She hated this society and their gossip. All she wanted was to return home where she could curl up in bed with a book.

The night couldn't end soon enough.

Chapter Three

L iana attempted to escape the ball and find a quiet corner to hide in. Before she could though, someone approached her.

"Excuse me, miss. May I introduce myself?" the man asked formally with a slight bow of the head. Liana gave him a respectful nod back.

"You may."

"I am Beta Mooncliff of the wolf pack." A shifter, and wolf at that. Liana was surprised that he bothered introducing himself. Although they lived in the same city, and Triaedian boasted itself as a kingdom of diversity, the species did not intermingle romantically. There were plenty of interspecies business deals. Even the neighborhoods of Sacta Valles had become quite mixed, in fact, the Monroe's neighbors included a shifter to the right and a vampire family at the end of their block. Despite that, the various species had not dared to cross the line of romantic involvement. At least not publicly where the gossip mongers could spread the news.

"I am Lady Liana Monroe, daughter of Lord Michael Monroe."

"It is an honor to meet you, Lady Liana. I noticed you sitting alone and thought you might like a dance. Would you do me the honor?" Liana hesitated to take the man's outstretched hand. It wasn't forbidden to dance with someone outside of their own kind, but it certainly was not approved of. He sensed her hesitancy and added on, "I know it is not exactly proper, but I could not stand to see such a beautiful young woman missing out on the fun. Please, just one dance."

She'd already garnered enough attention this evening, especially from the king, but the man asked so kindly and was bold enough to do so. Liana nodded, not meeting his golden, vibrant eyes. Her mother would faint when she saw them dancing.

Her body remained stiff as they began the dance, holding the man's hand while the other rested on his shoulder. "Relax, Lady Liana. No one is paying us any mind."

That dragged a laugh from her, and she met his eyes with humor. "I sincerely doubt that, Beta Mooncliff." He was a tall man, as all shifters were, which worked in her favor considering her height issues.

"Why is that?" he wondered. He smirked down at her, his golden eyes twinkling with humor, golden curls falling into his eyes. The man was handsome to be sure with his square face and blond hair that made his light eyes stand out all the more. The rough stubble along his cheek and unkempt curls gave him a rugged exterior, vastly different from the stuffy mage males she was used to.

"Not only are you a shifter and I a mage, but I am also the city's pariah. I believe all eyes are on us." She could feel them too, even if she forced her own to stay on his.

"A pariah? Surely because your beauty is too great for anyone to be around for too long in fear of becoming ensnared forever," he teased.

"Hardly," she scoffed right before he twirled her in time with the music. "They think me inept because I do not wish to spend my time dawdling with stitching or gossip. They protest my opposition to their conformist and oppressive society."

"Strong words from a lady," he pointed out with a curious brow raised.

She sighed, looking away from the shifter. Liana thought he might be different from the mage males. That he might value a woman like the shifter culture was rumored to do. It must have been gossip as usual.

Liana gave a simpering smile. "But of course, I speak too boldly as usual. Do not let me bore you with my woeful tales. How are you enjoying your night?" she asked, settling for a neutral topic.

He frowned as they split and exchanged partners for a step. When they came back together, he said, "I didn't mean to offend, my lady. I was only caught off guard by your brazen honesty. I find it rather refreshing, especially from a mage female."

She tried to hold her tongue, yet again insulted by his sexist remark. "Are you surprised that a female could have a mind of her own, or specifically a mage female?"

He sighed heavily. "I believe I keep fumbling my words. Please, forgive me, Lady Liana for I am simply too caught in your enchanting mind to create sentences that are not insulting. I care not what you are, nor do I find females inferior. Shifters worship females, as should mage males."

Liana nodded. Her tongue was causing trouble yet again. She needed to move on and quickly. A ballroom was not a place to assert her independence with a man she didn't know. "There is nothing to forgive, Beta Mooncliff. Let us move past this."

He smiled. "You are a wonderful dancer."

"Thank you. I enjoy dancing very much. You are surprisingly light on your feet for such a large man. I didn't think I would have any toes left by the end of this dance."

A deep and rumbling laugh erupted from him and caught far too many stares. "And here I thought you hesitated to take my hand because I was a shifter."

"Not at all. I was worried about my delicate feet and slippers. They are new and I do not wish them ruined."

He chuckled again. "Then I shall endeavor to keep your new slippers and delicate feet free from damage."

He twirled her on cue then took her hand again and she noticed how warm he was. Concerned for the shifter as he dripped with sweat, cheeks a deep red, and probably near to passing out, Liana wondered what was wrong.

"Beta, if I may be so bold again, are you alright? You feel very warm and are sweating profusely."

He tugged at the collar of his formal jacket. "Shifters run warmer than everyone else and these formal clothes are stifling."

"The room is rather warm," she agreed. Glancing around demurely, Liana checked to see how many were still looking their way. Most had returned to their conversations while some still stared in open distaste. "If you may permit me, Beta Mooncliff, I could perform a spell to cool you off," she whispered so quietly that she could barely hear herself.

His eyes widened in surprise before shuttering back to neutral. "I wasn't aware a lady would know of such spells, but I am beginning to understand that I should never underestimate Lady Liana Monroe. I'd be delighted if you assisted me."

It was true that most female mages didn't know many spells. Liana craved magic and spells though. It was what she excelled at. She backed herself into a corner though because there was no exact spell for what she needed. It needed to be far more discreet than the breeze she conjured in the carriage earlier, but it needed to last all night and not be noticeable by others which meant she also needed a concealment spell. This would require more magic than she thought and never should have opened her mouth. But the shifter had been kind to her and made her laugh, which apparently was all it took to garner her affections. She'd be cursing herself for this later when she wallowed at how pathetic she acted.

She'd have to come up with a unique spell which was unheard of in mage society. Only a Master could create new spells and even then, it was extremely difficult. Master Ranville only created two new spells during his five years as Master. Liana found it entirely too easy however and didn't dare speak of it to anyone for fear of becoming even more of a pariah.

If that weren't enough, she feared the indications of what such power would bring. If anyone were to discover that she was as powerful as a Master and had created dozens of spells, she couldn't imagine what would happen. Just the thought of anyone discovering her powerful magic had her heart beating in terror. Such thoughts always brought a rush of terror she couldn't explain.

If someone did find out, perhaps they would leave her alone. Perhaps the king would keep her for his own gain. Or perhaps someone would do something far more nefarious. People were unpredictable when it came to power. Liana knew though, that the only predictable thing about power was that everyone wanted more of it.

Holding his hand, Liana stared into his eyes and murmured the words under her breath so that no one else would be able to hear or understand what she performed in secret.

"Sweat be gone, temperature calm. Keep thy skin cool tonight and release this spell with morning light." He gave an instant sigh of relief as the sweat stopped and his skin cooled. She added a concealment spell afterward to keep other mages from knowing what she did.

The song came to an end as soon as she completed the spells. "Another dance, my lady?"

"Perhaps later. I do believe the people can only handle one dance at a time from such a scandalous pairing. Best give them time to settle." He laughed again then bowed, placing a kiss on her knuckles.

"Then allow me to thank you, the gods sent me a blessing in you. Sincerely, you have done me a great service and made my night far more enjoyable."

She blushed understanding he meant the spell but couldn't help imagining he spoke of her company as well. "You are very welcome, Beta Mooncliff."

"You are an unexpected delight, Lady Liana Monroe. Please, do find me later. I'd enjoy another conversation." She nodded before walking off the dance floor. Keeping her eyes on the floor, she didn't dare look at anyone as she passed.

Unfortunately, Liana walked right into her mother's path where she silently dragged Liana away. Anger poured off her mother in sinister waves which had Liana bracing for the scolding to come. When they were safely away from prying ears in the hall, her father lagging behind, Lady Monroe turned on her daughter.

"How dare you dance with that shifter, Liana! Your father and I were trying to find you a good match tonight, but you've ruined that completely."

"It is not a big deal, Mother. It was just a dance, not a marriage proposal," Liana countered with annoyance. All she wanted was to be left alone.

"It was not just a dance. Everyone saw it. Everyone is talking."

"Let them talk," Liana interjected angrily. "All they do is talk about me anyway."

"Because you give them so much to talk about," Lady Monroe countered angrily. "If you behaved like a proper lady, like your sisters, then they would not talk."

"Those idle ninnies would talk no matter if I were perfect or not."

Lady Monroe gasped even as her father coughed out a laugh. "Michael, do not laugh! This is serious. Your daughter is insubordinate, and she will never find a husband if she keeps up this behavior."

"Your mother is right, Liana," Lord Monroe said gently. "You must behave and find a husband that will provide you with a comfortable and safe life."

"I do not need a husband. I will provide for myself."

Lady Monroe scoffed. "Not this again," she complained. "And how do you propose to do that? Sell yourself on the streets?"

It was Liana's turn to gasp. "Mother! No, of course not. Why can't you understand that I don't want to marry one of these prissy gentlemen?"

"Argh! I blame this on you!" Lady Monroe accused Lord Monroe. "You spoiled the girl. You let her believe she could be something other than a wife and now look where we are."

"That is unfair, Mama," Liana said.

"No, it is not. I understand, Liana. I have a mind too. I know how to use it just as well as any man which is why I am telling you to stop with this foolish independence and find a husband. A woman is nothing in this world without a man to support her. Once you have a husband, do as you please. Learn all the magic you want. Do what you please as long as you have a husband to fall back on," Lady Monroe declared before walking away in a huff.

Lord Monroe hugged his daughter. "You know I do not like to admit it, but your mother is right, Liana. She usually is. Find a husband then do whatever you please."

"Why can't I just live with you forever, Papa? You don't care what I do."

He sighed heavily before pulling away. Keeping an arm wrapped around her shoulder he walked her back to the ballroom. "As much as I would love to never let any of you girls go, one day I will be gone and there will be no one else to take care of you. You need someone of your own."

Liana nodded. She always knew she would eventually marry. She knew there was no getting away from it forever no matter how much she resisted. As her mother said, if she wanted to continue on with her odd ways, she must hide it all behind a marriage.

"Now, pick someone you can stand before your mother picks someone for you," he teased but it held a merit of truth. He made a very good point on that.

Chapter Four

The Monroe sisters were the talk of the ball by the end of the night. Hannah and Charlotte danced with their preferred matches many times while Liana tried her best to repair the damage she caused and make a good impression on all the available mage suitors. The mage community flittered with talks of marriage for the three sisters. Most of all, gossip centered around Liana. This time though, it focused on how well she performed.

Ever the proper lady, Liana gave them all what they wanted. She didn't speak to Beta Mooncliff again, nor did she dance with him. If she was forced to marry, she would find the most bearable mage she could. There was only one man on her list, and he was not all that great.

Unfortunately, it was Keeper Olivier. The man was fifteen years her senior but still young enough to give her one child to add to the four he already had. He wasn't entirely disgusting. He kept himself fit and clean although his personality left a lot to be desired. Liana could deal with that as long as she could lead her own life.

Keeper Olivier was keeper of all records on the council which meant he kept plenty busy on his own. That would leave her ample solitary time and access to many resources the council sequestered from the females.

Her feet were sore and her stomach aching for food by the time she slipped away. Venturing outside of the ballroom, the guards didn't stop her as she walked to the end of the window lined hall. Torches held aloft in decorative iron holsters lit the way. Giggles erupted behind her before a couple hurried ahead and slipped through a door.

At the end of the hall, it turned left to continue on another window lined corridor with more mysterious doors on the opposite wall. In the corner of the hall, Liana noted an outcropping in the walls which held a grand statue. A boastful statue of a knight holding up a shield and sword with one foot lifted on his fallen enemy stood in the middle of the alcove which hid the bay of iron-paned windows and stone ledge. It probably wasn't made for sitting but she didn't quite care at the moment.

Leaning against the window, she pulled her feet up and sighed while staring out at the moonlit valley beyond. The cloudless night had her itching to be in the garden to practice a few choice spells which only worked on a night such as this with a full moon. Spells for the goddess Luna were always stronger under such conditions, she was the goddess of night after all. If they could leave soon, Liana might still be able to get some work in this evening.

Before she forgot, she summoned her special pen and pulled the sleeve of her left arm up. On her pale skin she began to write the spell she said earlier to cool down the shifter. She had to keep track of all the spells she created but it was far too dangerous to write them down for someone to discover. Hence why she decided to use herself as the book. She wrote the spells in her skin under a disguising spell where they would forever be safe. As soon as she was done writing, the words disappeared. Years ago, when she started this secret habit, she'd imbibed the pen with the spells to ink and disguise her skin, so she didn't always have to say the words.

"That is an interesting spell," a mysterious voice said from behind her. She gasped and stood while yanking her sleeve down and sending the pen back to her bedroom. Heart racing with terror at being caught using magic, Liana panicked, searching for an easy escape. The space was small though and the man blocked one exit. She surged toward the other side of the statue when he caught her by the arm.

"Let me go," she whimpered, yanking away. He let go instantly and she fell into the window, crashing back down onto the ledge.

"Calm yourself, female. I meant no harm," he assured, his voice low and soothing. Breathing heavily as her magic roiled within herself, Liana held a hand to her chest in an attempt to calm down. "I did not mean to scare you."

"Well, you most certainly did," she snapped, and a small flicker of golden magic hit the statue. She hid her hands in the folds of her dress to hide the uncontrollable magic.

"Does your magic always react so strongly to your emotions?" the man asked, his voice curious. Confused as to why he wasn't angry by her lack of control or the use of her spelled pen, she finally looked up. She stood with a gasp as her heart threatened to give out in shock.

Being so confined as she curtsied to the king, her backside bumped into the window which caused her to fall forward into the man's chest. Fumbling and apologizing profusely, she tried to right herself. "Your Highness, I am so very sorry. You startled me. I didn't mean to touch you.

I'm so sorry, Your Highness," she stammered, keeping her head bowed since she couldn't very well curtsy.

"It's quite alright, Miss. I did startle you after all." He took her vacated seat calmly. "Please, have a seat." Uncertain if she was allowed to refuse the king, she took a few hurried breaths and sat on the ledge with her back to the opposite windows now. This angle blocked her view of the hallway beyond. "That was interesting magic. What spell was that?"

Her galloping heart wouldn't calm down, especially not now the king had seen her peculiar magic. He was the last person she ever wanted to know of it. "Just a disguising spell, Your Highness." Liana clasped her hands together to keep them from trembling. She could do nothing to anger the king for not only did she not want to face his wrath but her mother's as well.

"Yes, but the one you wrote. What was that?"

"Oh, nothing special, Your Highness."

"Tell me," he ordered softly.

She gulped. There would be no denying him. "A cooling spell, Your Highness. It was rather warm while dancing." It was the truth, mostly.

"Interesting. I have not seen that particular spell before. Where did you learn it?"

Afraid to lie to the man, she deflected. "Are you familiar with many mage spells, Your Highness?" she asked in a rush hoping to divert him from asking more questions. She didn't dare look into those icy eyes for fear of becoming even more frazzled.

"Yes, all of them." If she weren't so nervous, his deep and smooth voice would put her at ease. "It pays well to know what all your subjects are capable of even if I cannot perform the same magic."

"Yes, of course. Very wise, Your Highness."

"And writing it into your skin, why did you do that?"

She planted her palms on either side of herself on the cool stone. She would have wiped the sweat on her dress, but the moisture would show on the silken fabric.

"As a reminder to myself. I am quite forgetful." Liana heard that vampires could sense if someone lied. She sincerely hoped that was a lie or else she was done for.

"I've never seen another mage do something like that… write in their skin. Not even Master Kinley on my council." Master Kinley was the most powerful mage in all of Triaedian and he served as mage council to the monarchs for the past fifty years. She gulped again. If the king said anything to Master Kinley about her new spell or the skin-writing, she would… Well, she wasn't exactly sure what they would do with a powerful female. It wouldn't be good, she assumed, and her magic agreed as it rebelled beneath her skin to escape this situation.

Fingers clenched around the stone as her heart continued to race, and her magic screamed that she was not safe. There was nowhere to go though. She was stuck beside the king.

"It helps me remember the spell, Your Highness," she told him again. Her brain fought too hard to come up with a decent lie and that pathetic reply became her only thought.

"Quite odd," he commented. Odd didn't begin to describe her but if he simply thought her odd, that was much better than the alternative. If anyone discovered her strength or skill she'd be punished. "And the magic sparks? Is that something that happens often?"

"No, Your Highness," she lied again. "You merely startled me is all."

He shifted, pulling one leg onto the ledge and resting his arm over the bent knee while staring out the window. Liana allowed herself a glimpse at the man as she tried to calm her nerves with slow, deep breathing, and focused on him rather than the terror in her veins. In this little alcove, he seemed even larger with broad shoulders and long legs. It was not just his physical form that took up space but his energy. He was powerful without even having magic. She couldn't ignore the need to stay at attention in his presence although he seemed relaxed enough.

"Tell me, Lady Liana, how are you enjoying your night?" he asked. Relief filled her as he changed the subject. It didn't escape her notice that he knew her name as well. He probably asked around after he caught her staring multiple times.

"It has been a wonderful evening. Thank you, Your Highness. May I ask how your night has been?"

"Stop with the formalities," he responded curtly.

Liana paused. Was she supposed to still talk with him? Should she leave? He didn't let her leave before, would he now? "Your night?" she prompted again nervously. He glanced over at her, and she glanced away under his all-too knowing gaze.

"I feel that it has taken a turn." He did not expand on that answer. As much as she wanted to ask about it, he moved on. "Have you found a suitable match?"

"There are many suitable men here tonight, Your…" she trailed off, not finishing his title as he demanded.

"That is yet to be determined and you did not answer my question," he pointed out. Liana fiddled with her dress as she thought of Keeper Olivier. The man was her best option.

"Keeper Olivier would make a fine match." Beneath her lashes she noticed a single brow rise in surprise.

"I did not expect that," he admitted. "He's rather old for you."

"You are one to speak of age," she quipped before she could stop herself. "My apologies, Your Highness. I…"

"Stop," he demanded with a rough chuckle. She sucked in a breath, forcing it into her tight chest. If he was laughing that at least meant he wasn't angry enough to punish her as was well within his right as king for her speaking out of turn. "You are right. I am rather old myself compared to you. However, I am not vying for your hand." Liana blushed twenty shades of red.

"Of course not, Your Highness," she said automatically then paused. "Sorry."

"What makes you think Keeper Olivier would be a good match for you?"

"He is a good, honorable man with a respectable family. He has an important job and would make me a fine husband."

"You sound as bored by him as I am," he sneered and surprised a laugh from her.

"There is nothing wrong with him," she defended.

"If you don't count a lack of personality as wrong, then perhaps you are right." She glanced at him from the corner of her eyes. He was already looking at her with a smirk on his lips. She wasn't sure what he was playing at but if he wanted to play, she would. There was a reason he sought her out and perhaps, if she dazzled him enough, he would forget about her magic. Letting go of her fear for the moment, she also let go of formalities and let her true self shine through.

"Fine, then. Who would you pick for me?" she asked, turning to face him fully. It was then that she noticed he no longer wore that intimidating crown of pristine gold.

"I wouldn't presume to know you so well as to pick a husband for you."

"You clearly have your opinions. I'm sure you could pick someone without knowing me." He raised a curious brow.

"Very well then, I would pick the shifter you danced with tonight." That gave her pause. Not only because they were not of the same breed but because he admitted to watching her.

She couldn't help herself from asking, "You were watching me?"

He frowned. "Everyone was watching you. They all had quite a bit to say on the matter too."

Liana looked out the window. Vampiric hearing was notoriously enhanced so there would be no doubt that he heard all the juicy gossip surrounding her. "They seem to find amusement in me for some reason or another," she admitted quietly, hating that he saw how the others ridiculed her. It was embarrassing that a man of his power and rank witnessed such petty gossip.

"They are simply jealous of your beauty," he commented. That was the second time in one night a male called her beautiful. It was miraculous enough that one man thought her such but for two males, the king in particular, was an impossibility.

She snorted. "You don't have to flatter me. I know I'm different." She looked toward him again. It was quick but she could have sworn she saw sadness in his blue eyes but was replaced quickly by that mask of indifference. "Is that why you chose the shifter for me? Because no other mage would want me?" To think that the king pitied her was unbearable. A man of such power and rank pitying her was exactly what she didn't want. She was strong. She was fierce and didn't need the approval of others.

"I meant no offense. I chose the shifter because he was the only one that made you smile."

"I smiled for everyone," she countered. The king went to say something but snapped his full lips shut. She waited for something more, but he said nothing while staring out the window.

Despite her earlier fear, Liana found she wasn't quite so nervous anymore, nor was she quite so eager to leave. The king intrigued her. All the rumors painted him as a lonely, bitter man focused on only protecting this kingdom. She should have known better than to listen to the same gossip that made her the outcast. Perhaps they misjudged him as they did her. Perhaps he was a man that simply knew the value of his own life and took the responsibility upon his shoulders seriously.

Liana didn't envy the pressure he must be under to uphold the peace in Triaedian. To keep a kingdom of vastly different people united under one monarch seemed like it would be a constant battle of wills and also compromise with a heavy dose of cunning in order to keep the three species placated. And to do it alone seemed even less appealing. The king never made his personal affairs known, nor did he have a harem of women as some of the foreign kings were rumored to keep.

"Do you never wish to find someone for yourself at these balls?" she asked, curious as to why he did not yet have a wife.

"I do not."

"Are you not expected to marry and produce an heir for the throne?" Her question was bold, but he didn't shy away from it.

"Of course, I am, I am king. The Ashwood line must continue. However, the last place I will find my bride is at one of these ridiculous balls."

She smiled. "You sound as revolted by all this as I am." He flashed her a wicked grin for her mockery of his earlier dig at Keeper Olivier. Before she could ask why he wouldn't find his bride here, he asked,

"Who taught you to dance?"

"A dance professor."

"Classically trained then. It shows. You are an elegant dancer."

She blushed again. "Thank you. I love dancing. Do you enjoy it? I didn't see you dance at all."

"I do not wish to be stuck with all the simpering ladies vying for my attention, so I avoid dancing." The king definitely did not enjoy high society then, especially power-hungry females. She hoped he didn't see her as such considering her staring problem from before. She felt sorry for him though. Dancing was such a wonderful activity.

"Oh, well that's a shame. Everyone should be able to dance if they wish."

He shook his head. "You sound very naïve."

Liana's eyes snapped to him in anger. "I beg your pardon. I am not naïve and how dare you for saying so."

"Ach, woman, calm yourself. I did not mean it in rudeness. Forget I said anything." She crossed her arms and looked out the window. Well, she certainly didn't want to continue talking to the hundred-year-old vampire now. As she thought that, she realized just how much life he had been through.

She shook her head at herself. "How naïve I must truly seem to you. A girl of nineteen compared to your hundred years." When her eyes met his, they seemed depthless, full of all that she'd seen lurking beneath the surface. She couldn't even imagine how much he'd witnessed and experienced. "You must find the courting season quite tedious after going through so many."

His face transformed into a mask of humor suddenly, their serious moment broken. "Quite accurate. They do entertain me a bit though. I get a good chuckle watching love-sick fools fighting over a woman."

She laughed humorlessly. "More like greedy men fighting over a sack of money."

"You are awfully harsh and judgmental. Do you believe all these people are only after status? What about love?"

She raised a brow at him. "You speak of love when not only minutes ago you spurned any chance of a match at these… What did you say? Oh yes, ridiculous balls."

A slow smile lifted the corner of his lips. "I did. That does not mean I don't wish to find love."

She huffed and crossed her arms, avoiding those piercing eyes. "Love. A fool's dream," she murmured. Leaned her head on the windowpane, she watched as the moonlight flickered off the waterfall far below their perch.

"So cynical for one so young," the king said quietly. She shrugged. She'd dreamed of love once. Dreamed that she could find it one day. But reality was harsh, and she knew that would never be in the cards for her. She would marry whichever influential man her parents picked.

Not wanting to discuss this further, she asked, "When was the last time you danced, old man?" she teased since he seemed to point out her youth whenever he could.

"The last time I was forced to," he replied with a quick grin.

"Fine, keep your secrets. But I was going to offer you a disguising spell so that we may have a peaceful dance. I'm not so sure anymore," she teased.

He raised that curious brow again. "A disguising spell? That's advanced." She shrugged a shoulder at her slip of the tongue even as she panicked internally. She was trying to hide her power from the king, not boast about it.

"It's child's play really. I'm not so sure I should though. You are so old; I'd be too terrified you'd break a leg."

He surprised himself with a boisterous laugh. "I'm a vampire. I don't break," he replied.

"Hmm, oh well. My feet are sore anyway from all that wonderful dancing I did earlier."

He chuckled. "You are a wicked little mage, aren't you?"

"I'm sure I have no idea what you mean, Your Highness." Her stomach chose that moment to growl loudly. "And I am in desperate need of food. Will you join me?" she asked, uncertain if she should even ask or if he would bother joining a lowly mage.

"Hold on." He leaned around the statue. "Bring us a tray," he said to someone. Liana glanced around but didn't see anyone.

"Who are you talking to?"

"A guard. He's been standing by. Couldn't have anyone eavesdropping. You were quite clever to find this spot. Very private." It was then that she noticed just how private and secluded this space truly was. Feeling uncomfortable now, Liana scooted away. King Ashwood noticed the move and squinted angrily. "I would never harm you, little mage. Nor would I spoil your virtue."

"Of course, King Ashwood. I didn't mean to imply you would. If someone saw us though…"

"Then they would mind their own business because there is nothing untoward going on here and we've had a chaperone this entire time. Two in fact." Liana glanced around but could not find anyone. "Vampires have excellent hearing," he explained between clenched teeth.

"I'm sorry. I did not mean to imply that you are dishonorable. It's only that people love to gossip, and a mage woman's virtue is all she has. I'm sorry," she said again, afraid she'd angered him too much.

He sighed and scrubbed a hand through his long dark hair. "Do not apologize. You are right, unfortunately. A mage woman has no liberties in this world, and I would never dishonor you."

"Thank you," she said quietly. A tray appeared from around the statue. King Ashwood took it, handing it to Liana. He took one of the bite sized delights and popped it into his mouth, the tension in their secluded alcove dissipating. She followed his move, ravenous still.

"Why these functions don't serve full meals has never made sense to me," she complained. "I am always hungry, and it is not proper to hoard a tray all to myself like this."

"All to yourself? Am I not allowed to have any more?" He tried to grab one, but she blocked his reach with a shield. His hand bumped into the invisible shield; his eyes narrowed on her. She smirked.

"You did hand me the tray, did you not? Therefore, they are all mine."

His surprise dissolved into a smile. "Not even one more? I did get you the tray after all."

"Technically, your guard got the tray."

"Yes, but I told him to get it."

She scoffed. "That hardly deserves payment."

"It is my food. I paid for it, and I paid the chef to cook it," he countered.

"I suppose that is a fair argument." She picked one up and dropped the shield. "Here, you may have one tart."

"So very generous of you, my lady," he teased, reaching for it. Liana pulled her hand away at the last second with a giggle. He frowned and reached for it again. She evaded him again and again, laughing until he grabbed her wrist with vampiric speed and shoved the tart into his mouth. Warm, smooth lips closed around her fingers which had her gasping, the laughter cutting off. Something in her gut clenched and she gulped, watching wide-eyed as he pulled his mouth from her fingers and chewed. She licked her own lips reflexively.

King Ashwood dropped her hand suddenly. "I apologize, Lady Monroe. That was very nearly improper." She glanced away her face hot with... it wasn't embarrassment but something else entirely. A burning deep in her belly, a yearning for something more.

Out of nervousness, she did something foolish. She grabbed a pastry and chucked it at his head. The pastry topped with thick cream stuck to his cheek when it hit.

"Now that is improper," she said before breaking down into hysterical laughter. He laughed, pulling the pastry from his face. After eating it, he wiped his face clean.

King Ashwood grabbed another pastry before sitting back into his relaxed pose. "What other spells do you know? It was my understanding that females were only taught housekeeping spells."

Liana shrugged. She had to play it cool, had to convince him there was nothing special about her. "I like using spells. I've learned what I could on my own beyond what they teach us."

"From where?"

"My father and brothers have plenty of spell books."

"Ah, so you stole them," King Ashwood said in realization.

"I wouldn't call it stealing. Just borrowing. I always returned them."

"So, let me see if I've come to know you a little better. You're a ravenous thief and improper lady that is also a skilled mage." He said it teasingly, but Liana didn't find it funny. "That was meant to be a joke, little mage," he said lightly.

She nodded. "Yes, quite funny." It should have been, but far too near the truth for her to find his teasing amusing. The other mage constantly berated her for her oddities. No matter how hard Liana tried to be a normal female in society, they still teased her for being different, for daring to not be a part of the same mold every female was expected to fit into. The last person she wanted to know, or tease her about it, was the king. She also needed to get away from him. He'd already learned too much about her. This was the perfect excuse to flee.

She handed the now empty tray back to him. "Thank you for your time, Your Highness. I must be going before my mother comes searching for me. And trust me, you do not want her on your scent. She is part bloodhound." The king smiled but it did not reach his eyes. When he stood, Liana could not back up in the small alcove. He really was quite tall.

"It has been a pleasure, Lady Liana Monroe. The best ball I've attended by far. Should we ever meet like this again, you may call me, Damien." He took her hand and lifted it to his lips, leaving her breathless from his comment and kiss. She clamped her teeth together as a shiver ran down her spine. "Good evening, Lady Monroe."

"It's Liana," she said unexpectedly. "I mean, you may call me, Liana."

"Good evening, Liana," he said, his kingly mask already back in place.

A good evening indeed.

Chapter Five

L ady Monroe and her daughters were ecstatic during the carriage ride home. Pride filled her that each daughter found potential matches. Liana feigned happiness for her mother's sake and to not drag anyone else down with her. All she could think about though was her secret and unexpected meeting with the king.

She found it odd to think that the infamous, ruthless vampire king had sought her out. Or perhaps he didn't seek her out but merely stumbled upon her hidden spot. Highly doubtful with the multiple times he caught her staring. Nevertheless, he found her and stayed. Even insisted on shunning formalities and spoke as normal people. He made her laugh. He made her speak out of turn and even though she instantly regretted it, he seemed amused.

Perhaps that's all she was to him, amusement. But the way he spoke to her and allowed her to speak freely… It felt wonderful. They would never speak again most likely, but at least she had the memories. Memories of a stolen moment with a powerful man that let his guard down just a bit. Memories of his handsome smile and husky laugh. She dared not think of him beyond that though lest she convince herself that she favored him. That would never be possible anyway. Liana, the town's pariah courted by the king. What a ridiculous notion. Liana shoved the fluttering of her heart away and focused on Keeper Olivier.

The next morning brought with it much excitement as formal invitations for courting arrived. Custom had the men sending letters of intention to the female they favored. Each of the Monroe daughters received at least one. Charlotte received a maddeningly large number of letters. Six to be exact. Hannah received three. And surprisingly, Liana received two. The letter from Keeper Olivier was no surprise. It was the one from Beta Mooncliff that brought with it a shouting match to surpass all others before.

"No!" Lady Monroe shouted when she read the letter from the shifter while they gathered in the drawing room. "This is an outrage. I will not allow this! No shifter will be courting my daughter."

"Mama, he was a nice man. He holds the second highest rank in his pack. He is a good match," Liana argued.

"Good match?" she screeched incredulously. "He is a shifter. You are a mage!"

"There are no laws preventing our marriage, only social stigma."

"It is not just social stigma. Shifters are wild and dangerous. Their culture is vastly different."

"Ladies! Please, stop yelling!" Lord Monroe interrupted, screaming as well.

"They turn into animals, Mother. That does not make them wild and uncultured. They are human just as we are. Mostly," she added as an afterthought. Charlotte sprawled on the sofa reading and re-reading her letters with a goofy grin on her face. Hannah rolled her eyes at her mother and sister. The two always fought like this, both so opinionated.

"Isn't Mooncliff a wolf shifter?" Wesley interjected. No one responded to him.

"You have no idea what they are like, Liana. You don't know what you would be agreeing to. I forbid it!"

"I know perfectly well what I will be agreeing to. I will be agreeing to a kind man that sees beyond social status to find a partner he is most compatible with." That's all Liana could ever ask for. A partner in life. Someone that would be her friend and possibly a lover if they were so lucky. She gave up on that dream years ago. Perhaps she could dream again.

"Liana, please, don't do this. It will bring ruin upon our family. Think of your sisters. They still need to make their matches."

"Oh, Mother. You are far too dramatic. This will not ruin our family. My sisters have plenty of suitors anyway. They will shackle one down one way or another."

"Don't be disrespectful, Liana," Lord Monroe cautioned as he reclined on the sofa with his youngest daughter and middle son, Carlisle.

"I've heard stories about them, Liana. They are… they are rough with their women."

Carlisle snickered. "I heard the shifters breed in their animal forms under a full moon," he sneered before howling like a wolf. Lord Monroe reached around to smack Carlisle upside the head. Lady Monroe gasped, nearly fainting while young William asked,

"What does 'breed' mean?"

This set Hannah and Charlotte to giggling while Liana helped her mother to a chair. "This is ridiculous, all of you. It was merely an intention of courtship, not a marriage proposal. That doesn't mean he will propose and even if he does, I'm sure he will be a gentleman and understand that I am a mage not a shifter. There will be no breeding under full moons. Well, if that's their culture maybe, but certainly no animal bits involved."

The boys planted their hands over their ears faking sick while Lord Monroe jumped off the couch in an outrage. "Daughter, don't speak of such things in front of me again. I cannot allow any man to marry you if I think of such things." He shuddered before forging ahead. Liana shrugged. It was nature. It was how babies were born. "Enough of this arguing. If Liana wants to accept the courtship, that is her choice."

"Excuse me!" the butler, Henry, shouted to the room. Everyone spun around and froze. Henry stood red-faced and agitated by the doorway. "I've been trying to get your attention. You have a guest," he said but this guest needed no introduction. The family dropped into bows and curtsies at once. "King Ashwood is here to see you," Henry said unhelpfully.

"Thank you for the introduction, Henry," King Ashwood said with a sly grin, leaning against the door frame beside the embarrassed butler.

Dressed in simple cream-colored riding pants and a black tunic he looked like a normal male, not a king. Although, one could never call Damien a normal male with the overwhelming confidence radiating off him or the way the collar of his tunic expertly fell open to reveal tanned skin. Or perhaps it was that sinister smirk and expertly raised brow that had him standing apart from the rest. Liana bit her lip when she noticed his long locks had been pulled back into a knot at the crown of his head. Last night his black hair hung straight down to his shoulders as was the current style, however, she much preferred this rugged look. It didn't escape her notice either that he no longer wore the ostentatious crown of the Ashwood line.

"Your Highness, what do we owe the honor of your presence?" Lord Monroe asked, still in a bow, his head nearly touching the floor. Liana watched the king closely as he pushed off the wall, his movements lazy and unhurried.

"Rise, everyone. As you were," he instructed then chuckled. "Well, perhaps no arguing but please, relax." Henry offered him the best cushioned seat in the room. Only after the king sat did everyone else. Liana's face would be permanently red from the total embarrassment she'd never forget. "As entertaining as it would have been to let you go on, I have come with a purpose." The king pulled a letter from his pocket and handed it to Lord Monroe. "I have come to make my intentions clear. I intend to court your daughter, Liana."

Lady Monroe swooned and no one bothered to move from their own shock to aid her. She lay safely on the couch anyway.

Liana looked at him in surprise. Icy blue eyes stared back brazenly. A courtship. She couldn't believe it.

"What an honor, Your Highness," Lord Monroe managed to say as he opened the letter. Lady Monroe shot up in her seat, resurrected with wide eyes.

"Is it true? Do you truly wish to court Liana, Your Highness?"

"I do, Lady Monroe."

"Oh, what an honor, Your Highness. An absolute honor. We will gladly accept," she said greedily. Liana crossed her arms and glared at her mother. "How wonderful and unexpected. I didn't even realize you knew of our little family, Your Highness."

"I met your daughter last night. We had a pleasant conversation."

Mary looked to her daughter. "A conversation? When? Did you have a chaperone?"

"We did, Lady Monroe. I assure you nothing untoward occurred. Your husband and my guard were both present."

Both daughter and wife gave Michael surprised looks. "He asked me to chaperone discreetly."

"You heard everything?" Liana accused.

"Don't use that tone with me, young lady," her father replied.

"The better question is why are you so mortified? What did you and the king talk about?" Carlisle teased. Liana glared daggers at her little brother.

"Well, then. I will say again how honored we are that you will consider our daughter to be your wife, Your Highness."

Liana harrumphed; her arms still crossed. King Ashwood raised a questioning brow at her. "Is there something you would like to add, Lady Liana?"

"No not at all, Your Highness. I just find it very odd that my mother is so keen to accept your proposal. I mean, you are a vampire after all. We can't have our courtship ruining our good family name as mage."

Her mother elbowed her hard in the ribs. King Ashwood looked down to hide a smile. "Please forgive my daughter. She can be a bit stubborn when she is passionate about something."

"I shall count myself lucky then that she has passions about something other than fashion and gossip." A surge of pride filled Liana at the compliment. For once, her bold views were something to be praised, not ridiculed. "I must take my leave. It has been an unexpected pleasure visiting your home, Lord Monroe. I look forward to the coming weeks." The family bowed to the king.

"Is someone going to tell me what breeding is now?" young William asked at the most improper moment. Liana found it to be the perfect moment however and snorted as she tried to confine her humor. Holding her hand over her mouth, Liana's shoulders shook with laughter while Carlisle fell back on the couch laughing outright.

"Unexpected indeed," the king reiterated with a smirk before leaving.

As soon as he was out the door, the hysterics started again.

"How could you all embarrass me like that?" Lady Monroe wailed. "Gods above! The king must think me an awful mother with such misbehaving children."

"That is not true, my dear," Lord Monroe said in a half-hearted attempt to calm her.

"Everyone to your rooms, right now!" Lady Monroe declared, sending her children fleeing. "Not you, Liana." Reluctantly, Liana turned back around, the sound of her siblings' retreating footsteps mocking her.

"How could you not tell me that you met with the king? I am your mother," she declared, aghast.

"He found me, mother. I had nothing to do with it."

"Found you? Where were you?"

"I was just sitting in an alcove of windows."

"Oh gods!" Lady Monroe cried. "My daughter, hiding in an alcove. What he must think of us."

"It is fine, Mary. He seemed enamored by Liana. He sought me out before he even said hello to her. He must have watched her and waited for a private moment away from prying eyes. You know how people like to talk."

Mary nodded. "You're right. He wanted privacy. What did they talk about?"

"Mother," Liana complained.

"I didn't hear everything, but I can tell you he is intrigued. Who wouldn't be? You've raised such wonderful and unique children, my love." Lord Monroe captured Mary in a hug.

"I did. I did raise wonderful children," she repeated. Michael waved at his daughter to escape while she was distracted. The man loved his wife, but she was a handful to be sure.

Liana ran up the stairs to her bedroom and locked the door so her siblings wouldn't barge in to berate her for details about last night. She jumped onto her bed and sighed.

She wasn't sure what to think of the king's proposal. On one hand she adamantly opposed all things related to marriage because it meant the end of her limited freedom and privacy to perform magic. On the other hand, she enjoyed the king's presence, as impossible as that seemed to her.

Her head fell to the side, and she found a bouquet of flowers waiting on her nightstand. A vibrant bouquet of white lilies and bold blue irises were artfully placed in a simple glass vase. Their fresh aroma filled her room as if they'd been freshly picked minutes ago. She grabbed the card and read the elegant script.

May the statue forever keep our secrets.

Damien

Surprised at herself, she smiled like a fool at his words. She was not the romantic type or the one to swoon over simple words.

"I thought you would appreciate the colors." She startled at the sound of his deep voice. She looked over her shoulder to find the king standing just inside the doors to her balcony and gasped. Liana scooted off the bed as gracefully as possible in her gown and gave him a quick curtsy.

"Your Highness, what are you doing here?"

He took a few more steps into the room, knee-high riding boots making his legs appear even longer. "I wished to speak to you. I found myself thinking of you all night after you departed."

She blushed. She had thought of him all night as well. However, she wouldn't admit it, especially not to the powerful king. Glancing around, she noticed yet again that they were without a chaperone. "We should not be alone in my bedroom."

"No one will discover us," he declared. He took a few more steps toward her then took her hands in his. Gentle fingers tipped her chin up so she would look him in the eyes. She wasn't sure she was even breathing with him so near. "You have enchanted me, Liana. I needed to see you again. I need to know you better."

Liana didn't know what to say to that. She could hardly believe he was here right now. "So, you sent a letter of intention for courting me? I would have said yes to afternoon tea."

He chuckled, his smile quick and easy, such a contrast to the stern look he wore most of the ball. One hand cupped her cheek and his thumb brushed over her soft skin. "You bewitched me so thoroughly I had no other option."

Liana blinked. Was the king truly confessing his feelings to her? Perhaps she was dreaming. That must be it. She lay on her bed after finding the flowers and fell asleep. There could be no other explanation because no king would ever want her. Her family was not rich enough. They were not powerful enough. Despite her father being on the Council, they did not own vast estates across the country. The king would gain nothing from marrying her.

"I thought you said the ball was the last place you'd want to find your bride," she challenged.

"That was true, until last night." His hand drifted from her face down to her neck where his fingers caressed across her collarbone. Breathing became difficult as fire followed the line of his fingers.

"I am only a mage. You are a vampire," was all she could think to say.

"It doesn't matter. The moment our eyes locked I knew there was something different about you." Hearing those words was like a bucket of reality doused upon her. Different. She'd always been different. She was odd. All her life that's what she'd been told. They meant it as an insult yet here the king stood, appreciating those differences.

Taking a deep breath, she collected her nerves and stepped out of his hold. "We should not be alone in my bedroom," she repeated, keeping her voice even. King Ashwood stood before her again and took her hands.

"Tell me you accept my offer," he demanded softly as his thumbs brushed over the backs of her hands. She didn't dare get lost in those striking eyes again and instead observed their hands. His deep skin made her tanned skin look pale in comparison. His fingers were long and thin like an artist but marred by scars and callouses from fighting and holding a sword.

"My parents already accepted your offer," she said. She didn't get a say in the matter.

"I am asking you, Liana. Do you accept?" Lifting her head, she narrowed her eyes on him. The ruthless king did not act so harshly now. In fact, Liana would say he seemed quite vulnerable at the moment which was so at odds with how she imagined him, even after last night. He gave no indication that he was interested. On the contrary, he said he was not looking for a wife at all.

And although he asked her directly, she still did not have the option of denying him, the king of Triaedian. She could not say no. And despite the inevitability of it all, Liana found that she did not want to say no. King Ashwood intrigued her. She wanted to know more just as he claimed of her. And a courtship wasn't a definitive marriage proposal. They could at least get to know each other.

"Why me?" she asked, curiosity outweighing reason.

"Because you are intelligent and witty, and you made me laugh."

She smirked. "For a king, you don't have high standards." He smiled back. Letting go of her hands, he wrapped his arms around her waist and pulled her into his body. Liana gasped at feeling his body against hers.

"You are also the prettiest female I've ever beheld."

She snorted. "And a terrible liar. Are you sure you're a king?" she teased.

His hand cupped her cheek again, his brows furrowed, and lips pursed. "I did not lie." A blush crept up her neck. "What is your answer?"

"I accept."

King Ashwood held her tighter. "You've made me very happy. Now, I must go before someone catches us. Until next time, Liana," he said, then bent as if to kiss her. She froze, not knowing what else to do. She'd never been kissed, nor was she allowed to. But the king did not kiss her. Instead, his head dipped into the curve of her neck where he brushed his nose along her throat. Liana's head tilted back of its own accord as her eyes fell closed. That burning in her core scorched her with a vengeance.

"You smell wondrous, my little mage," he breathed against her skin which had her biting her lip. When his lips pressed against the pulse in her neck, a noise escaped Liana she'd never made before, one full of longing.

The king chuckled darkly as he stood to his full height. "I am certainly going to enjoy this, Lady Liana," he said as her eyelids fluttered open. He smirked down at her then he was gone. Liana stumbled onto her bed at the sudden loss of his support. He moved with vampiric speed, faster than she could track, and exited through the balcony doors.

Falling onto the mattress, Liana's fingers went to her neck, the feel of his lips lingering. Her heart pounded fiercely as she wondered just how much trouble she'd gotten herself into. This was the king. He wanted her. And despite all her protests against society and marriage, she wanted him.

There was no denying the butterflies in her stomach. Liana Monroe, was, for the first time in her life, smitten.

Chapter Six

D ressed in their modest and pristine worship gowns, the ladies of the Monroe family trailed behind the men in their equally garish suits. As with all things high society, even the proper fashion to attend worship was dictated by the top trendsetters. Although they deemed the finest fabrics and jewels the only attire worthy of the gods, no consideration of the gods went into the decisions at all.

If the gods truly cared about the attire, they'd all likely be dressed in simple fabrics with modest designs while all the finery and jewels were offered in worship to them. As it were, Liana wore a gown of sky-blue satin that covered her from her chin to her toes. She hated the gown despite the beauty of it. The collar sat too high on her neck, as did the bow tying the collar together, giving her the feeling as if she were being strangled. Tight sleeves cuffed at her wrists making it unbearably hot while the endless layers of fabric added to the burden weighing her down.

Liana truly did love the look of the gown. Loved how the designer created lapels of the blue fabric that created a V-shape toward her waist with elaborate embroidery along the edges in shimmering silver thread. Loved the ivory ruffles cascading from her neckline and the way the scalloped edges of the gown flowed downward from the right side of her waist across the front. She still hated how uncomfortable it made her.

Phillipa knew not to tie the corset too tight, but it still irritated Liana. And after convincing her maid to reduce the volume of the petticoats beneath, it was far easier to walk in. Which is why she didn't stumble while walking to the temple.

The temple for high society members sat in the middle of the city. A monument to the many gods, the structure boasted three arched entrances to its domed cathedral on the west, north and south sides. To the east stood a wall of stained glass that lit up with the rising sun to worship the many gods.

A dais stood proudly in the center of the circular place of worship, wooden benches surrounding it. Along the perimeter of the room, grand statues of each of the gods watched over them. Taller than any other building in the city, it was said to have taken one-hundred years for the church to be constructed and the statues carved. The domed ceiling glinted with dark gold trim and intricately painted scenes from, *The Book of Worship.*

Although the species shared a temple, their services were held separately. The vampires were first, followed by the mage. The shifters performed their rituals and worship during the evening hours for which the temple would be open only to them.

The Monroe family took their usual seats near the front in the fourth row while everyone bustled in. Liana sat with her hands neatly in her lap as she tuned into the conversations around her. News spread fast, and everyone gossiped about how the king finally decided to court a lady. Liana kept her head down even as a secret smile played on her lips.

The king had chosen her.

All of yesterday she spent floating on a cloud. After the king left her, she couldn't stop smiling and for the first time, she understood how Charlotte and Hannah felt. Understood why they yearned so badly to find a match. They wanted to feel this too.

Although she'd given up hope on marrying for love, she still dreamed of it. Dreamed that she would one day find it and live happily ever after. Liana wouldn't call it love just yet, but she was surely attracted to the man and the way he made her feel so special. As much as she rebelled against all things expected of her as a woman, she hated to admit that it thrilled her to know that she caught the eye of the king. The thought of actually marrying him horrified her still, but it certainly boosted her ego.

The last thing she wanted was to be a willing pawn in the game of men and if she were to marry the king, she would be the ultimate pawn. There was no greater position that would put her on the board as a piece to be used. At least as a simple Keeper's wife she would be inconspicuous. She'd be able to hide from most gossip and social climbing. As queen though, it would be the only thing she'd be a part of. She'd rather take her chances as a spinster than endure that.

Then again, Liana felt comfortable in his presence. She also liked the look of him, and the mysteriousness of him intrigued her. What little interaction they had she could only discern that he liked to shun formalities as much as she did. If that were the case, perhaps she could learn to live with the man. That was, if he decided to eventually propose, which was highly unlikely. It would be far better for her safety if he didn't. Not only did she hate the public eye, but the fear of anyone discovering her magic overshadowed any fear of retribution if she turned him down.

"But did you hear about the other two?" a female whispered none too quietly. Liana's interest perked. The temple was always a fantastic place for the ladies to gossip.

"What other two?" another female asked.

"He sent letters of courtship to three females, not just Liana Monroe."

The woman gasped. "Who?"

"A vampire and a shifter. Both from Sapphire Cove!"

"No!"

"Yes. Quite the competition those girls are in for," the woman said smugly. Liana clenched her teeth, her fists balled in her lap even as her chest squeezed with an uncomfortable tightness.

That lying, conniving bastard, Liana thought, her feelings of infatuation rapidly turning towards hate. He played her.

He said he wasn't looking for a wife at the ball. That he only decided to court her because he was too intrigued by her. He manipulated her. Each word and caress of his fingers expertly chosen to make her feel special, only to turn around and court two others. She felt betrayed not only by him but by herself. She knew better than to have believed a man. They were only ever after one thing, power. And she was full of it.

Terror struck her heart as she thought of the spell he'd witnessed her write into her skin. Perhaps he spoke to Master Kinley. Perhaps they now knew she had considerable magic and that's why he chose to court her.

How stupid and reckless she'd been by performing magic in such a public space. And then to carry on with the king during their conversation… She truly had been a fool. She'd let herself be swept up away by his openness, his false vulnerability. Scolding herself for being so naive as to believe he could truly be interested, she wondered if he had private conversations with the other females that night as well. Why choose her at all when he had other, far more suitable options?

Charlotte set a hand over Liana's fists. "Calm yourself, sister. The other courtships mean nothing."

Liana shook off her sister's hand. "I don't know what you mean. I am calm," she lied, then took a deep breath. Her magic was anything but calm. It surged in her veins, angered and vengeful. There was nothing to be done though. She could not spell the king and risk punishment.

"He is king, Liana. He had to choose many for courting. I'm surprised he didn't choose more. Don't be jealous."

Liana huffed. "I am not jealous. I would never be jealous. In fact, I don't want to marry the king, nor anyone else."

Charlotte's eyes darted around quickly before turning on her. "You cannot say that. You're in this now, sister. You must marry someone and with the king's attention you have little choice in the matter."

Much to Liana's dismay, Charlotte was right. If the king truly wanted to marry her, she would have little say. The only opinion that mattered was the king's and her father's. They would negotiate the terms of their marriage and she would simply arrive at the altar to say her vows.

Simmering, Liana barely listened to the priest as he led them in worship to their many gods. They started as usual with the god of earth, praising his name, followed by the god of the sun. There were many more gods that followed until the goddess of the moon was mentioned, the only goddess mentioned during weekly prayer. Even the female gods didn't receive respect from the male mage.

Liana didn't pay much attention anyway. Upset at herself for letting a man rile her so easily, she added that to the mental list she constructed on reasons why she could not marry King Ashwood; he was a manipulative liar and irritated the calm out of her. Most detrimental of all, he was king. She wanted to hide from society, not be put in the center-stage.

Any feelings of favor she held for the king vanished in light of her realizations. He may have intrigued her, may have seduced her, but that was all. She would not fall for him or his games.

The only divine information Liana gleaned from their day of worship were the names of the two other females the king offered courtships to. Ms. Yvonne, the vampire female, and daughter to the head of the vampire on the council in Sapphire Cove. Omega Willow was daughter to the Alpha panther and head shifter on the council in Sapphire Cove. It was no surprise that Liana also had a connection to the same city, her uncle, a Master mage and head council in Sapphire Cove, who unfortunately had only one son and no daughters.

To call it a coincidence would be idiotic. King Ashwood strategically chose the three girls. Sapphire Cove, a hub of international trade and directly on the coast, sat in the ideal position for a wealth of international trade. Being such an influential city, the king likely knew he needed to keep closer ties to it. Apparently, he thought there was no better way to keep people on his side other than marriage. If the rumors had it correct, the king also liked death threats. Liana wished he'd stuck with that modus operandi instead of dragging her into the running for who shall become his wife.

For now, she'd been entered into a higher stakes game where the men controlled her fate which is exactly what she'd sought to avoid.

***

Still fuming about the king's manipulation, Liana didn't sense anything amiss as they approached their home until Lord Monroe halted them all. Standing upon the stairs to the front door, Liana sensed with her magic that something was wrong inside their home. She couldn't pinpoint what it was, only that her magic sensed danger.

"Mary, take the children next door. Do not return until I retrieve you," Lord Monroe declared before shoving them all back out the front door. Only Wesley remained with their father.

Charlotte questioned their pale faced mother. "What is it?"

The older woman plastered a fake smile to her face. "Nothing, dears. You heard your father. Off we go." She shooed them onward. Liana let them go first because her magic twitched, yearning to be used, and when her magic felt like this, she listened. It hadn't steered her wrong yet. Sprinting up the stairs, she snuck inside, leaving the others to flee as they were told.

Liana held still at the door, taking in the scene. Henry lay unconscious in the foyer amidst broken furniture, her father and Wesley nowhere to be seen. She rushed to Henry's side, kneeling beside him. Magic poured out of her unbidden to inspect the man. When her magic latched onto the dangerously fractured base of his skull and the blood pooling there, Liana took a few steadying breaths to keep from panicking. This was a severe injury and one that would require great skill to heal. Normally, she would allow the trained mage healers to tend to Henry, but he didn't have much time. The blood accumulated quickly as she inspected him, his life fading with it.

Liana had no spells for this so she would have to make something up. As she rambled words to make a coherent spell, her magic lurched out of her control.

"Oh no! Not again," she pleaded. More often than she liked to admit, her magic lashed out on its own without any spells or directions from her. It had been harmless so far, aside from fraying her nerves, but she hoped it wouldn't cause more damage now as it poked and prodded at Henry's wound.

She felt the surge of energy as it worked to heal the man. First, it stopped the bleeding then it rid the skull of the blood. And finally, sealed the fractures. Henry moaned and rolled onto his side but did not wake fully. Liana pulled her magic back with a relieved breath and stood. He would be fine, thankfully.

As soon as she stood, her vision wavered, and she collapsed into the wall. Breathing heavily, Liana waited for the dizziness to pass. That magic took more out of her than usual but that wasn't surprising considering the severity of the injury.

Listening intently for any sounds of struggle, she stood slowly before stepping on silent feet toward the stairs. If she couldn't hear anyone down here, perhaps they were upstairs. Thoughts of doubt plagued her as fear threatened to drown her. She should have gone with her mother, but someone had broken into their home and nearly killed Henry. She wouldn't let them hurt her brother or father either.

She made it to the second floor which housed all their bedrooms. Glancing both ways, she didn't find her family, nor any sign of the intruder. Everything was in its place. She took a few carefully placed steps to avoid the particularly creaky floorboards and walked toward the back of the house.

Heart pounding out of her chest, Liana had the terrible thought that the intruder might not be a mage. If it were a vampire, there was no use being quiet. It would hear her heart beating from the front door. Not letting herself panic, she took quiet breaths and focused on avoiding the squeaky steps. She placed her hand on the door handle to the back balcony but did not open it yet. Through the curtains, she peeked outside. Nothing seemed amiss.

Not a single boot shuffling or creak of wood alerted her to anyone's presence right before she was shoved from behind. A jilted scream erupted from her as she was shoved into the doors, her hand pressing the handle and stumbled through.

Skin scraped and tore as she caught herself on her hands and knees, her back bumping into the iron railing. Before she could get her bearings, someone launched at her from the doorway. Liana curled into a protective ball just as her magic lashed out on its own. A shield formed around her, the person thudding into it with a sickening crunch.

Muffled cursing reached her ears, and she dared a glance up. A man in shabby black and brown clothes held his face, blood pouring between his fingers.

"I'm going to gut you for that!" he yelled, his eyes full of fire and vengeance. Liana scrambled to her feet, holding onto the iron railing as if it would save her. The man came at her again, a dagger leading the way. He went slower and when he reached her shield, the man mumbled a spell. The dagger burned with blazing red magic before he slammed it into her shield and sliced through it with ease.

Liana didn't know that spell, but if she survived, she would be learning it straight away. Backed into a corner, Liana glanced over the railing then back at her attacker who now smiled viciously, his crooked teeth stained with blood. She threw a stunning spell at him, but he was too quick and dodge out of the way.

Panic had her frozen to the spot as he advanced again. Although she studied defensive and offensive spells, there was a difference between practicing them and using them in a real fight. Never before had she been involved in combat, but for all her confidence and bravado, she found that she couldn't move from the fear plaguing her.

Footsteps pounded up the stairs, relief making her knees wobble. Someone was coming for her. Two men ran onto the balcony, both equally dressed in black and brown tatters. Relief morphed into dread. They weren't here to help.

"We have to go! They are coming back!" one of them shouted to their comrade. Both panted heavily. "We led them through the city but lost them a while back. They will be here any second. We have to go!" he urged, pulling on the man's shirt when he wouldn't move.

Her attacker didn't care. His eyes stayed locked on her own. "A girl shouldn't be using spells like that," he growled. Her magic surged, protecting her as she could not do so for herself. The shield molded to her body because he was that close when he drove the blade into her stomach. It bounced off the shield uselessly, the blow still physical as her power wavered beneath the force.

The man muttered his breaking spell again, the dagger lighting up with a red glow. Liana gripped the iron railing. She could not fight her way out of this. Her only options were to flee or somehow hit him with a spell.

Her decision was made for her as his dagger sliced through her shield and right into her belly. Liana screamed from the pain, her entire abdomen burning as pain radiated outward.

Sensing her pain and fear, her magic flared hot and fast, an explosion of power erupting from her. The force of her magic blew the three attackers away and pushed her against the railing. Another scream tore from her throat as she slipped over, hurtling toward the ground.

It was not a far drop so it likely wouldn't kill her. It would hurt though.

Chapter Seven

Her scream cut off as her body jolted against something that was far more forgiving than the bricks below. She peeled her eyes open to find a woman she did not recognize. The stunning female held Liana effortlessly before settling her into one of the patio chairs.

A braid of shimmering blonde kept her hair out of her sharply framed face while wide, sapphire eyes and lush lips gave her a more feminine appeal. The oddest thing about her, aside from the excessive strength, was her outfit. Dressed in black trousers and a black blouse, she looked like a man.

"Who are you?" Liana questioned through gritted teeth. The wound from the dagger still burned fiercely.

"Sasha, your guardian," she said in a clipped tone.

"Guardian? Who sent you?" The woman turned to look up at the balcony and that was when she saw it. A patch on her left arm with the king's crest. The king sent someone to guard her. Or perhaps she was a spy for him. Maybe both. Either way, Liana didn't appreciate her presence because it meant the king thought he had the right to intervene in her life.

Although, the woman did just save her from a lot of pain, possibly death, so perhaps her presence was welcomed in this one instance.

The woman moved faster than Liana could track as she leaped onto the balcony. She disappeared from view followed by manly grunts and groans.

"Liana! Liana!" her father yelled, running through the house. Red faced with sweat dripping from his matted hair, he scurried down the patio stairs and to her side. Leaning over her with one hand on the chair, the other on his chest, he gasped for breath. Wesley followed closely and was far less winded.

"Gods, Liana. What happened? We heard you scream," Wesley explained.

She lifted her hand away from the wound which was steadily bleeding.

"Oh gods! Fetch the healer! Wesley, go!" Lord Monroe shoved his son toward the house, but she stopped him.

"Wait! I can fix this myself," she declared.

"Don't be a fool, Liana. You cannot heal yourself," Lord Monroe spat angrily.

Jaw clenched, Liana held her hand over the wound. Glaring into his eyes, she recited the spell. "Magic of the gods, I call upon thee to heal. Find thy wound, make me not feel. Knit the skin together, make a good seal." Her hand burned bright white for a moment before the pain disappeared. She inspected the hole in her dress to find scarred flesh.

"You shouldn't know that spell, Liana," her father scolded. She brushed him off and stood. The vampire female was back. She stood a respectful distance away with her hands behind her back.

"The perpetrators are unconscious and tied up on the balcony," she informed with a slight bow of the head toward Lord Monroe. "I have already sent word to the king about the attack."

"I can deal with this on my own," Lord Monroe declared then turned to Wesley. "Go to Master Ranville. Tell him about the attack and that we have prisoners." He grabbed Wesley by the arm before he could race away. "And don't mention anything about your sister, do you understand me, Son?"

Wesley nodded, his lips pulled into a thin line at the severity in his father's tone before rushing off. Lord Monroe was a stern but gentle man with his children so to see him so aggressive was disconcerting.

Lord Monroe released him and turned on the vampire. "And not a word about her involvement either. No one must know of her magic."

"I only take orders from the king," she replied coolly.

"And he orders you to forget everything you saw here today," a low, steady voice commanded, joining the group which had Sasha's head bowing once more. Liana turned to find the king striding out of the house, Wesley trudging behind him. He stalked straight to Liana, those glacial eyes roving over her body multiple times, and each time getting stuck on the bloody rip in her dress. He stopped inches away from her which had her taking an instinctive step back. "Are you okay?" he asked quietly.

Staring up into his genuinely concerned face had all thoughts fleeing from her mind. She merely nodded. It was the truth, mostly. She could use a nap and a hefty plate of food, otherwise, she was fine.

Intense blue eyes stared into her emerald ones for another moment before she watched his entire face transform. Gone were the furrowed brows and clenched jaw. All that remained of King Ashwood was anger as he turned to the others.

"I will take the prisoners to be interrogated. More guards will be sent until the nature of this attack can be determined."

"Your Highness, these men attacked my home. I have a right to interrogate them myself."

"They attacked my subjects, and I protect my subjects. I will handle the investigation," King Ashwood declared. "We keep this quiet. If anyone asks, it was a simple break-in. Not even Master Ranville will know of this."

Lord Monroe rubbed a hand over his bearded jaw, his eyes briefly flicking toward Liana. "Do you think they came after my daughter because of you, Your Highness? Or is this an attack on a council member?" Liana's curiosity peaked. Why would they come after her because of the king? They certainly weren't engaged so why would anyone care about her relation to him? Who would attack a council member either? She hadn't heard of any unrest in the city.

"It is too soon to tell." He looked around, taking in the scene then up toward the balcony. "What happened?"

Lord Monroe started. "When we returned from worship, I found our butler unconscious in the foyer. I sent the ladies next door as we chased the culprits out of the house. We lost them soon after and returned, then we heard Liana scream."

The king turned to her. "Why were you in the house?"

Under that powerful gaze she didn't quite feel like answering at all. In fact, she wanted to ignore the manipulative king and go take that nap. "I believe your guard can fill you in. I'm rather tired after this ordeal and would like to retire to my bedroom."

What was he doing there anyway? Liana was no one special, nor did she warrant a visit from the king after an attack like this. As her father said, he should be the one to deal with the perpetrators.

He raised a curious brow. "It will take but a moment to relay your tale. Tell us what happened," he pushed. Gone was the male that spoke hushed, romantic words to her in her bedroom, words of beauty and hopeful promises. Standing before her was the man she thought him to be, the ruthless king of Triaedian.

"Liana," Lord Monroe prompted when she still didn't answer. Keeping her eyes on her father, she gave them a brief synopsis of what happened, brushing over the parts where she used magic. The king did not need to know how powerful she was.

"I told you to go next door. Why don't you ever listen, Liana? You would have been safe there," Lord Monroe complained.

It was a good thing she had returned, or else Henry would probably not be alive. Nor would they have caught the attackers. If the king and his lackey weren't standing there, she would have argued her point. As it were, she kept her mouth shut.

King Ashwood glanced toward the guard and Liana's eyes followed. The female gave one short shake of the head and Liana felt those eyes snap back to her. "You are leaving something out," he declared confidently. "How did you defend yourself against the males?"

Liana crossed her arms. She knew he was searching for information. If the vampire was nearby, she would have seen it all anyway. He already knew she could perform magic beyond the normal female, so she told him honestly, "A shield. I only used a shield to defend myself."

"How were you stabbed then?"

"A shield breaking spell, obviously," she retorted. A wave of dizziness swept over her, threatening to force her to rest after using so much magic. Locking her knees and gritting her teeth, she stayed upright.

Her father nudged her with an elbow. "Be polite," he whispered angrily. Again, the king looked to Sasha who shook her head.

"Out with it then. What did she do?" he asked in exasperation.

The female kept her head up and spine straight as she told her side of the events which was far more detailed than Liana would have liked, especially in regard to the magic performed. Especially when she recounted how she first stopped to heal Henry.

Sasha glanced nervously at Liana then at the king. She cleared her throat. "Then," she paused, shifting on her feet. "Then her entire body glowed a bright gold before blasting everyone, including herself, backward. I caught her before she could hit the ground."

All eyes were on her.

In defense of herself, and attempting to get the attention off her magic, she accused the guard, "Why didn't you step in sooner if you were watching me from the start?"

"I was given explicit instructions not to interfere or show myself unless you were in immediate danger," Sasha answered.

Liana glared at the king before landing back on her guard. "And the man with a knife attacking me wasn't enough danger for you to step in?"

The guard didn't show an ounce of remorse. "You protected yourself with magic. I didn't need to step in."

"Liana, is all this true?" Lord Monroe questioned, his surprise at how truly powerful she was lingering.

She shook her head, causing the dizziness to return full force. Reaching out a hand to steady herself, she found only the king's arm. She gripped it tightly, taking deep breaths but the dizziness did not abate.

"I did nothing," she denied. Her other hand reached out and clutched his arm, the only thing keeping her from completely collapsing.

"What's wrong?" he asked softly, gripping her arms as she closed her eyes to lessen the dizziness. That made it ten times worse though and her wobbly knees finally gave out. Strong arms lifted her off the ground before her knees could hit.

"Liana?" her father called worriedly as a hand cupped her forehead. His familiar magic soothed her a little before pulling out. "Likely shock and magic depletion. She used too much. All she needs is rest and she'll be fine," he explained.

"I will get her settled," King Ashwood declared to which no one argued, not even her father. If Liana could have protested, she would have. As it were, her head lolled against the king.

"What shall I do with the two bodies, Sir?" the guard asked.

Liana picked her head up off his shoulder for a moment to look at the guard. "Two? There were three men on the balcony with me."

The king cursed. "Get the others to help. Track him down and take the prisoners to my dungeon." Before Liana could argue about being carried, she found herself lashed in the face with wind, then it was gone just as abruptly, and she was in her bedroom. The king laid her on the small bed and remained sitting beside her.

"How did you even know which is my bedroom yesterday?" she snapped then rolled onto her side.

"I followed your scent to it," he explained calmly, his voice deep and soothing.

"Are you sure your spy didn't tell you?"

"She's not a spy. I sent her as extra protection."

She wanted to throttle him. Throttle him and every other man that ever underestimated her. "I can protect myself without your help."

He hummed, not quite believing her. "You seem rather angry with me, Lady Liana," he commented.

"How could I not?" she scoffed. Only his deep, even breathing filled the room for long moments.

"I am at a loss. What have I done to deserve your malice aside from protecting you?"

Liana opened her mouth to berate him but held off. This was the king she was talking to. A king that now sat beside her on the bed.

They had a few stolen, private moments together and she was acting as if he professed love to her when in fact, he had been manipulating her. He seduced her and she let herself dream of something more as she so often did. Always with her head in the clouds, her mother said. This time she was on the verge of not returning her feet solidly to the earth if she didn't temper her attitude toward the king.

She had loved their secret rendezvous behind the statue and when he came to her room. It made her feel special. Made her feel like he liked her simply for being Liana and nothing more. Then the letters came, and she knew she was just a pawn, just as she always would be in this world made by men.

Liana curled away from the king. "I apologize, Your Highness. I am shaken by the ordeal and did not mean to speak to you so harshly."

"That does not answer my question as to what I've done to irk you."

She bit her tongue. This was not the man to challenge for her independence. He was the monarch of their entire kingdom. He didn't care for her feelings, nor did he care what she wanted. All he wanted was an advantageous marriage.

"Nothing, Your Highness. I am grateful you assigned a guard to me, or I would be in a lot more pain currently." She would have healed herself perfectly well, but he didn't need to know that. He already knew too much about her magic.

"Will you not even look at me, Liana?" he questioned softly, his voice a beautiful cadence she wanted to play on the piano over and over again, which made her hate him all the more. Everything he did was a seduction, a manipulation, to get her to do as he pleased.

"I am very tired, Your Highness. And we should not be alone in my bedroom."

"You are correct, Lady Liana." He slowly stood. "I wish you a speedy recovery."

After she heard his quiet steps retreat, and the soft click of her door, Liana buried her face in her pillow. Sleep called to her drained body, but her mind reeled. And it wasn't stuck on the attack that landed a dagger in her belly. It was stuck on the handsome king and his machinations. She hated him for intriguing her. Hated him for getting the better of her. She knew better than to think a man thought of her as more than a piece to barter for. The king played for power and somehow, she ended up as a pawn on his board.

Chapter Eight

Liana took a short nap and refueled with a large plate of food at supper before joining her mother and sisters for the rest of the day's worship activities. While the men went into her father's workshop to complete their worship, the women gathered in the solarium, not one of her sisters or mother questioning what happened that morning. Her father fed them a story of a simple break-in, nothing more.

The moon was not quite full this evening, nor had it crested to its full height, so a few candles lit the dark space. Windows surrounded them on all sides which gave a perfect view of the gardens during the day. The four females sat around the iron table in much simpler tea gowns while a silver tray rested before them. A small cauldron sat in the center while small vials and dishes of herbs and liquids surrounded it.

"Alright, my girls, tonight we shall worship the gods as usual with additional prayers to the goddesses now that courting season is upon us. Let us begin," Lady Monroe said and held her hands out. They performed these extra rituals commonly on certain worship days of the year. Usually, they would worship a single goddess on each worship day, but with the courting season upon them, it was custom to pay homage to them all.

Charlotte sat to their mother's right and held her hand, slipping her other into Liana's, who followed with Hannah. Once the youngest sister completed the circle, the women began to recite the prayers of the many gods.

The prayer catered to all gods, worshiping their greatness and offering themselves as servants. Worship at the temple already went through detailed prayers to each of the gods, starting with Jupiter, the king of gods. The mage worshiped him most of all, the god that gave them life and the power of magic. Next came Neptune as they'd prayed for calm seas and swift currents to aid their trading businesses. A long list of gods followed for one reason or another, which is why they did not worship them individually during their private practice.

Tonight, the ladies focused on the goddesses. Lady Monroe began the night by whispering a spell to set a flame within the cauldron.

"Goddess Juno, mighty queen of the gods, accept our offerings of this goat's blood and these lilies. We pray for your divine blessing for favorable and fruitful marriages." Liana and Charlotte used their clasped hands to pour the cup of goat's blood over the flame. As soon as the liquid touched the flames it sizzled, the scent of iron filling the room. When the lilies burned, the flame flared higher than the cauldron's rim.

"Praise Goddess Juno," the girls prayed. "Bless us with favorable and fruitful marriages."

"Goddess Venus, we pray to your generous soul for your blessings upon my daughters. We offer this crown of myrtle and wine so that you may find them a proper love match this season," Lady Monroe intoned, while Liana and Hannah reached with their connected hands and lifted the small crown of white flowers into the burning flame.

"Praise Goddess Venus," the girls chanted as one. "Bless us with love."

"Goddess Fortuna, we offer this wreath of narcissus flowers and a goat's horn." Lady Monroe and Hannah dropped both over the flames, all of it turning to ashes within seconds in the magical flame. "We pray for your good fortune in securing their husbands, and to bless my daughters with fertility."

"Praise Goddess Fortuna. Bless us with good fortune and fertility."

"Goddess Luna, we humbly sacrifice our blood to you, and offer our finest wine. Grace my daughters with fertile cycles." Lady Monroe and Charlotte tipped a mug of their combined blood into the cauldron. They all still bled from the wounds on their right palms beneath the makeshift bandages they hastily wrapped it with. The flame flashed a deep red and held for a few seconds, the largest Liana had ever seen their flame get during these worship rituals, and it certainly never turned a wine-colored red. Hannah's hand tightened on her own, surprised by the change.

"Praise Goddess Luna. Bless us with fertile cycles," the girls intoned once more. Then together, with their mother, they said, "Gods bless us all."

"Did you see the flame?" Lady Monroe questioned, bouncing out of her seat. Hannah and Charlotte dropped their hands. "We must build altars to the goddesses, girls. They have answered our prayers, which is why the flame changed color," her mother raved. "We must start tonight. Charlotte, go to the cellar. We need more wine. Hannah, fetch your lady's maid and gather bushels of myrtle and narcissus flowers. Liana, you'll need to go to the butcher. Get as many goat's horns as they'll allow, and the blood."

The girls scampered off at their mother's bidding while Liana remained seated.

"Mother, the butcher is closed on worship day, and it is already late in the evening."

Lady Monroe glanced at the darkened windows. "See if our chef has either of those. If not, we shall wait for tomorrow."

Reluctantly, Liana dragged herself toward the kitchen where Charlotte already carried two bottles of their finest wine. The last thing Liana wanted to do was help with these altars. Not only did she not want to waste her time, but she most certainly did not want to hasten her chances of being sold off to a man for marriage. She'd pray to the gods with every breath she took if it meant living a peaceful life alone with her magic. If Lady Monroe had any say in it though, or held any sway with her incessant prayers, Liana was doomed.

****

Their chef did not have any goat's blood or horns last night which is why Liana now walked toward the market district to buy some. Phillipa trailed one step behind her, while Sasha stayed four steps behind Phillipa. Liana didn't enjoy the guard's presence even if it made her feel safer. She didn't like that the king could interfere in her life already and they weren't even engaged.

Ignoring the female, Liana didn't directly go to the butcher. That would be her last stop of many this morning. She had a long list of things to deliver to others that took precedence.

Liana stopped first at a bakery owned by a mated pair of shifters. The older couple ran the business for over thirty years and had always been so kind to her. The moment she walked in Helen gave her a warm smile. Walking out from behind the counter, the greying fox shifter pulled her into a hug.

"Congratulations, dear," Helen said, squeezing her tightly. "We couldn't believe the news when we heard. Courted by the king," she said on a whistle. "You couldn't do any better."

Liana blushed, glancing at Sasha who stayed silent by the door, her eyes fixed forward as if she weren't paying attention. She knew the vampire could hear everything though.

"Thank you, Helen. It was quite unexpected."

"Just remember us once you are queen. We still want to see you."

Liana huffed. "There is no chance he will pick me, Helen. You've seen Lady Yvonne. That vampire is the intelligent choice."

Helen wrapped an arm around her shoulders and pulled her to the back of the store. Walking behind the counter, she said, "Nonsense, Liana. You are the only choice. With your talents, selflessness, kindness and beauty, there is no other option." Liana shook her head in denial. They paused as Helen declared to Sasha, "You're not allowed back here."

The blonde vampire stood her ground. "I am Lady Monroe's guard. Where she goes, I go."

"She is among friends here. You wait out there, she is in no danger."

"I take my orders from the king. I am to never take my eyes from her," Sasha persisted.

Liana rolled her eyes. "You can hear just fine. Please, wait out in the shop."

Sasha shook her head. "I am duty bound. I cannot disobey orders."

With a heavy sigh, Liana looked toward Helen. "If it's not too much trouble, Helen, let her in. Or we can sit in the shop."

A frown marred her friend's brow. "It's your choice, Liana. We can do this another time." In private is what she meant.

"I'm already here." Helen led her through to the kitchen which was at least ten degrees hotter than the shop. Helen's mate, Bacchus, kneaded a ball of dough on the long wooden counter, his apron already covered in flour and a fresh batch of bread baking in the hot stove filled the room with its delicious aroma.

"There's our girl," Bacchus chimed, a smile lighting up his face when he saw them. "Liana, Phillipa, how are you lovely ladies?" He always was quite the charmer. It was part of the pull for his customers, he made them feel appreciated and welcomed with no effort at all.

"Very well, thank you," Liana replied, quickly followed by Phillipa's similar answer.

"You two have a seat, I'll bring us biscuits," Helen offered. While the two took their usual seats at a small, round table in the back corner of the kitchen, Sasha hovered nearby.

"Who's the vamp?" Bacchus asked. No malice edged his words, only curiosity.

"My new guard," Liana answered.

"Ah, right. Engaged to the king now. Suppose you would have a guard."

"We are not engaged, Bacchus. He merely sent a letter of intention for courting."

He smiled, the deep laugh lines around his mouth and eyes standing out all the more. "Yes, but anyone that meets our Liana cannot deny her anything." Liana rolled her eyes at the sappy shifter.

"Smother your own children with that nonsense, shifter," she quipped. Bacchus guffawed, slapping the ball of dough.

"He has a point, Liana," Helen commented as she returned with two plates. Each carried a small cup of tea and a biscuit. She didn't comment on their thoughts. Before they went any further, Liana conjured a shield to block the vampire from hearing them.

"I've got a shield up. Just a warning before I make it opaque." Helen nodded. Phillipa needed no warning as she was so used to her charge's frequent magic use. Once her shield turned a pure white so that no one could see in, Liana summoned a small burlap bag. Glass clinked as she set it on the table gently.

"I have to ask you a favor, Helen," Liana started.

"Anything, Liana," the woman offered without hesitation.

"With my new guard, I cannot easily deliver all these orders without the king learning of what I do. Would you be able to deliver these? They come from shifters, and I left a list of the orders in the bag. Each vial or jar is labeled appropriately." Liana spent all of the previous evening finishing the orders and creating the list knowing that she would not be able to deliver them herself today.

"Of course, sweetheart." Helen looked inside the bag. "What of payment? Who has paid already?"

"Do not worry yourself about that. Just please get them delivered soon. Today if you can."

Helen glared at her. "Liana, you must charge something. You don't have to charge a lot but at least for the cost of supplies."

She sipped at her tea and picked at the biscuit.

"She is right, Liana. Your father is noticing that his supplies dwindle too quickly," Phillipa pointed out. "At least with the money you can buy your own supplies."

"Sometimes I charge. Sometimes they don't have any money."

Helen sighed. "Gods bless you child; you have a heart of pure gold. Of the ones that I know can afford it, I'll make sure they pay. As for the rest, you be careful. We don't want you getting into trouble for this," she warned.

"Thank you, Helen. But I'll be fine." Her father would never harm her. He might punish her in some way if he discovered what she'd been doing all these years, but he'd never physically harm her. "Hide that bag behind the leg of the table until we are gone." Helen hid the bag then Liana released the shield. No one startled at the vampire that hovered just beyond, her face thunderous.

Arms crossed, she glared down at Liana. "You can't shield yourself from me."

Liana stood, putting herself nose to nose with the fierce soldier. Raising a brow, she challenged, "And how are you going to stop me?" The blonde had no answer to that. Stepping around her, Liana led the way out. She still had more errands to run.

On an early morning such as this, many people were not out yet which served her well. Liana walked three doors down to the fabric and thread shop.

Claudius didn't bother glancing up as the door opened, the needlework in his hands far too enticing. "Welcome. If you need any fabric cut, ask me before you touch, thank you, kindly."

Liana laughed at the lackluster greeting. "I don't think I can shop here after that pathetic greeting." Finally, his head snapped up. A smile filled his thin, angular face while dark brown eyes lit with humor.

"Well, if I'd known it was you, I'd have put on more of a show," he lied. He stood to embrace her. "Congratulations on the engagement. You are all anyone is talking about these days."

Liana sighed. "We are not engaged. And when are they not talking about me?"

"Fair point." He pulled away. "I have some gossip for you though." Claudius led her over to a display table of small strips of fabric that were used for decorative hats. Sasha and Phillipa stayed near the checkout counter. "Mrs. Florence came in yesterday near to closing time in a tizzy. She ranted about a certain vampire female needing new gowns for her engagement."

Mrs. Florence was Sancta Valles's most skilled dressmaker, who all the elite females went to for their gowns. "If you're talking about Lady Yvonne, I do not care in the slightest." Liana spoke the truth. She didn't care what that female did, nor did she care that she vied for the same man because Liana had no intention of pursuing the king.

Claudius gave her a pointed look. "If you say so, my dear. Now, come look at this new shipment that just arrived from Chimerion. They sent this blue silk so vibrant I don't think I've ever seen another color like it." He pulled a pair of clean satin gloves from his pockets, donning them before touching the brilliant fabric.

Liana gaped at the color that reminded her so much of the crystal blue waters in Sapphire Cove. "This is stunning."

"It would look stunning on you with that dark hair," he said, tempting her.

Dresses were the last thing she needed more of, but this fabric made her want another. "It is far too much, Claudius. I have too many gowns as it is."

Claudius huffed. "A female in high-society can never have too many dresses. I will hold the fabric for a few hours. Bring your mother back and I can guarantee she will buy this for you."

"Maybe," she acquiesced. She truly had no need for more dresses. Lowering her voice, she glanced back at her guard. Sasha stared directly at her, her gaze sometimes darting out the shop window. Liana turned her back to the guard and erected a sound shield. "The vampire cannot hear us for now. I've brought your order, and a few others. I cannot deliver them. I need you to do that for me. Everything is in the bag." She removed the spell and turned to look at a table. A small, wooden chest sat open, fabric artfully draped on or around it.

"What is in here?" she questioned, sticking her hand into the chest. It was not very deep but enough to hide the bag of vials and jars that she summoned directly into it.

"Just some thread," Claudius said, lying as he saw the bag.

"Thank you for the early look, Claudius. I shall return later with my mother." Claudius gave her arm a squeeze in farewell before Liana led Phillipa and Sasha to one more place. This one would be far trickier to hide but she couldn't figure a way around it. She had to visit. It had already been two weeks since she'd been there last. If the ball that marked the beginning of the courting season hadn't gotten in the way, she would have been there sooner.

The only problem with her visit today happened to be the female vampire trailing her.

Chapter Nine

One street over and a few doors down, Liana veered toward the next shop.

"Lady Monroe," Sasha called, rushing to step in front of her. "Do you know what this shop is? Who it is catered to?"

"I know very well what this place is, Sasha. You have no need to worry." An idea perked in her mind. "In fact, you should take a moment to yourself while we are here." Liana pushed past the vampire and entered into the private establishment. As the day got later, more people were out, and this shop was far busier than the previous two.

Tables scattered about the room were filled with patrons enjoying an early morning cup of tea with another mug close by. The scent of fresh bread filled her nose as the warmth inside chased away the morning dew clinging to her skin.

Sasha stepped close, their shoulders brushing as some of the patrons eyed them. A woman stepped out from the back with a tray full of mugs and bread. Her eyes caught on Liana.

"Ah, there you are, girl. Give me a moment," she called, then set down the tray onto a nearby table. As she served the guests, Sasha leaned down to whisper in Liana's ear.

"What are we doing here?"

Liana narrowed her eyes on the vampire. While the others could hear, she would not be saying a word. "Come with me," the server said and led them through an archway toward the back of the shop. They stepped into a smaller room lined with simple chairs, each with an even smaller table. A few people sat scattered about, other vampire servants flitting around.

The majority of those sitting looked a bit worse off with tattered clothes and dirty faces. There were a few that were freshly washed with decent clothing, as was the nature of establishments like this. Blood cafes provided vampires with the much-needed sustenance of blood. The donors were paid well for offering their blood which is often how some survived.

They were led through the shop and up a set of stairs in the back. The first level above the shop held a modest living room. The room was large but sparsely furnished. Scattered about were mismatched sofas and mattresses. Some hid lumps beneath, the vamps still asleep.

One more level up is where Liana's true destination lay. "He's waiting for you," the younger vampire said, gesturing to the attic living space.

"Thank you," Liana said. A nervous glance at Sasha showed that she inspected the new area intently. Liana erected a sound shield and slipped the server a bag of her creations as with the other bags. "Deliver these, please," she said quickly, also shoving a few coins into the female's hand, then dropped the shield and stepped in front of the woman so she could escape before Sasha looked their way.

"Liana, is that you?" a deep voice called, his voice hard to pinpoint in the empty, echoing room. Sasha stepped in front of her.

"Show yourself," the guard demanded. Darkness consumed the room which had the guard on high alert. With a wave of her hand, Liana lit the candles she spread about the room so she could see during her visits. Flames ignited which illuminated the empty attic except for a bed, a private bathing space, and a tea table. Beside the table rested two cellos in simple stands.

"It is me, Felix. I've brought Phillipa too." Liana walked to the table where he sat with a mug of blood and a scone.

Felix scented the air. "There is someone new with you."

Liana took the seat beside the straight-backed, unwavering Felix and placed her hand atop his. "Against my will, I've been given a guard by the king."

The male smirked. "You've become the talk of the city, my dear. It is all my students talk about."

Phillipa took the seat opposite her and patted Felix's other hand. "Gods bless, friend," Phillipa said.

"Same to you, my dearest Phillipa," Felix reciprocated, turning his hand over to clasp Phillipa's. The older vampire had a soft spot for her lady's maid that warmed Liana's heart.

"Do they not talk about the other two? I am only one of the ladies the king is courting," Liana complained.

Felix chuckled. "They mentioned the others, but everyone is more interested in you. They all want to know about the mage I teach."

"I hope you're telling them a bunch of lies," Liana teased. She grabbed one of the cellos and rested it on the floor between her legs, shoving the cumbersome fabric of her dress out of the way.

"Of course. I told them you are a humble, kind, and selfless mage that would make the most perfect wife."

Liana grinned wickedly. "Excellent."

"Oh hush, you two. Liana is exactly all those things," Phillipa scolded. "Well, except for the wife bit." That set them all to chuckling.

Felix stood and held onto the back of Liana's chair, guiding himself to pick up the other cello. Carefully, he sat back down. "There is another seat, guard," Felix said to Sasha.

"I will stand," Sasha declined. Felix halted and sniffed again.

"Is that you, Sasha?"

The woman actually cracked the hint of a smile. "It is, Felix. It is good to see you again, old friend."

"I wish I could say the same," he jested, to which she chuckled.

"I'd wondered where you'd gone, after... after the attack."

Felix sighed. "King Ashwood rewarded me generously for my loyalty and offered to keep me in the army, but I had no desire to go through that again. Cassia needed a parent as well. I'd always loved the cello, so here I am. Thanks to Liana, of course. She started the business for me and brought me more students than I could handle."

Liana swatted at the man's arm. "I did not."

"You did. You dragged my sorry ass out of that alley and gave me purpose again. If my daughter were here, she'd agree." He laughed to himself. "I wish I still had my eyes in that moment because I can only imagine how ludicrous it must have been to see a ten-year-old mage girl dragging a drunken vampire and his cello through the alley and into this shop. She forced a few cups of blood down my sorry gullet and demanded that I teach her to play."

Liana shrugged. "Even drunk you were the best cellist I'd ever heard, and I wanted to learn."

Felix gripped her shoulder. "She saved both my life and Cassia's life that day." Liana studied the cello in her hands to avoid the praise. "The previous owner of this shop couldn't keep up with the demand, so with the money the king gave me, I bought it. Cassia and I moved in, and the girls helped me cope without my sight. Somehow, Liana urged more people to donate blood here and even found me more students. Our business has been thriving since."

"A ten-year old girl did all that?" Sasha asked incredulously.

Liana shrugged again. "I knew a lot of people that could use the money." Before she met Felix, she already snuck about the city using her magic wherever she could, which usually meant using it on people that needed it but could not afford the exorbitant prices mage usually charged. No one cared about her age or that she was female during those moments of desperation, and she always kept her face concealed to hide her true identity. Even that young, the thought of anyone discovering her sent terror racing through her veins. It wasn't enough to deter her from helping though. The people needed her more than the fear that consumed her. The need to perform magic constantly and learn as much as she could also far outweighed her fear of discovery.

As Felix reclaimed his seat, Liana noticed the new eye patches he wore. Desperate to change the topic from herself, she commented, "That is an impressive eye mask. Who made that?" The one he wore was new, and far more intimidating than what she was used to seeing on the man. The large vampire already intimated most he met with broad shoulders and soldier-like precise movements; he didn't need to add to his persona. Black cotton formed the new eye-mask which formed into points below each eye. Maroon thread lined the mask and shimmered in the candlelight.

"My lovely Phillipa made it for me," Felix answered, offering a smile to where her lady's maid sat. Liana smirked at the blushing maid. She hadn't realized how much they favored each other, although Felix always made it a point to dote on Phillipa while she accompanied Liana.

"Well, it looks fierce. It suits you well."

Felix gave Liana a bow of his head. "And I thank you, Lady Liana. Now, no more wasting time. We must practice." The pair started playing their cellos, a delicate melody filling the room. Liana had been studying the cello for nine years, ever since she met Felix, and her skill with the instrument grew each time she played.

They played song after song which pulled some of the vampires from their slumber below. They gathered around, sitting on the floor while the pair played. Sasha moved closer, standing behind Liana now. Once they were done, the room erupted in applause.

Liana set her cello back in the stand. "Thank you, as always, Felix." She turned her attention to the others. "Alright, who is up first?" They formed a line within a second pulling a laugh from her.

The first vampire offered up a pair of shoes that needed mending. The second requested an elixir to heal tooth pain. A third needed noise blocking earmuffs because she couldn't sleep with all the noise of the streets below.

"Gods bless you, Liana," the fourth and final vampire greeted, carrying a baby in her arms. Liana reached for the child while the woman plopped into the chair with her heavily pregnant belly.

"He's growing so quickly," Liana commented.

"He is going to be just as big as his father," Cassia said with a heavy sigh. "Just like this one, I'm afraid." She smoothed a hand over her belly.

Liana bounced the toddler with his adorable golden curls that matched his mothers on her knee. He smiled, giggling.

Phillipa reached over and did the same. "I sense she is healthy and strong."

"Thank you, Phillipa. Although, my father thinks we are having another boy."

"I said, I wanted another boy, not that it was," Felix defended.

"Yes, well, I threatened Marc that if it is another boy, he has to change all the nappies. He has been praying to the gods nonstop for a girl."

Liana laughed. "You should still make him change the nappies."

Cassia smiled fondly. "He does. Marc is a good father. He is a good husband."

Liana looked away from the woman's dreamy look. It felt private and she didn't want to intrude. It also made her heart clench in pain. That kind of love, that is what she wanted for herself. There wouldn't be a choice though. The king chose her and until he made a final choice between the three of them, there was nothing else for her to do except to accept her fate.

"Anyway, Dad, I brought more blankets and coats. Make sure they get passed out evenly among the others downstairs. They'll need them in a few months when fall rolls in. Ms. Pontius said she'll bring a few baskets of food leftover from the shop this evening. She'll bring whatever is on the verge of spoiling."

"Thank you, Cassia. I'll make sure everyone gets their fair share."

Liana set the toddler on the floor as he squirmed. "Light! Light!" he demanded, still unable to pronounce S's. Liana held her palm out and made a spark of golden light shoot from it. The toddler squealed and clapped his hands. Liana kept the light show going, varying the different colors.

"Do you have everything you need for the baby?" Phillipa questioned.

"We are set, thank you. We have a lot from when Constans was a baby."

Liana led the child running around the room chasing her magic while they chatted.

Sasha stiffened beside her just as Felix stood to his feet. "Something terrible has happened," Felix stated before he rushed around her chair toward the stairs. Liana grabbed the child and handed him to Phillipa.

"Stay with them," she urged the maid as she followed Felix downstairs. A group of men and women carried in two injured people, most of them worse for the wear as well. Sasha stayed at her back.

"What happened?" Felix questioned as the injured people were set on the floor. Liana sensed a mixture of people, shifter, mage and vampire alike. She went to the more seriously injured first.

The male mage bled out from a deep gash through his belly. When she lifted the cloth, Liana barely refrained from gagging at the organs that hung out of the wound.

"We were attacked. They came out of nowhere. We only had time to flee," a female answered.

"They burned down our home," a male growled. The shifter in him rode close to the surface, and if he shifted in here, they would all be in danger from his rage.

"Can you heal that wound?" Felix asked Liana.

"I can try." Aside from Henry's severe injury, Liana had not healed something so fatal. Her usual customers held only small wounds. Placing her hands on either side of the wound, she pushed her magic into the man's body. Not exactly sure how to heal such a large wound, Liana begged her magic to take over again. It responded easily, focusing all its strength on the wound.

"Why did they attack?" Felix questioned while Liana worked.

"We don't know. We were not doing anything."

"Someone must have discovered us," the shifter growled again. Liana didn't understand what they were talking about.

"How? I thought the house had been spelled?"

Liana panted as her magic worked quickly to seal the wound layer by layer, her magic doing most of the work as she did not know much of how to exactly heal this.

"It was. We don't know. The only explanation was that someone talked or was followed."

"Everyone can stay here for now. Do you think anyone followed you here?" Felix worried.

"No. They were too busy burning our home, and our mage shielded us."

Liana sat back on her heels with her magic receding from the healed male. She turned around to inspect the female shifter. "What happened to her?" The female lay unconscious, no obvious injuries.

"Hit with a spell," a random voice answered. Liana surged her magic into the woman, begging for help again. The shifter sprung awake, her eyes darting around wildly. Someone pulled her into a hug.

"They should both be fine," Liana said to no one in particular. When she stood, she ignored the dizziness and walked to Sasha. "Can you get Phillipa? We need to leave." The vampire nodded, surprisingly not giving any resistance to the request as it would require the guard to lose sight of Liana. Felix followed her. Liana reached for his hand as he searched for her. "I will leave a protective shield around these upper floors so that no one can scent or hear you all up here."

"That is generous of you, Liana. But we cannot afford to repay you for such a strenuous spell." Phillipa hurried to her, Sasha close on her heels. Liana leaned into the woman's support.

"You never have to worry about payment, Felix. Will you tell me who they are?"

He sighed and scrubbed a hand through his short hair. "They are a family. A family of shifters, mage, and vampires that chose to live together. Someone must have discovered them."

"Why were they hiding?"

"You know this world, Liana. People are judgmental and unfair. There are some that don't support intermingling of the species."

Liana's jaw dropped in disgust. "So, they burn their homes? Who would do such a thing?"

The vampire's lips pursed. "The same ones that took my eyes. The same ones that seek to destroy our kingdom." Liana stared at him in shock.

"What do you mean? You said you lost your eyes protecting the king."

He nodded his head. "I was on guard duty for the king travelling to Sapphire Cove when our convoy was attacked. They captured me and tortured me and took my eyes as punishment for supporting the king."

"Who?" she urged.

"The Separatists." Liana paused at Felix's words. She hadn't heard that name before. "They seek to destroy our unified kingdom. They think the races should live apart from each other."

"I've never heard of them before."

Phillipa wrapped an arm around her shoulders. "They don't teach the histories to the mage females, but I remember them. Their numbers grew about thirty years ago and posed a serious threat. They started a civil war that, gods bless us, ended very quickly under the rule of our previous king."

"So, they have returned?"

"Not necessarily. There are still those individuals that despise the mix of races. It could have been anyone to discover my friends' home." Felix patted her hand. "Don't you worry about it, Liana. You've done enough for everyone here. Get home safely and forget about this," Felix urged. There was no chance she'd forget any of this.

"We shall take our leave now. Stay safe, Felix." She squeezed the man's hand in farewell then hurried down the stairs. Halfway, she turned in the hidden stairwell and worked the spell to hide their presence. Phillipa supported her weak legs as they walked out the back door.

Forcing herself to stay strong, Liana only made it to the end of the alley before collapsing into a wall.

"What's wrong?" Sasha demanded.

"She's used too much magic again," Phillipa said, her tongue clucking in reprimand. "I told you not to do this to yourself, Liana."

Her eyes rolled as she tried to stay conscious. "I had to help," she said in a breathy whisper.

"Sasha, I need you to carry her home, discreetly. I still need to get the goat supplies or Lady Monroe will ask questions. I'll meet you in her bedroom. She just needs food and some rest."

Sasha nodded then picked the female up. "This may be disorienting," she warned before they moved faster than Liana could track. When she opened her eyes again, Sasha lowered her onto her bed.

"I will bring food." The vampire returned in the matter of a minute with linen full of bread and cheese. Liana forced herself to sit up and eat as the guard stood by.

"You do not have to watch me. I will be fine." Sasha made no move to leave. "You can't tell the king about any of this," she rushed to inform the guard.

Sasha raised a curious brow as she sat at the edge of her bed. "Why is that?"

"Because they are good people. They are innocent people. He doesn't need to know about them."

"I trained Felix. I know he is an honorable man. As for the others…"

"They are innocent," Liana urged.

"How would you know? You've never met them before."

"If Felix trusts them, so do I."

Sasha didn't look moved by her sentiment. "What if they are a part of the Separatists? What if they lied to you?"

Liana hadn't considered that. They couldn't be though. Separatists wouldn't be in a group like that, the species mixed together. "Like I said, I trust Felix. Those people have been through enough. They don't need the king harassing them as well."

Sasha shifted, lifting one bent leg to rest it on her bed. "What do you think the king would do with such information?"

Liana paused. What would he do? She didn't have a clue. "The king is a mystery. There is no telling what would happen."

"But he is a fair and just king. Or do you not think so?" Sasha questioned, fishing for a reaction. Liana couldn't very well insult the king to one of his guards.

"No matter what I think, we both know that if the king discovers them, he will question them at minimum. They don't deserve to be put under scrutiny simply because they chose to live as Triaedian wishes us to. They chose their family of mixed species, and they shouldn't be punished for it again."

Sasha stared at her unblinkingly. "And what of your magic? Am I to keep it a secret that you are perhaps the strongest female mage in history with far more knowledge than you should have?"

Liana's eyes widened in fear as her heart stopped in her chest. Of the magic that remained, it surged forth to protect her. "You can't. You can't tell anyone of my magic. Please. No one must know." She grabbed desperately for the vampire. Sasha moved quickly out of the way. "Please, Sasha, no one can know."

"You are the greatest threat to the king, in my eyes. Not that family. You are the one that is harboring powerful magic. No female should be able to perform the magic you've done."

Tears formed in her eyes from the sheer terror plaguing her. "I'm no threat. Please, Sasha. Oh gods," she cursed, her breathing coming too fast and tears pouring over. Magic surged in her veins as her skin lit from within. Something niggled in the back of her mind, something familiar yet far away. It made her cry harder. "Please, he'll hurt me again."

Sasha froze. "Who?"

Liana sobbed into her hands. "I'm not a threat. I'm no one. I promise. Stop hurting me, please."

"I'm not doing anything."

Liana curled into a ball just as Phillipa burst into the room. She took one look at Liana and rushed to her. Gathering the glowing girl into her arms, Phillipa rocked and soothed her.

"It's okay, Liana. I'm here, sweetie. You are safe." The next thing she knew, Liana blacked out.

Chapter Ten

L iana woke with a start, then startled again at the vampire that stood by the patio doors.

"Sasha? What happened?" she questioned, confused. Her head throbbed in pain.

"Phillipa had to render you unconscious. You were hysterical."

Liana barely remembered that. "The last thing I remember is asking you to keep those people a secret." Sasha nodded.

"And I will. As I will also keep your magic a secret."

Liana's brows rose into her hairline. "Pardon me, I don't believe I heard you correctly." Had she heard correctly? The obedient vampire would keep a secret from her king.

"Phillipa explained some things. I will keep your secrets for now."

She would have to speak to her lady's maid to discover how she managed such a feat. "I am grateful, however, what do you get in return?"

"Nothing, Lady Monroe. Now, you've slept through the previous day, and you have an event to get ready for. I will alert Phillipa that you are awake."

The guard disappeared in a flash leaving her confused and wary. What happened that could convince that stubborn soldier to relent? Phillipa was the only one that would give her answers.

Unfortunately, she didn't get to ask any since all the girls prepared for their next outing in Charlotte's room again. To continue the courting festivities, the king hosted an afternoon tea for all the couples at the castle. Against her will, and at her mother's insistence, Liana donned a lilac-colored dress that was far better suited to her tastes with lighter fabric and less ornamentation than the prior night's ball gown.

Her father and brother kept their word about keeping the attack on their home a secret. They didn't even tell Lady Monroe of Liana's involvement or else they would have had to deal with her hysterics. Surprisingly, the city never learned of the attack either, the rumor mills not catching wind of it.

She wondered if the attacks were connected as well. It seemed coincidental that her home had been attacked just after her engagement to the king, then one day later, a family of mixed species were attacked as well. Perhaps the Separatists were back.

Liana did notice the extra guards around the perimeter of the house which would follow any of her family that ventured beyond it. Which is why there were four mage guards hovering around the Monroe family for the day's outing. Liana didn't spy Sasha and guessed that she finally took a break from watching her all the time.

Liana questioned her father about the attack and the potential threat on their family, but he wouldn't speak to her about it. If only he knew how skilled she was with defensive spells perhaps he would have. Or perhaps if he knew of her talent, he'd allow her to know certain things and defend the family. That was not a lady's place though, nor did it help her case that she was stabbed during her defensive maneuvers, so she dutifully walked through the castle to the vast garden in the back.

All around the garden, tables and chairs and picnic blankets with cushions were set about. The Monroe's secured two tables and a blanket nearby one another for each of their daughters. Michael and Mary sat with Carlisle and William between the three daughters. Wesley had gone off to court his own ladies.

Liana's first guest, Keeper Olivier, reluctantly joined her on the blanket. Lady Monroe tried to insist that Liana take one of the tables in anticipation for the king, but she refused. Liana much preferred the ground to those uncomfortable iron chairs. Plus, she could feel the magic in the earth better while on the ground and her thick soled shoes weren't in the way. Not to mention she didn't want the conniving king to be comfortable either.

Keep Olivier was a rather boring first guest and as soon as he left, Beta Mooncliff took his spot.

"I must say, I am surprised you accepted my courtship," he said after formal greetings were exchanged. He snacked on the bread and cheese and Liana helped herself as well, adding wine to her consumption.

"I was pleasantly surprised you offered," she countered.

His smile came easily. His entire demeanor of nonchalance and effortless confidence seemed to be rather easy for the male. "You made a lasting impression on me, Lady Monroe. I was even more surprised to hear you attracted the king's attention. He hasn't ever looked for a wife during these courting seasons."

She ignored that comment. The king was toying with her, and she wouldn't stand for it. "Tell me about yourself, Beta Mooncliff. What do you enjoy for hobbies?"

"Please, call me, Evan. As for hobbies, I don't have many. When I'm not by my Alpha's side, I like to run as my wolf or cook."

"You cook?" she asked in surprise.

"I know it's not customary for someone of rank to do such a chore, but shifters enjoy food and the preparation of it. We see it as an honor to feed our loved ones."

"Oh, that sounds sweet. What kind of dishes do you make?"

"Anything and everything. I do not bake though. I am a horrid baker."

She chuckled at his self-deprecating tone. "That makes two of us. The chef tried to teach me to bake a pastry. I made bricks worthy of our home's foundation rather than flaky dough."

Evan threw his head back with laughter. "You are a witty female, Liana. I enjoy that."

"And you laugh at my jokes, Evan. I enjoy that."

He smiled again. "What about you? What kind of hobbies do you enjoy?"

If she were to tell him the truth, she'd tell him of the magic she practiced daily or the many magical orders she supplied. Those secrets were best left unsaid though. "Seeing as I have no job to keep me busy, I enjoy many things. The piano is my favorite and reading of course. I enjoy gardening as well. Sometimes I even like to paint."

"What sort of paintings?"

"Nothing presentable. I mainly just like to put color onto the canvas."

"Oh, so no people or landscapes?" He popped a grape into his mouth then reclined on his hands.

"No. I'm not a very good artist. I've never been able to create the images I see. My people end up looking terrifying, hence why I only color the canvas."

"Do you hang your work around your home?"

Liana laughed outright. "Gods, no. Mother would have a fit if I ruined her perfect artwork by putting up my own."

"If no one sees them, isn't it a bit of a waste then?"

Her brows furrowed. "No. I enjoy doing it, so I do not find that wasteful."

He didn't say anything in response. "What types of things do you cook?"

"I don't cook. We have a chef."

"Not at all?" he asked aghast. She shook her head. Things were quickly taking a turn for the worse in her opinion considering he acted rather affronted by her habits. "All shifters know how to cook. I thought mage females were trained in cooking."

"No, my family has a chef," she repeated. "I'd be open to learning though. I am a quick study and find that I work very well with my hands. Aside from the baking, of course. And drawing," she added reluctantly.

He nodded, seemingly disappointed. "What about your magic? You must be able to do some incredible things with it. I've seen a few rare things from others."

"The females are not taught much magic. That is reserved for the males."

"I've heard they are given a better education, which is awful. Our females run just as freely as our males do." Liana barely refrained from scowling. There was no need for him to boast over something he already knew she lacked. Freedom was her only desire, something she envied the female shifters for.

"What magic can you do?" he asked.

So much. She could do so much, and none of which she could tell him. "Housekeeping things. Summoning water for the wash or mopping. Flattening clothes of wrinkles. Dusting, sweeping and cleaning windows. Repair clothing and such."

"Is that all? No defensive or offensive spells? No healing spells?"

She knew plenty. "No," she answered crisply, getting the feeling that this courtship was going nowhere quickly.

"How do they expect you to protect yourself or your children if you do not know basic magic?"

"What is there to protect them from?" she asked just as angrily even though she was in complete agreement.

"From anything. A burglar, disease, wound rot. I could go on."

"How do you suppose shifters and vampires do it without magic?" she countered, her irritation growing quickly.

"We protect them with our fighting and strength and call upon mage healers when there is need of magic. It seems wasteful to have mothers that cannot heal their own children."

She did her very best to keep calm, an effort worthy of applause truly. What she couldn't understand was how the kind and open-minded male at the ball turned into the judgmental ass in front of her.

"If you have a problem with my education, you may take it up with the mage council."

He shook his head. "I don't think I understood how different we really were. What kind of wife would you be? Would you even be able to provide for me like a shifter wife could? Is there anything special you can offer?"

Liana couldn't believe the nerve of this male accusing her of not being worthy. Forget composure, she needed to set this bigot straight. "How dare you accuse me of being insufficient when you do not even know me. I will make an excellent wife. I will keep my house as is expected and protect any children that I may have with my life. The real question is what do you have to offer me? Because I can find any man to provide a house and sire me children. Gods know there are plenty of horny men around here. So, what makes you so special? Why should I waste my life taking care of someone that so easily judges a culture they do not fully understand and makes a woman feel less than valuable when she has done the best she can under the suppression of ignorant men like yourself?"

Someone took her shoulders in hand from behind before she could climb to her feet and pummel the guy. "I think that is all for today, Beta Mooncliff. I believe this courtship is over," her father said sternly to the male who merely looked confused.

As he walked away, Lord Monroe rubbed Liana's arms up and down.

"What did he say?" he asked, not entirely sure he wanted to know. As soon as he heard Liana's voice rise enough for him to hear clearly, he knew there was trouble.

"He accused me of being unworthy, of not being good enough for him like a shifter wife. He asked what made me so special, Papa. That fool has no idea who I am or what I am capable of." Her father didn't quite know either considering she kept most of her magic a secret.

"I know, sweetheart. Do not let him ruin your day any further. You still have one more suitor to meet with."

Liana didn't hear his words over her own rage. "He even acted like it was my fault that this misogynistic society intentionally stunted my magic training. As if there was something wrong with me that I couldn't do anything more than mundane house chores."

"It's okay, Liana. You know who you are. You know your worth and so do I. Don't let him take that away from you. You should also not be saying such things allowed. Now, buck up. Your last suitor is walking this way." He gave her another hug. "And sweetie, if I hear you mention one more sexual thing, you're grounded until marriage. Young ladies should not have such knowledge, nor should they ever speak of it. And your poor Papa will most certainly die a tragic death of shock."

"Sorry, Papa," she said contritely. She did get rather improper with that one comment.

He patted her on the shoulder then walked back to his spot on the blanket with her mother. Liana took a calming breath. She was going to need to keep her temper in check far better for her next guest. And he walked toward her now.

"Lady Monroe," King Ashwood greeted with a slight bow of his head, that sparkling royal crown glinting in the sunlight. She dipped into a curtsy.

"Your Highness," she greeted politely even though her anger at him for his schemes remained and the rage she had toward the shifter still simmered. "Please, join me for afternoon tea," she said politely.

He sat upon the blanket looking relaxed in all black trousers and a blouse. He appeared rather casual again aside from his crown. An odd look for the king. She imagined him in another decorated coat similar to the one at the ball, but he seemed to favor the more discreet clothing. "I must say, I was highly entertained by your last suitor. I think he is still trying to digest the tongue lashing you gave him," the king said with a cocky smirk before biting into a sliver of cheese.

"You heard all that?" she asked incredulously. "Where were you?"

"A few hedges over. Vampires have excellent hearing," he commented as a way of explanation.

"Did you eavesdrop on my entire conversation then?"

That roguish smile didn't falter. "Of course. I wasn't going to let my competition have it that easy."

Her jaw dropped. "You listened the entire time? Even with Keeper Olivier?"

He nodded, completely unapologetic. "I must say, my chances are looking positively splendid right about now. One down, one to go," he said with a smirk. Liana did her best to pick up her jaw.

"This may be a game to you, Your Highness, but I assure you, I'm not interested in playing. Whatever schemes you have you may play them with your other two ladies. I will not be your pawn in a political scheme."

He chewed more slowly, his eyes narrowing on her. "Why do you say I'm playing games and scheming?"

"It is quite obvious that you planned this all along. Your courtships are with three very advantageous females that would help you maintain strict control of Sapphire Cove."

Those glacial eyes didn't move from hers as he sipped his wine. "You've got me all figured out then, don't you?"

She scoffed. "I would never presume to know you at all. A powerful man like yourself, especially one far older than me, is not one to anger or get involved with. I have no lofty ideas of becoming a queen and I have even fewer of becoming a pawn in whatever this next power move will be. Please, just leave me alone and focus on the other two women."

When he simply stared at her, those icy, depthless eyes giving away nothing, she feared she had gone too far. A smile filled his face but this one was not pleasant. It was sinister and terrifying. When he lay down on the blanket with his hands behind his head, she didn't know what to do.

"Lay down, Liana," he commanded. She hated that she told him to call her that the other night. Using her name seemed to give him more power. Reluctantly, she lay down. "Put up a privacy spell," he commanded. "No one can hear us, nor can they read our lips. Lay down."

"I don't…"

"Do not bother lying to me, mage. I know exactly what you are capable of, and it was all too easy to discover yesterday after just an hour of searching for answers. It seems that there are a great many people that are grateful to you for offering free services that a Master would normally charge exorbitant amounts for. You were right the other night; the people do love to talk about you."

She gulped, her eyes stinging from the bright sun. Or perhaps they were tears of fear. He knew. The king knew she was powerful. Even though Sasha kept her secret, she shouldn't have been surprised that he tracked down every move she made, even when she disguised herself and snuck out of the house. She'd been doing so for years. Ever since she discovered her talent with magic, she snuck away to the less fortunate parts of the city where she could use spells to help those that couldn't afford normal mage services. She did everything for them from healing spells to mending clothes, no task was too small. It helped her magic grow and it aided those that needed it the most.

But now the king knew of her power and skill. What did that mean for her though? She was terrified to find out.

"What do you want?" she said through gritted teeth after erecting the silencing spell so that no one, not even a vampire could hear them.

"Ah, there's a good girl," he said, a smile in his voice when she put the shield up. "I want you to be my wife," he declared outright.

Her heart skipped several beats.

Surely, she heard him incorrectly. Surely, he was joking. Surely, she'd lost her mind because there was no way that the king wanted her. No one even wanted her as their friend lest they also become the city's pariah.

"Why me?"

"Why not you?" he countered. "I believe I answered that question in your bedroom the other day as well," he reminded her. "You enchanted me." Liana's cheeks filled with shame as she remembered how easily he manipulated her, even kissed her neck.

"The vampire female is of your kind and far more valuable. Her father is the lead council of Sapphire Cove."

"I do not want the vampire female. I want you."

"Nobody wants me. I'm stubborn, rebellious, improper at the best of times and vulgar at the worst. I will not make a good wife nor a good queen."

"Ah, but that is precisely why I want you. You are everything that this society teaches against." She closed her eyes as horror drew the breath from her body. All her life she was different. All her life she was shunned for not being proper. In the end, she accepted herself if it meant she wouldn't have to marry. Here she was though, stuck to the worst of the worst. "I think you are exactly what I've been looking for."

"Looking for what?" she asked, her voice cracking from the tears. Magic sparked from her fingers as terror gripped her again.

"Do not cry, little mage, for I have a wonderful proposal for you. I will make you my bride and in return, you will become my queen."

"That was self-explanatory. Obviously, I would become queen," she remarked snidely. All pretense of decorum fled in the wake of her desperation. "What do you want from me as queen? Complete devotion to your oppressive, patriarchal society?"

He growled which had her tensing. "Aren't you being just as judgmental as the shifter about things you don't understand? Do not presume to know me or my plans."

Liana sat up and hugged her knees to her chest. The world felt like it was caving in on her. All the things she wanted for herself, for her future, gone in an instant. It took everything she had not to cry.

King Ashwood sat up beside her. "Your main role will be to serve as my secret, personal guard." That had her glancing at him in confusion. "I will get you the magical education you so desperately want and in return, you will guard me and my kingdom with that magic. It would be advantageous to have your support on certain matters, however that is of little consequence to me if you agree to that part or not. I have been king on my own for two decades and do not require your support."

After all she'd done to hide her power, in a few short days, the king had discovered her too easily. Now her worst fears were coming true. He was going to use her and her power. She should not have been so naïve, should not have been so forthcoming with him.

Magic surged through her veins urging her to run far away from all this. Panic threatened to steal all air from her lungs which made the world around her go fuzzy. Her chest refused to expand, her body tight with tension.

"You do not need to fear me, Liana," the king said. Out of the corner of her eye she caught the motion as he reached for her, and she flinched. A flash of pain had her recoiling despite the fact he didn't touch her. He growled again. "I would never hurt you, Liana." His voice was low and dangerous, but not aimed at her. "I will kill anyone that tries to hurt you," he declared.

Hugging her legs, she stared out at the garden. She had to calm down. That was nearly impossible with her magic battering at her skin to be let out to protect her.

"What has you so scared?" he asked. She did not completely know the answer to that question. The mere mention of anyone discovering the extent of her magic always sent her into a spiral of fear and the need to flee.

Liana scooted away from him and forced herself to breathe evenly.

"You saw my power at the ball. That's why you want me. That's why you are playing this charade of courting the three of us and finally decided on a wife… because of my power," she accused.

He shrugged, looking away from her as he reclined on his hands. "Partly. I did not lie that you intrigued me. Nor did I lie that I find you beautiful. Your magic was an added surprise and advantage."

She couldn't fault him for that explanation, if it were even the truth because he could very well be manipulating her once more. It still stung that he tried to manipulate her into this situation.

"That's it? You just want me to be your magical guard? What about other wifely duties? Children?"

He smirked cockily, a favorite expression of his she was beginning to realize. "Didn't your father tell you to keep such matters out of your mouth? It is improper for a woman to speak of sex. Do you want your father to die of shock?"

"Didn't you tell me to put up a privacy charm?" she mocked.

"Yes, but you clearly have no clue how to be obedient. As for children, I do not expect them from you or any woman. There is no guarantee that we are able to have children. I will not blame you for a lack of an heir. Your wifely duties will be whatever you want them to be. I am not aroused by unwilling women in my bed." She blushed furiously. "Surely you are not embarrassed by my talk when you so brazenly called out all the lonely, horny men in this garden that would gladly sire children upon you."

"I may have lost my temper a bit," she admitted through gritted teeth. He threw his head back with laughter.

"Lost…your…temper…a bit," he mimicked through laughter. "I have seen very few women speak their minds so openly and eloquently. But you, little mage, surpassed them all. You truly are a riot. I look forward to our future."

"I haven't agreed to anything," she said out of spite.

His amusement fled in a flash. "You would deny me?"

She bit her lip, looking away from his intense and terrifying gaze. "Do I have a choice?"

"I'd like to lie to you and say that you do, but no. I do not think I could let you go even if you asked."

"Then, no. I do not agree to this marriage," she said boldly, testing his theory. She had nothing to lose.

His face was stony, his eyes unreadable. "I cannot accept that answer. Even if you are to hate me forever, I will not let you go."

She buried her face into her knees. "Fine. Take my life. Do what you will with it. I always knew I would end up at the whims of a man."

"Do not sound so forlorn, my little mage. I will provide a good life for you." She didn't argue that their ideas of a good life varied greatly. "For now, we pretend that nothing has happened. I will continue to court all three of you until the time is right. Until then, pretend to be deeply infatuated." He kissed her hand courteously. Unfortunately for her, she still felt that shiver down her spine when his lips caressed her skin. "See you soon, my little mage. And behave," he warned.

"Never," she declared as an act of rebellion. The vicious vampire merely laughed as if she were an adorable puppy threatening to bite his hand off.

What had she gotten herself into?

Chapter Eleven

A storm rolled in during the late afternoon and hadn't lessened during the night. She spent most of the evening playing out her aggression on the piano, thoroughly angered by the king. She hated him for what he forced upon her, a marriage for power. She hated him because she couldn't get those soft lips out of her head either. He was a cruel man forcing her into this.

Thunder shook the house as Phillipa helped her out of her gown. It was a terrible night to leave the safety of her home. Liana had to go though. People were relying on her to show up and despite the fact that the king now knew of her secret activities thanks to his spies, she was going. After Phillipa bid her goodnight, Liana locked her door and donned her cloak over the trousers and shirt she stole from Carlisle's wardrobe, Liana snuck onto the balcony. She'd been lucky that her bedroom looked out over the backyard and afforded her some privacy as she snuck out weekly.

Sasha hadn't made an appearance since that morning, which was good for her sleuthing. With the new guards looming around, she had to plan for the moment the guard walked to the back perimeter of their property. She'd watched him a few times as he did this and there were a few moments when a large oak blocked his view of her bedroom. That's when she made her move.

Liana climbed over the iron balustrade while still hugging the side of the house and bent down. Gripping the slick railing, she braced herself as she lowered one foot at a time. Directly beneath her balcony sat the patio. It would not be a cushioned fall but there was no other way. Having done this a hundred times, she dangled as low as she could then let go of the railing and dropped. Her boots thudded on the stone. Luckily the rain covered the noise.

She sprinted around the side of the house, through the gate and down the sidewalk. No one was out tonight. Not with the rain coming down in sheets. Already soaked through, she didn't bother erecting a shield. It would have been worth it if she did it sooner. Even her hair was drenched despite the hood concealing her face.

Liana ran through the rain, down back alleys and side streets to get to her destination. She didn't mind the long journey to the edge of town which consisted mostly of slums, not when she knew how much these people needed her help.

The further she ran, the more she kept alert. This part of town didn't boast the best safety, nor did it claim to have the finest buildings. They couldn't even claim their buildings were intact. Liana cringed at their living conditions and hated herself for it. They couldn't help it. Most couldn't afford to eat, let alone pay for a sturdy home.

Keeping her eyes ahead and her magic on alert for any danger, she slinked down a narrow alley. Her vision altered to the low light with a spell she learned long ago. She kept her steps light as she avoided the filth lining the alley, even a man sleeping in the rain. Heart aching, she kneeled over him. Letting her magic inspect him first, she discovered the male to be middle-aged, riddled with disease, and not a threat in the slightest.

She shook him awake. "Hey, wake up," she declared, deepening her voice. Not many respected her when they thought her to be a woman, not even the homeless. "Come inside. Stay dry and I'll get you some food."

"Piss off!" he spat before curling into a ball. Sighing, she shook her head and stepped over him. At the end of the alley, sandwiched between the two buildings waited a single wooden door. Liana undid the lock with a spell and snuck inside. Warmth hit her cheeks soothing the chill the rain brought, quickly followed by the stench of human waste which wasn't a surprise.

She locked the door again and stepped into the open space. The building had once been a shipping yard for lumber but closed decades ago. Now it functioned as a home for the homeless and an infirmary.

An older woman approached when she saw Liana walk in. "You shouldn't have come tonight," she scolded. "You'll catch your death with those soaked clothes

"It's just a bit of rain, Grace. Besides, I am capable of doing this." Liana used a spell to dry every crevice and stitch of clothing on her. Grace frowned.

"Cocky mage," she murmured. Liana ensured that the hood of the cloak was pulled low over her face to conceal her identity before they got started.

"What do we have tonight?" Liana asked, ready to work.

Grace shook her head. "Far too much for just you to fix."

"So, the usual then," she joked humorlessly.

The old woman snorted. "Let's get started, girl."

The energy in the room remained bleak as always. These people suffered greatly, and her small acts of kindness made little impact in the grand scheme of it all. Still, she came here once a week to help them.

Grace took her to the most critically ill first. She healed their ailments with little effort then moved onto the minor aches and pains. Once they were taken care of, she went from space to space asking what she could do for them. Some things were as simple as mending clothes. Some asked for things beyond her capabilities such as a new home or food enough for everyone. When she couldn't deliver, they settled for a spell to clean their clothes, beds and bodies.

"You did well tonight, child," Grace commented softly, leading her back to her makeshift cot.

"I wish I could do more," Liana complained. All she did for these people seemed so useless when what they really needed was far beyond her reach.

"Don't think that way. You are doing more than you should." Liana could only think of other things she wished to do for them. They both paused when they spied a form huddled beneath the heavy blanket on Grace's bed.

"Alright you thieving animal, out of my bed," Grace demanded as she yanked the cloak off. Two children whimpered, hugging each other tightly as they cowered below Grace. She stepped away. "Sorry, kids. I thought you were a squatter."

Liana kneeled before them, grabbing the blanket from Grace. She wrapped their sodden bodies in it before drying them each with a spell. "You are safe here," she told them firstly. "What are your names?" The boy looked to be the eldest, his younger sister looking to be not quite five years old yet. Neither of them answered.

"That's alright. My name is Liana. This is Grace. You are welcome to stay here as long as you need. Are either of you hurt?" The boy shook his head as the young girl stuck her left leg out. Liana lifted the tattered dress up to her knee finding a long scratch down the side of her calf. Red puffy skin lined the scratch, infection setting in. Liana performed an easy spell to burn the infection away then another to heal the wound. The little girl stared up at her wide-eyed.

Liana smiled gently at the girl, noticing that neither of them wore shoes and their cheeks too sallow. "Grace will get you some food. You'll be safe here."

Grace walked Liana to the door. "I have no food," she told the skilled mage.

Liana pulled a single coin from her pocket. It wasn't much but was all she could manage to steal from her parents. "Buy yourselves some food tomorrow after the storm has passed." She closed her eyes and pictured the loaves of bread their chef prepared. He made three per day, two for the day's consumption and one for the next morning until more could be made. Liana knew exactly where it would be and what it would feel like in her hands. If she didn't, she wouldn't be able to summon the object. That was how she was able to perform such advanced summoning. She had to picture precisely the object she wanted and where it was in that exact moment.

The bread appeared in her hands, and she shoved it toward Grace. "Split that between yourselves tonight."

"You truly are a miracle, Liana," Grace whispered as she slipped out the door. Bracing against the chilling rain, she didn't bother to hurry. There was no point when she was already drenched again. Nor did she have the energy to run or conjure a shield to block the rain. She'd never admit it to Grace or show it in front of the others, but all that magic took a toll on her. Although the spells came easily to her, the power they required could become overwhelming and she feared she'd overdone it again. She tried to not make a habit of draining herself, however, it seemed selfish to refuse help when she had plenty of power to give. Especially yesterday morning when those two were injured from the attack on their home.

Her steps slowed, her energy waning along with her spirit. She didn't know how they survived it, living in such horrid conditions. The guilt weighed heavily upon her more than the exhaustion. And those poor children. They were all alone and starving.

Liana turned the corner, walking a few more blocks before giving up and sinking to the ground beneath a canopy in front of a shop. She leaned against the brick wall, her knees drawn into her chest while her head dropped back with exhaustion and guilt.

She sincerely hated this world. A world where children starved while fighting to survive on the streets, where people were burned out of their homes because of who they chose to love and where women were treated as possessions. If she were allowed to have any say, to take a political position, there would be nothing to stand in her way as she fought for the rights of females, of everyone.

Perhaps that would be a possibility if she truly became queen, if King Ashwood gave her any allowance to do as she pleased. Something to consider at least. Currently though, all she yearned for was her bed. She could sleep for days.

"Someone could easily sneak up on you like this," a haughty voice commented. She startled at the shock but quickly relaxed, recognizing his voice. Slowly, she peeled her eyes open.

"What are you doing here?" she sneered with as much venom as she could muster.

The king sat beside her, his plain black clothes soaked and plastered to his muscular form while his hair was pulled back yet again.

"Keeping you safe apparently. Anyone could have come upon you like this. There is no telling what would have happened," he scolded.

Liana rolled her eyes and closed them again. "Then leave me here to die, King. I would hate to inconvenience you."

He growled over the sound of the rain. "You have no care for your own safety. I will not stand for this when you are my wife."

"Even more reason to leave me here to die," she snarked.

"You'd rather die than be my wife?" he questioned seriously. She didn't respond but it did seem like a good option at the moment. Liana gathered whatever strength remained in her bones and pushed to her feet. A shiver ran down her spine as the rain pelted her face again.

"What were you thinking, Liana? You cannot sneak out of your home and walk alone at night, especially in this part of the city. Especially not in this weather!" he yelled over the rain. Vision blurring, she couldn't tell if it was the rain clouding her eyes or the exhaustion hitting her. Strong hands gripped her shoulders, halting her. "Gods, you can't even walk straight. What did you do in that building?" he accused.

She shoved him away and took a few hurried steps away. A gust of wind whirled between the buildings strong enough to knock her off balance. She stumbled into the side of a building and slid to the ground. That was it. She'd had enough. Come what may, she wasn't walking another foot. Rain drown her or criminals stab her, she was going to sleep no matter what.

"Liana?" Damien called. Fingers tapped at her cheek. "Liana, wake up," he demanded. Sleep hovered just out of her grasp. "What's wrong with you?" She groaned and slumped to the side. He hefted her into his arms. A strong wind blasted her side as her body rocked with motion. It all came to a sudden halt along with the rain. She blinked her eyes open to find herself beneath her patio.

"What's wrong with you? I don't smell any injuries or disease. You're not drunk either."

"Magic depletion," she whispered, resting her head on his shoulder to soak up the warmth radiating from him.

"How do I help?" he asked at a loss for what to do next.

"Sleep." Beyond the patio, sounds of the rain slowing filtered through the haze. She still felt droplets on her cheeks as he jumped to her balcony without making a single sound or jostling her. He set her on the chaise before taking her right foot in hand. He untied each boot then slid off the soaked stockings. Sounds of him ruffling around things in her room weren't enough of a curiosity to make her open her eyes to monitor his movements.

When she felt his fingers skimming over the flesh of her sides to lift her shirt, her eyes snapped open, narrowing on him. "What are you doing?"

He smirked at the fierceness that returned to her. "You'll catch your death if you go to bed in these clothes, and seeing as you can hardly open your eyes, I will change you. I'll be quick and I even promise not to peek," he teased. She glared at him, her eyes squinting so much that she could barely see out of them. In the blink of an eye, her shirt was replaced by a sleeping gown. He slid her trousers off, pulling the gown down with them.

"You're awfully skilled at taking a woman's clothes off," she remarked. He carried her to the bed and tucked her in.

"Did you forget that I also dressed you and didn't expose any part of you? Doesn't that count for something?"

She shrugged. "I wouldn't have cared if you looked. You are my fiancé, are you not?" In truth, she would have cared a great deal. Her body was still hers to control, for now anyway.

"Well, if you're offering," he countered with a cocky smirk, one finger pulled down on the blanket covering her. Liana hugged the fabric closer.

"You missed your chance, vampire. Better luck next time."

"As much as I would wholeheartedly take you up on that, little mage, please do not let there be a next time," he said. His fingers ran through her hair, nails scratching lightly against her scalp. Her mood sobered.

"Those people need help. I have to help. You have to help, you're the king."

He sighed heavily. "I know." He leaned with one arm supporting himself over her legs. "What would you do as queen?" Damien asked.

Her brows furrowed at the random question. "What do you mean?"

"As queen you will have power over the people. What will you do with it?"

She'd briefly pondered the idea a few minutes ago before he showed up. There were so many things she wanted to do though. Only some of them were realistic goals. "I'd create a community home for the homeless. They'd have sanitary living conditions and access to food. It would offer a safe place for everyone and help them toward building a proper life. I could be a resource to help find them jobs."

"That would require a lot of resources. A lot of money."

She raised a brow. "I think you have plenty to spare. Is there not also a fund in the royal budget for helping your people?"

He nodded. Shifting, he suddenly pulled off his soaked shirt, revealing chiseled muscle, and climbed over her, stretching out beside her on the bed. His shirt landed with a wet plop on her floor. A blush stole over her cheeks at the intimacy of the situation and his shirtless torso. "Indeed, there is. I shall inquire with my keeper of coin where that money is being used." That was more than she thought he would do. She thought he would laugh her off. "Enough business. Tell me, do you always sneak out in the middle of the night?"

Ignoring their proximity, she erected a privacy shield with the little magic she had left so that no one could hear them and dried his pants so that he didn't get her bed all wet.

He raised an impressed brow. She knew she should have insisted he leave, but she couldn't find the willpower to do so. She blamed it on the magical exhaustion. Laying back, she sighed. "I try to go once a week to help them."

"How else do you enjoy spending your days?" he asked.

"Why are you so curious?"

He grinned, a hint of sharp teeth peeking out. "I am interested in getting to know my future wife. The wife that knows how to track my guards and sneak out when they are blinded for only seconds."

She grinned at his statement which almost felt like praise. "They made it too easy."

His frown said he didn't appreciate her comment. "Yes, well, it would have been if I didn't also have a guard hidden in the tree to specifically watch your room.

Liana scoffed and rolled her eyes. "So overbearing."

"I wouldn't have to be if you weren't so reckless." She didn't bother arguing with him, his mind already made up. "Now, tell me how you spend your days when you're not saving the less fortunate."

"Why don't you tell me how you spend your days, my king?" She rolled onto her side, burrowing beneath the warm blankets, which also happened to be closer to his broad chest.

"During the day I am bogged down by kingly duties. When I do find myself with free time, I enjoy swimming." That was unexpected.

"Swimming? Where do you swim?"

"There is a small lake beside the castle." He supported his head with one hand which had her looking up at him. "Do you enjoy swimming?"

"I do not know how to swim." There was never a place to learn. There were no lakes in close proximity to Sancta Valles, only shallow rivers unfit for lessons. When they visited her uncle in Sapphire Cove, no one bothered to teach her then either.

"We shall remedy that someday soon. It truly is wonderful. What do you enjoy?" he asked again.

"I do enjoy gardening."

"Were you pleased with the gardens at the castle?"

"Yes, they were quite grand and well-kept with a variety of plants and flowers." Not thinking clearly at all, she scooted closer to his warmth as he asked,

"Your favorite food?"

She smiled at the thought of it. "It will make my breath smell for days, but Chef's onion and garlic bread is the best thing you will ever taste." He smiled at her confession.

"You will have to bring me a piece sometime."

Sleepiness had her smiling like a fool and nodding, her forehead brushing against the warmth of his chest. "What is your favorite?"

"Custard pie." A laugh escaped her. "Why is that so funny?" he asked, his eyes sparkling warmly in the candlelight.

"I thought you were going to say blood."

His laugh shook her small bed. "While we do drink small amounts of blood to survive, it is not my favorite. It is like drinking water. We need it to survive. Now, drinking blood for pleasure is another thing." He licked his lips, and she couldn't help but gulp as she remembered his lips on her neck.

"What do you mean, for pleasure?"

"Vampires taste blood differently. Mostly, it is a simple drink. However, it is a treat as well as our sustenance. When we indulge in blood outside of fulfilling our hunger, it is a very pleasurable experience."

She cleared her throat, his low voice doing odd things to her body. "And how do you drink the blood for pleasure? From a glass or…" She couldn't say it. Could hardly think of it without her body tensing.

He breathed in deeply, his eyes closing for a moment before they pinned her to the spot. A sinister smile filled his lips. "My little mage, you are aroused at the thought of me biting you."

"I am not," she denied. Is that what she was feeling? Surely not. She was not enjoying the idea of him sinking fangs into her neck. Not at all.

"I can smell your arousal. You cannot lie to me." He leaned forward and pushed aside her hair to breathe in at her neck. She froze, not knowing if he would bite her or not. More importantly, she didn't know if she wanted to tell him no. "After we are married, I will show you just how pleasurable the bite can be for both of us."

"I will never let you bite me. I will run away if you ever try it," she declared. Some part of her knew he was right. She would enjoy what he offered. Another part of her rebelled at the thought simply out of principle. She was a mage. She shouldn't be letting him drink her blood.

"Oh, my innocent little mage, I can smell your sweet blood from a mile away. There will be no running from me." She shivered, terror sliding down her spine. What had she gotten into with this powerful creature? "Do not be scared, Liana. I will never force you to do anything." She wasn't sure she could believe him.

She fought to keep her eyes open even as each blink weighed heavier than the last. The warmth cocooned in her bed didn't help any. He pressed a kiss to her forehead before whispering, "Sleep, my little mage."

His heavy arm pulled her against his smooth, muscled chest, his warmth seeping into her bones. Despite how improper the situation, blissful sleep finally claimed her.

Chapter Twelve

"Why did you insist on sitting outside during this horrible weather, Your Highness?" Liana complained as they sat under the gazebo while it poured rain around them.

It had been three days since he helped her get home during the storm. Three days of recuperating and wondering how he'd found her. Not to mention how he so gently and discreetly dressed her. It was odd to think the king did that for her, such a private thing. Not only because he was king but also because his rumored brutality didn't fit into the gentleness and respect he showed her. Nor did it track with the situation he forced her into, a marriage of power. Yet he had done those things and held her gently as she fell asleep that evening. He was gone long before she woke, but his scent and the feel of him holding her remained in the morning.

It had also been three days of fantasizing about the king and his fangs. She dreamed of him biting her. Dreamed of this pleasure he promised which made her even more mad at him because she could not feel it for real.

Her mother and William sat at another table, as far away as possible while his guards were stationed in the rain. Phillipa and Lady Monroe's maid sat by themselves with a small table as well. Their personal mage guards stood under the gazebo near her family. Sasha had returned the morning after her trip to the slums which gave Liana ample time to question her. The guard swore that she didn't tell the king a thing about her magic, only that she gave a report on her daily movements. For now, Liana accepted that answer. She'd keep the rest of her activities as private as possible from now on.

"It makes it harder to eavesdrop. If you would do the honors of erecting a privacy spell so no one can hear us."

"Why do we need the spell if the rain is already making enough raucous?" she complained even as she did the spell. Not only did it protect their conversation, but it eliminated the sound of the rain.

"The rain is for your mother. She will assume she can't hear because of it. My vampires will be able to hear over it no problem, hence the shield."

She rolled her eyes. "And what is so important that we need such privacy?"

He gave her that sinister, terrifying smile. "Nothing at all, my little mage. I merely wanted to spend time with my future bride."

She gave him a droll look. "Then we could have done this in a warm room with cushioned chairs. Instead, I am uncomfortable, and my stockings are miserably wet."

"For being so opinionated against high-society women, you certainly complain well enough like them," he grumbled, taking a sip of his wine.

Liana smiled. "And does that annoy you, Your Highness? Because there is plenty more I could complain about. Like your wardrobe for instance. All black is so dull and unbecoming, especially for a man of your rank." In truth, Liana loved all the black. He looked deadly in that color, and it matched his thick hair which he had pulled back into a tight knot at the back of his head again. She liked his hair down, but the knot quickly became her favorite as it showed off the stubble of his beard and angular face.

He looked at her calculatingly. "It does not annoy me at all, my conniving little mage. You may complain all you wish."

She harrumphed, not nearly annoyed enough to voice all her complaints.

"Why are we really suffering through this luncheon?" The food was fantastic. The company was not.

"We must keep up appearances, as I told you. I've held luncheon with the other two females over the past two days. It is your turn."

"And how are those ladies doing? Either of them catching your fancy?"

"Not particularly. I've already made my choice anyway, or did you forget, Fiancé?"

"No, but a girl can hope."

"Hope is for children," he commented gruffly.

"Hope is for all those that have not given up yet."

"You still think there is hope for you? What do you think will happen, that I will change my mind?"

"Not at all. I have resigned myself to become your wife. I hope that when I do, I can still make some of my dreams come true."

"And what dreams are those?"

"I will not tell you so that you may turn around and crush them before I even get a chance."

He sat back in his chair, forcing back a swig of his wine. "How did I become such a villain in your eyes? Where did I go wrong after that first night?"

Liana wasn't going to say anything. He didn't deserve an answer. There was something so vulnerable in his voice just then though. As if she had truly hurt him. It confused her so much that she found herself speaking. "You made me trust you. You made me believe we were just two people enjoying each other's company. Then you showed up in my bedroom and made me believe there was something true between us."

"And what was so wrong about that? It was the same for me. I thought we had a genuine connection."

Liana glared at him. "Then I realized your schemes the next day with your many courtships. You told me you had no intention of courting, that I was the one that intrigued you, yet you sent three invitations."

"I am not allowed to change my mind then?"

"That is not what I am saying. I only mean that you made me feel special then tore that away. You were just manipulating me." She should not have been so forthright with him, but he riled her up so easily that she had to defend herself.

"It was not my intention to make you feel bereaved of that feeling. When I sought you out at the ball I did so without the goal of courting you. I merely wanted a conversation. It was not until after – after you intrigued me so thoroughly – that I decided to court you."

Perhaps she was reading too much into it, but he made it sound like he wasn't scheming. Like it was completely unexpected that he decided to court her. Like he actually wanted her for a wife and not as a tool. But she knew his games, knew his manipulations and seductions.

"Then what of the other women? They are oddly strategic matches for a king not intending marriage."

He shrugged as he reached for a slab of meat. He slapped it onto his plate and cut into it. "I am king. I cannot put all my money in one place, as they say."

"I'm an investment now?"

He sighed, resting his utensils. "Is it your goal to argue with everything I say?"

She shrugged, mimicking his aloofness as she inspected her fingernails. "I am a female. Isn't arguing what we do best?"

He smiled. "I knew I'd enjoy this courtship," he crooned, his mood changing in the span of a breath.

"That makes one of us," she mumbled before biting into an apple. The king was enjoying this far too much.

"Tell me more about yourself, Liana. What else do you like to spend your days doing?"

Her cheeks flamed as she thought of the other night when he lay beside her in bed. She told him of her love for gardening. Revealing anything more would betray her highly secretive work, not that he didn't already know most of it anyway. Still, as far as anyone knew, she did what all young ladies did, played piano, knitted and painted. "You listened to my conversation with Beta Mooncliff, don't you already know?"

He gave a tight-lipped smile with the food in his mouth. "Indulge me. I'd like to know the real you. Not what you told him."

"What makes you think I lied?"

"I find it hard to believe that a woman with incredible magic and talent that sneaks to the slums every week enjoys spending her time knitting and playing the piano."

She sipped on the wine ignoring the fact that he was correct. "I'm glad you find me so talented. Most men would not admit to the fact."

He choked on the meat from a surprised laugh. He swallowed quickly, still laughing. "Grace is very forthcoming with information when bribed. No one could deny your talent with the spells you do for those people."

Liana couldn't really blame Grace for giving her up. She was a survivor and Liana was sure Damien offered her a lot. "What did you bribe her with?"

"Food and new clothes." Liana nodded. That was good. She needed those things. "You don't seem upset that she turned on you."

"Grace needs those things to survive more than I need my secrets kept."

He paused, weighing her words. "How long have you been helping them?"

Liana considered his question. He seemed to only know of her time spent at the shelter but mentioned the other day that he had her followed and others spilled her secrets. "Who do you have following me? I know it is not Sasha. I questioned her."

He swallowed the food in his mouth. "What makes you think she told the truth?" Liana simply waited, crossing her arms. "Sasha is meant to guard you; another follows for extra protection and to gather more information on you."

"I'm surprised you admitted to it." Truly, she did not think he would answer.

"It is not my goal to hide from you, Liana. However, as my queen, I must know everything about you. Even the things you don't yet trust me with."

She narrowed her eyes on him. "Did you even think to ask me for answers first or did you assume I would be deceitful?"

He smirked at some hidden joke. "In the beginning I believed you might give yourself to me completely. After the attack on you at your home I sensed the change in your attitude. I knew I ruined your blind faith in me somehow, although I didn't know how yet."

She turned her nose up and looked away. "I did not have blind faith in you," she denied curtly. The denial stung her tongue because, against all resolve, she did put all her trust in the king that first night. Lesson learned though. She'd never be so naive again.

He didn't point out her lie. "With your lack of trust, I needed answers with or without your cooperation. I have to protect this kingdom, even if I want you more than anything in this world." Liana ignored that last comment even as her cheeks flushed. The man's manipulations knew no bounds. "Will you tell me what you did the other night to deplete yourself so thoroughly?"

She picked at her nails again. "Just a bit of housekeeping at the shelter."

He chuckled. "And see, you lie and hide the truth, leaving me no choice but to spy on you."

Glaring, she asked, "Why don't you tell me about yourself, King Ashwood?"

He held his hands up in supplication. "I'm an open book. What would you like to know?"

If he offered, there was no chance the gods could even hold her back from asking, "Have the Separatists made a resurgence?"

His smile fell, his entire body straightening. "What do you know of the Separatists?"

Smug, she shrugged. "People gossip. I heard there have been a few attacks over the years."

"My father decimated their numbers thirty years ago. As far as I am aware, there is no resurgence."

On one hand, she wanted the king to know so that he could investigate the validity of his statement. On the other, she wanted to protect Felix and his friends. If the king investigated, he would discover the burned house and search for the missing people.

"Is there something I should know?" he questioned. Liana shook her head. "Really? Would you like to tell me what you were doing at the blood cafe the other day, or should I tell you my theories?"

Liana's heart skipped a beat. He knew. He already knew. Of course, he did. And here she thought she'd gotten away with it. Forcing herself to calm, and her magic to rest, Liana raised a taunting brow. "You seem eager to tell me, why don't you do the honors."

"My spy saw you go in. They also saw a group of injured people enter." He paused, willing her to fill in the rest. She didn't give him the satisfaction. "He heard everything."

Liana's vision wavered. Gods, he heard everything. He knew about her powerful magic. Knew about the people in hiding. Body shaking, Liana wasn't sure if she even breathed. "What are you going to do to me?" she asked in a terrified whisper.

His brows furrowed. "Do with you?" he questioned. "Nothing. What do you mean?" Her eyes darted for an escape route. There were guards everywhere, vampire guards at that. She couldn't outrun them. Her magic surged to the surface, magic spiked out of her fingers onto the table, and she hid them in her lap.

"Please, don't hurt me," she cried, tears welling up in her eyes. Damien rushed to her side, kneeling so that she turned away from her family.

"Liana, look at me," he demanded softly. "I've told you before that I will never hurt you."

She couldn't think, couldn't respond. Terror consumed her at the thought that this man knew of her magic. Any moment he would cause her pain to incite her to use magic.

"Please, my magic is nothing special." She saw a hand reach for her face, and she braced for the pain. Instead of pain, a growl reached her ears.

"Liana, I will not ask twice. Who hurt you?" Flashes of pain bombarded her mind, and she squeezed her eyes against it.

"Liana?" a soft voice reached her, a comforting, familiar warmth of magic entering her veins.

"Phillipa?" Liana cried.

"Hush, sweetie. I've got you. You're safe."

Liana blinked, her vision clearing. Brows furrowed, she looked to the king in confusion. He kneeled beside her, his face a mask of deadly wrath. Phillipa held her with one arm, the other patting at her face with a handkerchief. "Phillipa?" she questioned her maid.

"It's alright, sweetie. You must have eaten something that didn't agree with you. You fainted." Confused, she looked to the king. She couldn't recall what they spoke of just now, nor did she remember feeling poorly.

"Oh. I apologize, Your Highness. I don't know what came over me."

"Liana?" Lady Monroe called, hurrying over at the commotion. "Are you well?"

"Yes, Mother. I am fine." A soft growl left Damien which had her eyes on him again. Still, he looked ready for battle, except now he glared at

Phillipa.

"Perhaps we should get you home," Phillipa suggested as she astutely ignored the king's glare. Liana nodded, still confused. As she stood, Damien did as well and reached out to steady her although she didn't require it.

"Are you sure you are well?" he asked, those icy blue eyes glaring through to her soul. Nodding, she looked away. Before he could question her more, a vampire ran through the rain and into the gazebo. She dropped her shield, the rain thunderous in her ears again.

"My king, there has been an attack on the wolf alpha shifter," the vampire relayed. "The beta died saving the alpha." Liana gaped. Beta Mooncliff had been killed.

Damien took her hand, pressing a kiss to the back of it. "I must go. Stay safe. My guards will accompany you home." With that, he ran into the storm, the messenger on his heels as they disappeared.

The journey home through the rain became torturous as their carriage stuck frequently in the mud. Liana still couldn't recall what happened, or that she fainted. She hated that he saw her that way, saw her in a weak moment once again.

She hated even more that, after a long, hot bath that evening, she dreamed of the king coming to her bedroom. She dreamt of him four nights in a row. He slid beneath her blankets, his hands caressing inappropriate places before fangs bit into her neck. She expected pain, but there was only a burning need for something more. A need for him that scared her beyond measure.

Chapter Thirteen

L ady Monroe worried over the king's abrupt departure the other day, not asking about Liana's health at all, but thankfully she still had Hannah and Charlotte to fuss over and keep her busy. The three of them were out shopping yet again while Liana stayed home. She worked in the garden behind the house when a visitor arrived. "King Ashwood is here for you, Lady Monroe," Henry called to her. She raced up the patio stairs, her dress filthy and her hands caked with dirt.

"Henry! I am a mess. How could you let him in?" she scolded before catching herself. What did she care? All the better if he was revolted by her.

"I'm sorry, my lady. Would you have rather I told the king to wait in his carriage until you are presentable?" The sarcastic butler didn't wait for a reply before walking off.

"Liana, join us," her father instructed, waving her into the drawing room. She was happy her mother wasn't here to see how abominable she looked because although Liana didn't care, Lady Monroe would punish her until the end of time for greeting the king in such a state. Brushing away the hair sticking to her sweaty face, she took a few deep breaths. Liana curtsied to the king who was still dressed in all black except with a decorative coat adorned with gold buttons and piping along the edges.

"I apologize for my state of dress, Your Highness. I did not expect you and was tending to the garden." Her cheeks heated but not because of her clothes. She recalled her dream from the other night and her eyes landed on his lips, imagining them at her neck. She shook that thought away.

"Do not apologize, Li… Lady Monroe," he added on hastily aware of Lord Monroe's astute listening. "Perhaps some music," he suggested abruptly. Liana caught on and started the piano with a spell before they took their seats on opposite chairs. She erected a privacy spell as well. This one would just make their words sound jumbled so her father wouldn't be so suspicious, which she explained to Damien.

"Good thinking, Liana," he complimented. "I came to apologize for the other day. It was rude of me to end our luncheon early. Let me make it up to you. I will host your family for supper tomorrow evening."

This caught her off guard considering the other day when he was so angry at her for being difficult. "There was an emergency, you were not rude. However, we would graciously accept your offer, Your Highness. I shall confirm with my mother that we are available to attend. As you know, my two sisters are also inundated with suitors at the moment."

He nodded. "Very well. It is short notice. Do let me know if we need to switch it to another night." Damien glanced toward her father then back to her, his eyes full of concern. "How are you feeling? Have you recovered?"

Embarrassed that he saw her yet again in a moment of weakness, she nodded, keeping her eyes on her clasped hands. "I am not sure what came over me. Truly, we were talking and then you and Phillipa were beside me."

"That is all you remember?" he questioned intently.

A vague tingling flittered at the back of her head, but she shrugged it off. "That's it. I apologize for my health yet again. You seem to always be near when I am not at my best."

His brows furrowed. "The previous times have been under altruistic intent from magical depletion and nothing you need to apologize for. This time was different, and still no apology is needed. I am merely concerned."

Liana was concerned as well, not that she'd admit to it. "Appreciated, Your Highness, but the healer examined me as soon as we returned home, Mother insisted on it. He said I was quite well, likely dehydrated."

His stare pierced through her, making Liana doubt the words. She might have believed them if her memory wasn't so addled, and her magic roiled beneath the surface any time she attempted to remember.

"I cannot argue with a healer," he acquiesced. "I am pleased that you are well, and I look forward to our dinner." He stood abruptly and she followed. When he simply stared at her, Liana wasn't sure where to go from there.

"You've come all this way, Your Highness. May I offer you a tour of our garden? It is not as grand as the castle, but I tend to it myself and am rather proud of it."

"That is agreeable. Lead the way." She dropped the spell and addressed her father. "Papa, we are going to walk in the garden. I will take Henry to chaperone."

"Very well," he agreed, bowing his head to the king. The ornery butler reluctantly agreed and he and one of King Ashwood's guards walked a good distance behind them.

Liana started the tour at her tulips. They were blooming so beautifully during this warm summer. "These tulips came all the way from our eastern neighbors. They have the best tulips of all."

"Why is that?" he wondered, inspecting the arrangement of colors.

"Their shape and colors. The shape is perfectly bell-like, and the colors are the most vibrant. You won't find prettier." He simply nodded. "Oh, and the wisteria is in full bloom this month," she informed him, walking toward the small trellis over the path. "Everything is blooming with the rain we've had and the warm summer."

"You are quite passionate about gardening," he commented, looking up at the dangling purple flower.

"I am passionate about a lot of things."

"And why is gardening one of them?" he asked, looking at her again while they walked through. In the back of her mind, she kept telling herself that he wasn't interested, he was just playing the part of courtier. So, Liana kept herself guarded even as she answered.

"It is rewarding. If you do it well, you get pretty flowers. It also calms me, grounds me. Feeling the magic in the earth, using my hands and shaping nature to what I want is freeing in a way." She shrugged. "It must seem silly to a man."

"Not at all," he said quickly. "This is your work, and you are proud of it. I understand." He paused, glancing back at our followers who studiously ignored them but also kept a close eye. "What do you mean you feel the magic in the earth?" he whispered.

She eyed him. "For claiming to be so knowledgeable about all your people, you don't know that much," she pointed out.

He frowned. "Enlighten me then," he demanded.

"There is magic all around us, especially in the earth. It is strongest in the soil and living things, less so inside homes or over the roads."

"Interesting. And why does that calm you?"

"The magic itself is calm. It is exactly as it was meant to be." She shrugged. "It is hard to explain."

He nodded his head. "I think I understand your meaning."

"I'm surprised your Master Kinley hasn't told you of this before," she commented wryly. He only hummed in response while his eyes stayed on the path they walked.

"Liana, I need to ask. Yesterday, at luncheon, before you fainted," he started. Liana wrinkled her nose at the reminder of the event yet again. "Do you remember what we spoke of just prior to it?"

"That's an odd question." She thought for a moment. "I think I had just asked you about the Separatists. Is that about right?"

He eyed her. "That is the last thing you remember? Are you certain?"

She stopped to face him fully. "Is there something I am missing? Just tell me, because that truly is the last thing I remember." Icy blue eyes searched hers before he turned away and started walking again.

"It is nothing. You worried me, that's all. As far as the Separatists are concerned, they were taken care of thirty years ago by my father."

As long as she had him here and he offered answers, she would use that to her advantage. "What happened with the shifters yesterday? Who attacked them?"

His jaw clenched. "We aren't sure."

"Why did they attack?"

He shook his head. "We don't know."

"It seems awfully coincidental that my father was attacked, then the alpha of the wolf pack. Both are key players on their council. It makes one wonder," she surmised, trying to egg him on.

He glanced at her sidelong. "You are about as subtle as a fox in a hen house."

She rolled her eyes. "Please, Damien, tell me something."

His feet stopped as he turned to face her fully. She waited eagerly for a single scrap of information. His brows furrowed. "You called me Damien."

Her mind skittered. Did she? She hadn't realized. "I apologize, Your Highness."

"No," he stopped her, holding up a hand. "Don't. I gave you permission to do so, and it is refreshing to hear." He began walking again, planting his hands in his trouser pockets.

"So, what of the attacks? Why are they targeting the councils?" she questioned trying to not be embarrassed by the fact that she liked using his name as well. It made things feel more personal.

"Why are you so interested?" he countered.

"Isn't it obvious? They attacked me. I want to know."

"What good will the knowledge do? You will not be able to change what happened."

"But I can aid you in keeping it from happening again."

One brow raised at her, he asked, "How so?"

They walked past the patio and kept walking, making another lap around the garden. She'd thought long about her proposal. Thought about what she was willing to reveal to him about her magic. The king already knew she had substantial power. He already wanted to own that power and was going to marry her to get it. There was not much left to lose at this point, and she wanted to help capture the bastards that nearly killed both her, Henry, and those poor people that only wished to live in peace.

"With my magic. You know I am skilled. I can help capture them and prevent anyone from being harmed again." He stopped once more, his gaze assessing.

"You speak of your magic so freely now?" he questioned which had her head canting to the side.

"You've already said you want me because I can use my magic. Why would I hide it?"

His gaze didn't leave hers for another moment, then his dark hair tousled in the sunlight as he shook his head. "A female mage aiding the investigation… that would not go over well with anyone, least of all your father. I do not want you in danger either."

Liana glanced back at their chaperones that were a hefty distance away but still erected a privacy shield. "You want me for my power. You specifically said that I would be your private guard. So, here I am. Use me. Let me help."

"You have not trained yet. I did not plan to drop you amongst the wolves without proper preparation."

Hands balled into fists, she refrained from screaming in frustration. "I have prepared myself. I know more battle spells than either of my brothers."

"Perhaps, but theory is different than action. Have you tested those spells? Have you fought against anyone before?"

Liana paused. Only the intruder the other day and she'd frozen when it came down to the moment. If her magic hadn't acted for her, there would have been a far worse outcome. "Perhaps I could use more training, but I do not expect to fight any battles soon. I just need information. There are plenty of spells I can do from the safety of my home to aid in the investigation."

"If there is anything I think you can help with, I will tell you," he said.

She huffed and crossed her arms. "That's not exactly what I aimed for," she grumbled.

"Yes, but that is all I am willing to offer at the moment." When they came to a simple stone bench, he gestured for her to sit. She took a seat first, keeping their privacy spell up as they settled in the nook of fragrant jasmine. "I do admire your tenacity, Liana, but until I know you are capable of defending yourself in a difficult situation, I want you safe."

There wasn't much to argue with on that point although she tried. Truth was, she knew she wasn't ready for true combat despite all her studying. "How do you plan on training me? Will Sasha train me?" As she said this, she wondered, "Do you have many female guards?"

He reclined on his hands, tilting his face up to the sun as he answered, his sharp jaw striking her eyes. "I have many female soldiers in my army.

Most of them are vampires, some shifters. I have yet to add a mage female to the ranks." He eyed her pointedly. "But I hope to change that soon." She shifted away from him, staring at the back of her home. No matter what he said, he was still just using her, she had to force herself to remember that. "As for your training, you will begin once we are wed. It will be easier to keep it a secret. For now, stay with your family and stay safe."

Liana mimicked his pose, absorbing the rays of the sun and breathing in the fresh air. This was not an ideal situation, her marriage to the king, but she could make it work. She'd finally get to use the magic she so desperately sought her entire life, so that made it an easier arrangement to follow.

"Your garden truly is beautiful, Liana," he commented softly as they both looked upon it.

She smiled. "Well, it's not strictly my garden. I only tend to some of these plants. It is far too much for just me."

"Nevertheless, it is beautiful." They lapsed into silence and Liana noticed that it had been a pleasant afternoon. The king hadn't annoyed her much at all. That was, until he opened his mouth again. "You are being quite agreeable today. Why are you being so nice to me?"

She sighed. "And you were being so courteous. I thought maybe you finally learned the meaning of the word humble."

He guffawed, her humor catching him off guard. "There she is. I must admit, I much prefer your ornery side."

"I am not ornery," she exclaimed. He simply stared at her. "Why do you think I'm ornery? Because I speak my mind?"

He chuckled. "You certainly speak your mind but that is not it. You find fault with every word I say."

"That says more about you than it does me, does it not?" she proposed.

His smile didn't falter. "Please, tell me what I do that bothers you so and I shall stop it immediately."

She rolled her eyes. "Do not condescend. And I don't find fault with everything you say. Only some things."

"Oh, then I shall rest easy tonight knowing I only somewhat annoy you."

Her cheeks blushed again as she thought of him in bed tonight. More likely in her bed among her dreams biting her neck again. She desperately needed to stop thinking of him in that way. It was nearly impossible though with the subject of her desire sitting in front of her. Those lips so close, all it would take was for her to lean in just so. If she arched her neck, he'd be able to easily access that spot he teased the other night and she'd be lost in him.

His smile fell as he took a deliberate breath in through his nose. "My innocent little mage, what in the gods are you thinking about?" he growled softly. She gulped, scooting away on the tiny bench.

"Nothing," she squeaked.

He breathed her in again, leaning closer. She watched as the irises of his icy blue eyes shrunk, the black consuming them. "I know that is a lie. Tell me, Liana, what is it that you're thinking to make your core weep for me?"

She shivered, her thighs clenching.

"Tell me, Liana," he whispered. "I hear your heart racing. I see your pupils dilating, your flesh quivering. You want me."

He hadn't even touched her, and she was near to melting into the grass. She could only imagine what it would be like for those long fingers to caress her skin, those lush lips to kiss her own. And how desperately she wanted to feel those fangs sinking into her neck.

"It seems my innocent little mage is not so innocent," he leered. He stood, gesturing for her to follow. "Let us walk some more." Appreciative of the change, she followed.

"You mentioned that you paint. May I see some of your work?"

Now she blushed darker than the reddest tulip in her garden for an entirely different reason, her arousal forgotten. "Oh, you wouldn't like to see that. I am not a skilled artist."

"I told you I would like to see them. If you do not wish to show me, that is fine."

She wasn't sure how to avoid this. On one hand he was being rather polite and accommodating, on the other, she knew he could turn into a demanding bastard within a second's time.

"If we return to the house, I believe there is one of my pieces hanging." She led him inside to the alcove beneath the stairs where two chairs sat. It was far removed from the rest of the house and her painting was difficult to see. "This is it."

Damien stared at the painting unblinkingly, his eyes glued to the small canvas. It wasn't large, just a small piece of canvas. "This was the only one my mother liked. She liked the colors." Liana used a navy so dark it was nearly black. With that, she added white, grey and gold. He stared silently for so long that she talked nervously. "It takes no skill. I just stroke the paint onto the canvas. I know a real artist would balk at my work."

"It's beautiful," he said quietly, which stopped her rambling. "Do you have others? I would like to take one with me."

Surprised, she nodded. "If you do not mind waiting, I shall fetch one." She curtsied half-heartedly before racing upstairs. Phillipa tended to a gown in her room when she burst in. "Oh, Phillipa, you must help me," she said in a panic.

"What is wrong, my dear?"

"He wants one of my paintings," she complained as she started flipping through the canvases resting against the wall on the floor.

"Why is that so distressing?" Phillipa questioned. It shouldn't have been distressing. In fact, she shouldn't have cared at all. Except that her paintings were private. She knew they weren't good enough to compete with a real artist, but she loved them just the same because they came from her heart. And to think that someone so cultured as the king would want it frazzled her nerves.

"Because they are terrible. He has portraits and murals aplenty in his castle that are so well done they look like real people. Mine are nonsense."

"Stop that right now, Miss Liana. Nothing you do is ever nonsense. And stop getting dirt all over the canvases. Let me pick one." Phillipa held one up. It was so different from the one downstairs. That one was all straight, short strokes while this one was colorful and swirling.

"No. What about the maroon one?" she suggested. Phillipa nodded.

"One of my favorites. The colors are perfect."

"Yes, that one will do. I hope. Thank you, Phillipa," Liana said, taking the canvas and hurrying back downstairs. Unfortunately, her mother and sisters had returned.

"Are you sure we cannot offer you a drink or something to eat?" Lady Monroe asked for what was surely the thousandth time.

"You are very kind, Lady Monroe, however, I must decline. I am late for a meeting and must be getting on my way as soon as Liana returns."

"I am here," she said, coming up behind her mother. "There you are, Your Highness." Liana handed him the small canvas. He took it but did not look at it, simply held it underneath his arm. He gave everyone a quick nod of the head.

"I shall look forward to dinner tomorrow evening. Lady Liana, please escort me out," he said then walked out. Liana followed. She closed the front door behind her. He stood one step below but was still too close to be proper. Especially when he leaned in to whisper in her ear.

"Whatever you were thinking in the garden, dream of it tonight," he demanded, then kissed the back of her hand.

"That's what started all this," she mumbled under her breath as he stepped away. He clearly heard with his vampiric ears as his foot slipped off the edge of the stair. He righted himself, glancing over his shoulder with a cocky grin.

"What do you dream of, my darling mage?" He already knew the answer to that.

"Good day, Your Highness," she said before slipping back inside.

"Was that one of your paintings you gave him?" Lady Monroe asked as soon as the front door shut. Liana nodded. "Why by the gods, would you ever give him such a thing?" her mother wailed completely aghast. "That is a man of royalty. He has famous artists paint things for him."

"I know, Mother, but he asked for one. Would you rather I denied him?"

"Oh gods, let us pray that he does not rescind his courtship," she said, overdramatic as usual before ushering her sisters upstairs. Liana crossed her arms and walked back into the drawing room.

"How did it go, sweetie?" her father asked.

"Fine. Why does mother hate me so much?" she asked on a huff.

"The two of you are exactly alike and your mother does not hate herself therefore she does not hate you," he explained factually while writing correspondence. "Why are you being dramatic, daughter?"

She sighed. "No reason. I'm fine."

"How are you liking the king?"

"He is an interesting man."

Lord Monroe grunted. "Of course, he is. He is a king. Do you like him well enough to marry?"

"Perhaps. We do not know each other all that well yet." Although she was beginning to understand him a bit better.

"Just be careful, sweetie. He is a man of power. No matter what he says that throne will be the most important thing to him. The throne will come before you and what you want. Don't lose sight of that." Liana sighed again and walked over to her father.

"I know, Papa. I know exactly what I'd be to the king." She kissed his head. "Love you, Papa."

"I love you, sweet pea."

When she went to bed that night, she welcomed him into her dreams. If she couldn't have the real thing, there was no harm in dreaming.

Chapter Fourteen

Lady Monroe dressed Liana in the finest gown she owned, which happened to be a navy silken gown with heavy layers to add volume to the bottom. Luckily, there was no petticoat beneath this gown because they were impossible to sit in. Phillipa structured her dark strands into a crown of braids atop her head, leaving her slender neck on display along with the iridescent string of pearls resting along her skin.

Liana added her own small touches of makeup to enhance the color in her cheeks and bolden her eyes with a thin line of coal. Charlotte and Hannah looked pretty in their muted gowns of grey and brown. They wore only thin gold necklaces, and their hair was simple. Everything about them looked simple compared to Liana. Lady Monroe designed them that way so the king's eyes would only favor Liana. The woman was diabolical, but Liana had to admit she was smart for doing so.

Once they arrived at the castle, their guards following, they were brought to a sitting room to wait for everyone's arrival. The ladies sat on the sofas while the males stood about inspecting and commenting on the trinkets and décor about the room. Master Ranville and Lord Dietrich arrived together and were served drinks. Shortly after, King Ashwood arrived, and they were led to the formal dining room. The same style of the stone castle permeated this room as well with arched walkways and alcoves while the length of the far wall consisted entirely of windows. It made for a stunning backdrop to their dinner with the mountains as their scenery.

Seating arrangements were preset by society which meant Lord Monroe sat to the king's left followed by Wesley, Carlisle and William. To the king's right sat Master Ranville and Lord Dietrich. The ladies were left to fill in the remaining seats. Lady Monroe sat beside Lord Dietrich followed by Charlotte and Liana. Hannah sat on the opposite side beside William. Liana hated that this put her so far away from the king but hated even more that they were put last in the pecking order.

Servants brought the first course of a roasted tomato soup which Liana sipped properly yet quickly as her stomach grumbled.

"How are the wolf shifters after suffering such a loss?" Lord Monroe questioned, getting into the political talk. The ladies stayed silent as was expected.

"They are mourning in their way. Once the mourning period is over, they will select the next Beta."

"Such a terrible loss for the community," Master Ranville chimed in. "Do you yet know who is behind the attacks?" he questioned, his voice loud and expectant.

"Not quite. As best we can tell, they are a group of rogues."

"Do you mean rebels?" Master Ranville countered. "Could they be making a resurgence after the last rebellion?"

Liana's curiosity perked. Damien wouldn't tell her much yesterday, and it looked as though he did not enjoy talking about it now either. To the untrained eye he probably looked unperturbed, but Liana made it a point to study every twitch the king made. And now, his carefully blank face and the slight raise of his left brow didn't bode well for the mage.

"My father crushed the rebellion before they could cause too much trouble. If that is the case here, I will deliver swift justice and be done with them."

"You would condemn them to death without even a proper trial?" Master Ranville accused.

Liana rolled her lips inward to keep from smiling because it was much more fun to see the king's ire directed at someone else other than her. There was no mistaking that sharply raised brow aimed at the mage. "The rebels seek to destroy everything that Triaedian stands for. We are a country of peace. A kingdom of equality among all breeds. Thousands of men and women, shifters, vampires and mage alike, fought to create this kingdom a thousand years ago because they knew that a kingdom of unity among breeds was far stronger than separate kingdoms. If there are any that seek to destroy the peace we've cultivated for so long, I will not hesitate to destroy them."

Everyone else at the table studiously ignored the pair instead focusing on their soup but Liana brazenly stared. Which is how she noticed Master Ranville's hand tightening around his spoon so that his knuckles went white. The man was known for his diligence toward justice, it was one of the many reasons the mage community worshipped him. Aside from his Master status, he fought for the notion that all were innocent until proven guilty and held countless trials whereas most would simply throw a thief in jail or cut off a finger.

Liana didn't think he'd attack the king, with a spoon no less, but she had her magic ready to throw up a shield. She didn't dare put one up now for fear that the Master would sense her magic.

"Well said, Your Majesty," Master Ranville commented, his hand relaxing around the silver. "It is such a shame that there are those that would disrupt the peace our forefathers gave their lives to create."

Damien spooned the soup into his mouth, his eyes burning with ire. When he finally flicked his glance away, it fell on her. She finally released her lips and let them spread into a smile. He raised a silent questioning brow to which she only shoveled more soup into her mouth. She gained far too much joy from seeing him berate another.

Wesley chimed in, changing the topic to less tense conversation. "My uncle writes that trade is flourishing with the other kingdoms. Sapphire Cove is bringing in double the revenue with the increased merchant vessels you helped build."

King Ashwood nodded. "I merely loaned the merchants the money to build quality ships. You have to invest in order to make any return," he counseled the younger man. "And that return is greater than I expected within the first year. It will tide us through the storm season which has already begun."

"What is the most profitable export?" Liana questioned without thinking. Lady Monroe leaned around Charlotte to pin her with a deathly stare. Ladies were not to engage in such discussions unless specifically asked a question.

King Ashwood paid Lady Monroe no heed as he answered. "Wine. Our climate is perfectly suited to cultivating the finest grapes and our vintners are some of the finest in the world."

"Why are they so skilled, Your Highness?" she wondered. "Surely Triaedian doesn't have a monopoly on wine making."

He smirked. "We do not. But our vintners have many years of experience passed from generation to generation, each one creating better and better wine. That, along with our superior crops gives us the edge."

She picked up her glass and took a sip of the wine, her eyes never leaving his. "And is this some of the finest wine the world has to offer?" she quipped. Charlotte elbowed her via her mother, but she ignored them both.

"It is, and it happens to be a barrel from my own vineyard to the north of here."

"Quite delicious. And what is our most profitable import?"

"Fabrics and silks from the Chimerion Kingdom. Their silk production is the largest in the world and the easiest to obtain. They are also the only ones capable of creating such vibrant colors like your dress, Lady Monroe."

She thought of that alluring blue Claudius showed her and which her mother went back for at Phillipa's suggestion. Liana had passed out from all the magic used that day and Lady Monroe bought the fabric for a dress for Charlotte instead. "Fascinating. Have you ever been to the other kingdoms, Your Grace?" she wondered.

He glanced at the head butler and nodded, ready for the next course. While the servants took away their soup bowls and replaced them with the main course, he answered. "I visited a few when I was still Prince. They are vastly different from our own but similar in some ways. If anyone ever has the opportunity to visit, I recommend going."

Liana wondered if she would ever get to visit another kingdom once she became queen. It likely would never happen if she were to marry anyone else. Not many people left Triaedian, at least not that she knew of. Not all kingdoms were welcoming of all breeds either. They had to be careful if they did decide to travel.

Lord Monroe cut in to say, "This courting season has brought with it unexpected benefits, Your Highness. I am told that there is a promising young mage that came in search of a wife. He is the son of a farmer, but his magical talent is unparalleled. The mage council is discussing a possible charity seat for the boy to study magic, possibly even become a Master. Of course, that is if he passes our testing."

Liana focused on the plate of roasted pig and vegetables that now sat before her. The lighthearted mood she was in disappeared in an instant with the news. In the history of mage education, she didn't know of a single male that was ever given a free seat. She was thrilled for the boy but also disappointed that no one ever saw her talent and thought she'd be worth the effort of training. This boy was a step in the right direction though. If they were willing to offer one talented mage a free education, then many more could follow because more than the rich deserved to learn magic. It was their birthright.

The men took over the conversation after that, even when they retired to the drawing room, the ladies were left out. Liana and Hannah played a duet on the piano for everyone's entertainment until it was time to leave.

Liana wished she'd had more time to speak with Damien alone before they left. As it were, he stole a few moments at the end of the night. As her family walked toward the carriages, he held her back atop the stairs. She erected a privacy shield out of habit.

"What were you so smug about at supper?" he questioned.

"I simply admired someone else being on the receiving end of your kingly ire for once. It was a pleasant change of pace for me."

"When have I subjected you to such treatment?" he asked, affronted.

"Oh, so many times, my King," she said with a teasing smile. He huffed in annoyance.

"I would never speak to you like that. Nor could I ever want to throttle you like I did that man."

Her smile widened. "You wanted to punch him, didn't you?" She would have liked to see that.

His brows rose. "Does my little mage like the idea of me fighting?" he whispered huskily. She bit her lip not knowing why she yearned so desperately for this man when she did her best to swear him off. He growled softly. "Perhaps I shall invite you to a sparring session soon and show you what I'm capable of."

Gods forgive her, but the image of him shirtless, sweaty and fighting made her entire body flush. He growled again, stepping closer. Her back was to the carriages, and she hoped no one would tell how improperly close they were. His guards certainly could see but they studiously ignored them.

"Did you dream of me last night, my little mage?"

"That is a bold thing to ask of a lady," she quipped even as her blush betrayed her. She did indeed dream of him. They were in the garden under the light of the moon. Neither of them wore any clothes as he kissed and suckled at her neck. When his teeth scraped along her skin, the dream abruptly ended leaving her begging for more as she woke.

He bent to kiss her hand and breathed in her scent. "It must have been an excellent dream," he surmised with pure male satisfaction. "Tell me what you dreamed of so that I may join you in your pleasure."

"You want to control my dreams now as well?"

He chuckled. "I doubt there is anything about you I can control."

She smirked. "Tell me, my king. You have fangs to bite with, do you not?" He nodded. "Show me," she demanded in a whisper. If he could seduce her, manipulate her, she would do the same to him.

His lips parted slightly as four canines lengthened into lethal points. She shivered.

"Different than I imagined," she admitted.

He pulled his fangs back. "Tell me of your dream last night," he demanded quietly.

She smiled secretively. "It seems like a nice night for a stroll in the garden beside the tulips. It would be a rather quiet spot I would think for privacy."

His eyes fell closed on a groan. "Mighty temptress, you are trying to get me killed."

"How so?"

"Because your father will surely kill me for the images you are painting in my head."

She laughed at his torture. "Goodnight, my king." She couldn't wait to get home so she could sleep and discover what else her dreams brought.

Chapter Fifteen

As their clandestine relationship heated up, so did the gossip. The city couldn't get enough of their rumors and went wild about their courtship. The king often stopped by the Monroe home and invited them to dinner or afternoon tea. They wouldn't get much alone time, but he would always find a way to sneak her aside to tease her. She reciprocated just as much though and flirted with him unabashedly. It became an unspoken game between the pair to see how much they could rile the other and Liana loved every second of it. It made her feel in control of the life she actually had no control over.

She chose to engage with the king. She chose to accept him and drive him mad with lust. It was a small win, but a win just the same.

During their flirtations, another attack occurred. This time on the vampire council. They were attacked by mages, likely the same group that got the others. Luckily, no one was killed although there were some serious injuries. Vampires healed quickly though. Damien refused to give her any information about it, nor would her father. It was impossible to ignore that the councils were being targeted. For what reason, Liana could not discern.

Liana and her sisters were in the city shopping for more supplies for their shrines to the goddesses, gossip following their every step, while their mother took William to his dance lessons. Lady Monroe made the girls pray to the goddesses each night just as they did on worship day. The new altars they created in the sunroom remained day and night to worship the goddesses and gain their favor during this courting season.

The ladies stopped in the market perusing the wares before getting the supplies while Liana wandered off to the plants to see what new bulbs they might have.

Inspecting the lilies, she sensed a pair of vampires stop behind her. An invisible shield encompassed her without even a thought, her magic reacting to the unknown threat.

"Can you believe the king chose her?" a snide voice said to her back. "She is so frumpy."

Another female laughed. "She takes no pride in her appearance."

Liana looked down at herself. Her mother made her change out of the dirty gown she'd been wearing before they left the house. She supposed her hair was a bit of a mess. After walking in this humid heat, her hair was bound to be out of sorts though.

Surreptitiously, she tucked a loose strand of chestnut hair behind her ear as she turned to face the females. "May I help you with something?" she asked calmly, despite her anger. Normally she did not engage with those that chose to ridicule her. Normally she would walk away and forget about it. However, today she didn't want to listen to it. She didn't want to let these women purposefully whisper in her ear about how different she was. If they wanted to talk about her, she would be all too happy to give them something real to talk about for once.

The ladies looked like every other vampire female; tall, thin and beautiful.

"You do not deserve the king," the blonde said.

"Lady Yvonne is such a better match for him," the brunette beauty informed. Yvonne, the gorgeous vampire courtier, of course they were here to boast their lady. "She is so beautiful and poised."

"Yes, so perfect. And look at you, always covered in dirt. And that hair. Ugh, I can only imagine what is living in there."

"Well, when your mother allows you to spend all your time in the garden or your nose buried in a book, you don't learn how to be a lady. They are lucky they have your sisters. At least they are normal."

Liana wasn't sure why she bothered to stay and listen to them berate her. It was always the same. They would try to tear her down for being different, and now they are doing it out of jealousy.

"The king needs a vampire as his wife anyway. Cut your losses, mage before you regret entertaining the idea of marrying him." Her magic surged against her skin, begging to be let out, to attack these vicious women for their hurtful words.

"Are you threatening me?" she asked, her voice lethally calm.

The women scoffed in unison. "We don't need to threaten you. There is no way the king will ever choose an outcast like you."

Liana gave them an evil smile. "Then clearly there is no need for you to warn me against him if my chances are nonexistent."

The brunette stepped closer in an attempt to tower over Liana. It would have worked if Liana didn't stand at the same height and didn't raise her chin at the move. Staring into plain blue eyes, Liana didn't back down.

"You are nothing. He is only stringing you along for appearances. Everyone knows Yvonne is the next queen."

"If you truly believed that you wouldn't be standing here threatening me." Liana waited a moment longer for her point to sink in before stepping back. She pushed between the pair and let her magic out for a bit of play as she walked away. It took them a few moments before she heard squealing and screaming once they realized what she'd done. She chuckled darkly right as someone fell into step beside her.

"Your Highness?" she greeted, confused as to why he was here.

A smile played on his lips while his hands clasped loosely behind his back. "Good afternoon, Lady Monroe."

"What are you doing here?" she whispered, looking around to see if anyone noticed. Everyone did and stared openly.

"Well, I was going to come to your rescue with those vile wenches, but it seemed as though you did not need my help at all."

She huffed indignantly. "Haven't you learned by now, King Ashwood, that I do not need a knight in shining armor. I take care of myself."

"That you do, my little mage. Orange hair... downright diabolical," he teased, making her laugh. It had been a petty move but well worth it. He continued to walk beside her, drawing all attention their way, and causing people to stop and bow as they passed. "May I ask you to join me for some tea?"

"Now?" She wondered if he would take her all the way to the castle or if he expected her to lead him back to her home.

"There is a lovely café up the road that is a favorite of mine. Will you join me?"

She glanced around for her family but could not see them anywhere. With the recent attack on council members, she did not want to leave them alone. "I must find my sisters first."

"I assigned two of my guards to them. They are protected. I was hoping to get a few moments alone with you."

"As long as they are protected, I will join you."

He led them a few streets over to Café Convolo. She'd never been inside before, although she'd walked past it many times. It always appeared to be a quaint place that she'd enjoy. Her mother refused to go inside though claiming it was beneath them and she certainly couldn't go alone. Excited to finally visit, she hadn't realized she gripped the king's arm. He bent it at the elbow and placed his other hand over hers.

"You enjoy this establishment as well?" he questioned.

The feel of his warm fingers over hers had her blushing which she found embarrassing. Especially considering all the shameless flirting they'd engaged in. All it took was an inconspicuous touch to rile her which was ludicrous.

"I've never been, although I've always been curious to dine here."

One of his guards opened the door for them and Damien led her inside. They walked into a square antechamber crafted with wood paneling painted a muted green. Double doors with paned windows stood before them, the glass painted green as well to hide whatever lay beyond. White and black checkered tiles covered the floor and only a single podium stood in the room with a male butler. A spell kept the air at a refreshingly cool temperature compared to the weather outside.

He bowed his head, not surprised in the slightest to see the king.

"Private seating today, Nathaniel."

He nodded. "Right this way, Your Grace." The young man opened the doors and gestured them through. He closed them once their party was through, Damien halting to allow the man to lead them again.

Liana's heart skipped a beat as she took in the main room. She had been right that it was a quaint café but also wrong because it was far more. The large room held many smaller tables with only two chairs and a few larger tables with at most six chairs. Sporadically, a sofa and chairs with only a coffee table were laid out giving it a more relaxed feel. The walls held most of her attention though. Rows and rows of inlaid bookshelves filled the walls broken up by private alcoves with cushioned benches. In the center of the room stood a circular bar complete with a stove whose vent shot straight up through the ceiling and was fully stocked with liquor and wine. The patrons sat quietly reading a book while picking at a pastry and tea or relaxed on the sofas, talking quietly with their companions.

Liana recognized some of the patrons in her mage community, however, most were unknown to her. A few glances shot their way but veered away lazily as if not caring that the king was in their midst. It helped that Damien did not wear his crown today as well. He seemed to wear it only for special occasions such as, the ball, and supper the other night.

The butler led them to the back right corner of the café and gestured to an alcove decorated with a vibrant purple velvet cushion along the bench seat. The walls above the bench contained more shelves overflowing with books.

Damien gave the man a slight nod before sitting Liana on the bench. She breathed in the overpowering scent of freshly brewed coffee and baked bread, a complex mix of spices and faint hints of tobacco layered beneath. Two guards stood on either side of the alcove while the other two sat at the table directly in front of them.

Liana felt the telltale shift of energy in the air right before the butler summoned two menus and handed them to the couple. "I shall return shortly to take your order."

"Wow," Liana exclaimed, not bothering to look at the menu yet. She turned in the seat, her fingers running along the spines of the books. She didn't recognize a single title. "This is magnificent."

"I thought you might like it," he admitted softly.

She couldn't help the smile on her lips as she looked into those stunning eyes. "I'd hate to inflate your ego even more, but you were right, Damien. I love this place." The wicked grin he gave her had goosebumps rising along her arms then down her back.

"My ego does not exist when you are around, my little mage. You knock me down every chance you get."

She nodded. "You're welcome for keeping you humble, my king."

He chuckled then nudged her menu. "What would you like?" Their food options were limited but they all sounded delicious. As it was midafternoon and a bit warm, she chose a light salad. With her tea, she chose an orange scone. Damien ordered a plate of dried meats and cheeses with a glass of wine.

Her tea and scone were delivered first. Liana erected a privacy spell before they spoke again.

"Are you often berated on the streets like that? My guards have not reported a similar incident."

Liana sighed. "The other mage females have ridiculed me since I was a child, mostly when my back is turned, and sometimes to my face." She shrugged. "They need entertainment. I also think it makes them feel powerful, which I understand in a way. The only way they can do that is by putting other females down because they cannot do that with men." She shrugged again. "Those vampires though, they've never outright approached me. They have more freedom than mage females and I figured they would leave me alone."

He took her hand in his, threading their fingers together. Her heart raced at the move. "That sounds difficult to endure, especially when you were so young."

"It was not easy, but I became stronger for it. If it weren't for their vileness, I never would have started venturing out on my own. I never would have learned as much magic. Never would have met Felix or Grace. I wouldn't have helped as many people as I have if they didn't shun me."

"I sincerely doubt that, Liana. You have a pure soul. You would have helped them no matter if they alienated you or not." Uncomfortable with his praise, she pulled her hand away and focused on her scone. "You handled yourself well with them," he complimented.

"Yes, well, as I said, I've dealt with this for years." She put on a smile and turned to him. "Any particular reason you nabbed me off the streets for an impromptu luncheon?"

Reclined on the bench, both arms hanging over the back of the seat with his glass in one hand he answered, "I believe I asked you to tea, not luncheon. That was your decision."

She rolled her eyes. "It is past midday, and I am hungry which I am sure you accounted for before finding me."

"You assume I planned this?" he asked with that damned expertly raised brow. He must practice that in the mirror, she thought.

"I don't need to assume. I know you have carefully planned out every moment of this courtship." Which he most likely did. Liana didn't think the king left a single thing up to chance, not even when it came to her. He was a master of seduction and manipulation and a master of his kingdom. There was nothing in this land that he didn't control.

"I'm not sure if I should be flattered by your observation or offended."

She popped a bite of the scone into her mouth and chewed. "Both," she murmured behind her hand. He shook his head and laughed.

"You give me too much credit. As much as I've tried, you continue to surprise me at every turn, my little mage. How can I plan our courtship when I cannot anticipate your moves?"

"Don't play ignorant with me. This whole courtship is like a game of chess, which I'm sure you are a master at as well. You play all your pieces perfectly and are leading the rest of us in a game destined to be defeated."

Amusement left his eyes as he slugged back his drink. "You truly think the worst of me," he surmised.

"I would not say that."

He growled lightly as he leaned forward, his hand resting on his knee as he invaded her space. "Then what would you say because you explain my character so confidently as one that leaves much to be desired?"

Remaining calm, she nibbled on another piece of the scone. "I merely see who you truly are, and that is a man with great power that must fight every minute of the day to keep that power. As for me, I am just another piece in your fight to hold control of the kingdom."

Scowling, the king caught the attention of a servant and gestured to his glass before sliding it onto the small coffee table before them. "You make me sound very narrow-minded."

"I did not mean any offense, my king. I only pointed out that I have accepted my position in this world and have accepted who you are. There is much more to you than the throne but nothing quite as important." Glacial eyes glared into her own. She refused to back down. Everything she said was the truth.

A servant delivered the glass, breaking through her privacy spell for a moment.

"You think this way of me and still attempt to seduce me?" he questioned.

She copied his devilish smirk as best she could and leaned closer, their lips nearly touching. "Did I say that I did not favor you, Your Grace? Did I say that you repulsed me? Because I thought I'd made it clear that despite everything, I still desire you." His eyes went nearly black before her eyes were drawn to his parted mouth where his fangs slid out.

She didn't cower from him. Instead, she brushed her fingertips over the hand he gripped his knee with. Sliding them along his skin, she danced to the back of his wrist.

"Your pulse is racing, Damien." She whispered his name, drawing it out.

"How could I plan any of this when you are so unpredictable, my tempting little mage?" he growled around his fangs.

She pulled away, laughing as she did so and scooted over on the bench. "I am predictable to a fault. Whatever a lady would do, I shall do the opposite."

He took a moment to compose himself, swigging back more wine as his fangs receded and his eyes returned to normal. "Gods, I knew I shouldn't have tempted myself today." He shifted on the bench to close the gap again. He didn't touch her, but he didn't have to. Just the scent of him and the awareness of his presence had her head swimming. "Each moment I am with you becomes more and more tempting to taste your luscious lips."

Said lips tingled as she forced herself not to wet them. Gods, but she wanted that so much as well. This is exactly what she explained though. He was turning her own desire against her.

Liana reached for the rest of her scone and bit into it, the king's eyes tracking every movement and fixing on her lips. It tasted like dust as her mouth went dry. She forced it down with a gulp of tea.

"May I inquire about the investigation?" she asked, flipping the conversation. Damien sat back adopting his relaxed pose again. He cleared his throat before answering.

"It is ongoing," he revealed, purposefully obtuse. She gave him a droll look just as their plates arrived. Feeling relaxed, Liana shifted on the seat to draw her legs beneath her and placed the plate in her lap while facing

Damien. He plucked a slice of meat and cheese from his platter, leaning back again.

"Again, I offer my services. You know I am skilled with magic." She desperately wanted to be included. She wanted to prove that women were just as useful as men.

"Master Kinley is more than capable."

Liana shoveled the salad into her mouth to keep from arguing. Master Kinley was capable, but she could do things no other mage could. Not that she'd be revealing that to him. Not yet anyway. "Just a hint of what's happening. Tell me something. Is it the Separatists?" That reminded her to ask about the first rebellion, the one his father quelled.

His jaw clenched. "I believe it is."

"What of the rebellion with your father? I could not find any mention of it in the bibliography of your father's reign."

There went that damned brow again. "You researched my family?"

"Of course. After the attacks, and what Master Ranville said at supper the other night, I looked into it."

"Do you often research things?" he asked, intrigued.

She knew he did so to avoid answering her. "We were taught nothing of history or the monarchy during our lessons to be perfect ladies in high-society, so I often read on my own."

"And where did you find such taboo information?" His smirk said he already knew.

"My father's study." She leveled her fork at him as he chuckled. "And before you call me a thief, I returned each one after I completed it."

Hands held up in supplication, one still held his wine which he sipped. "I wouldn't dare. I was going to say that you are very determined and resourceful."

She nodded in agreement. "Thank you. Now, tell me about the rebellion," she demanded.

"Determined, indeed," he grumbled, then sighed. "Rebellion is a strong word considering it never amounted to anything. They are really a group of people that aim to split the kingdom by species. They believe we should be like the rest of the kingdoms and be segregated, left to rule over our own kind."

"And your father defeated them?"

He shook his head. "The separatists cannot technically be defeated. There will always be those that believe we are better apart than together. That particular rebellion thirty years ago was squashed by my father however."

"And they have gathered again," she surmised to which he nodded. "All the more reason to let me help. They would never suspect me to be capable of it."

"How would you help that would be a surprise? Everything you can do, Master Kinley can also do plus much, much more."

Liana stilled, her hand fisting around the fork as her teeth clenched. He sighed, rubbing a hand through his hair. "I did not mean to sound so harsh, Liana. What I meant is that there is nothing for you to do. Nor do I want you involved in this. You are already in danger because of your father's position. I do not want to further endanger you."

Nodding, she picked at the salad. His fingers brushed her chin to make her look at him, but she swatted them away. "Don't be mad, Liana. I only wish to protect you."

She gritted her teeth. "And I told you, I don't need your protection."

He sat back on a heavy sigh. "Until you are properly trained in combat, I'm not letting you anywhere near conflict. I cannot lose you," he declared. Liana set the plate on the table and didn't turn back to him.

"Fine," she sneered. "I am through. If I may take my leave, Your Highness?"

He cursed. "Stop acting like a child that didn't get her way."

Liana's back stiffened and she held her shoulders back leveling the king with a stare that could burn cities to the ground. He flinched. "I would like to go home, Your Highness." She was done with this conversation. All she needed right now was to vent her anger on the piano or in a painting. She was so tired of having to fight for even a scrap of acknowledgement or trust in her abilities.

"No. I am not done with my food yet," he countered. "Stop pouting. You are ruining my meal."

Sparks of magic erupted from her fingers as she curled them into fists. Her magic reacted to her anger and that did not usually end well. If it surged out of her control here, she would never be able to show her face in public again. Taking deep breaths, she focused on anything other than the king. Images of her tulips flitted through her mind, music lilting through her ears. Slowly, she calmed.

"What just happened?" Damien questioned. "I felt the rise of power. It was stifling."

"Nothing," she spat angrily then took another deep breath to calm.

"Does it truly anger you so much that I want you alive?" he growled.

She whirled on him. "That is not what angered me. It's you, and every other male that belittles me, that assumes I am not capable. I am the most skilled mage in this city but time and time again, I am beaten down, told to hide my power and be a proper lady." Damien's eyes widened the barest bit at her outburst before blanking.

"I lost count of how many times I pleaded with my father to pay for a spot beside my brothers in their magical education. When he refused, I begged him to teach me on his own. Still, he refused. And when I begged on my knees to even look at one of his spell books, he gave me Wesley's beginner's guide to magic. Now, they plan to give a boy free education simply because he shows a speck of talent when my family could have paid handsomely. I'm sick of being looked over, Damien!" she seethed.

His hand reached up to cup the side of her face. She hadn't realized she was crying until his thumb brushed away her tears. Pulling away, she dabbed at her face, embarrassed. Clearing her throat, she forced the tears back.

"I apologize, Your Highness. That was uncalled for, and I should not have yelled at you."

"Liana," he whispered brokenly, which had her facing him again. "You may have whatever your heart desires once you are my queen. I will force them to accept you into the mage school or I'll burn it to the ground and Master Kinley will teach you himself. Whatever you want. Please, just stay out of harm's way a little while longer."

How could she argue with that? What other male would offer to burn down buildings just for her sake, or offer her anything she desired? She didn't know if he truly meant it, although she found herself believing him. Capitulating, Liana nodded. There really was no other choice. As much as she rebelled and wished for a different way of life, this was her reality. There was no changing it.

"I will take you home," he said softly, tossing a few coins onto the table. Liana made herself presentable again and followed him out of the café. Guilt plagued her as they walked in silence.

"I'm sorry for ruining our lunch, Damien," she whispered.

"Don't apologize. I am sorry for making you feel inadequate. Truly though, there is not much information we've discovered from the rebels. We have one in custody, but he's taken too much of the antidote prior to capture for Master Kinley's truth serum to work. We wasted most of it on our previous prisoners and it takes too long to remake. There is nothing for you to do."

A guard held the gate to Liana's home open as they walked through. A sinister smile twisted her lips before she chuckled. "For being a master manipulator, you are too easy to fool, Your Highness." He paused, facing her with furrowed brows. She murmured a summoning spell while picturing her stash of potions. Two small vials with cork stoppers appeared in her hand. One held a vibrant purple liquid, the other a clear liquid.

She held the purple vial up. "Give this to the prisoner three hours before you give him the clear one. It will burn the antidote out of his system then you can use the clear vial which is truth serum." The king simply stared at her as she tucked them into his coat pocket. "And perhaps next time you can save me the dramatics and just tell me what I want to know," she suggested with an evil grin.

His mouth opened and closed then frowned. "You faked all that at the café so I would reveal information?"

"Oh no, it was real. But did I also use it to my advantage? Most certainly." Turning on her heel, she shot him a wink over her shoulder before walking up to the front door. "Until next time, Your Highness," she promised with more heat than was proper. He still stood there staring at nothing when she closed the door.

Liana chuckled. Two could most certainly play the game.

Chapter Sixteen

L iana still smirked as she reclined on her chaise lounge reading an adventure novel later that evening. She'd well and truly fooled the king into revealing information and there would be no forgetting that anytime soon. He fell right into her trap, proving that she could play just as well as the males. It was all too simple to play the simpering female in need of saving. She knew he wouldn't be able to resist an attempt at making her feel better. She hadn't expected him to reveal the information so easily though.

He wouldn't forget it either which meant she'd have to be diligent about keeping her guard up around him. It had been a strategic move giving him those potions. It revealed that she was capable of difficult magic but also did more to prove her usefulness in the future. It was worth it to give up that bit of information to gain future success.

Her body jolted as the door to her balcony opened. She wasn't all that surprised when the king slipped through.

Putting down the novel beside her, Liana waited for him to speak.

Dressed in all black yet again, she noticed the riding boots added to his outfit and the lack of a crown. Curiosity had her speaking first. "Going somewhere, Your Highness?"

He nodded, his long legs eating up the room as he walked toward her. She didn't move from her reclined position as he gently pushed her legs to the side so he could sit. "Your potions worked wonders. The man spilled his secrets. I thought you should know."

"I am pleased to hear that. But you could have sent a letter. Why are you in my bedroom, yet again?" she questioned smoothly despite the slow heat churning in her belly. The vampire was too attractive for her own good, especially with his hair pulled back in that tight knot again.

"May I inquire as to what you will be wearing to the next courtship ball?" he asked, throwing her off.

"An odd question. Did the king suddenly take up sewing and like to create me a gown?" she quipped.

"Simply curious. Besides, I've tried my hand at sewing. I'm dreadful."

She smiled. "It will be an emerald gown."

"Excellent. I shall see you at the ball then."

"That is a week away. Why shall we not see each other before then?"

The devious smile on his lips didn't bode well for her. "Am I to believe that the stubbornly independent Lady Liana Monroe is going to miss me?"

She sniffed. "I do not believe I said any such thing."

"Oh, but you certainly implied it." Her cheeks flushed. "Because I am so flattered, I shall tell you that I must travel to our neighboring city for a few days. The information the prisoner gave us was invaluable, so thank you. But do not fret, I shall return for the ball."

"A lady does not fret, Your Highness," she said primly. He merely smiled down at her. "What did he tell you? I could get you more potions, or perhaps I could go with you. I know plenty of torture spells."

"I told you not to fret." He paused, one brow rising. "What kind of torture spells?" he asked, intrigued. She only grinned back.

"Pray to the gods you never find out," she replied softly. He moved quickly as his hands caged her in, resting on the chaise. She leaned back, her head falling onto the chair as her chest rose and fell too fast. He leaned in, his chest pressed against hers, their lips nearly touching.

"How can my sweet little mage be such a tempting vixen?" he questioned, his breath hitting her lips. She placed her hands against his chest, feeling the hard planes of muscle.

"It's easy when my fiancé is so handsome."

He huffed a laugh as his mouth danced around hers, their noses bumping in an attempt to keep himself from actually kissing her. All she wanted in that moment were his lips on hers. If anyone ever found out, it would ruin her forever, but with his body hovering over her, his intoxicating scent filling her nose, she didn't care at all. Gods of virtue and virginity be damned, she wanted this man with every part of her body.

"You sound as if you truly like me," he quipped.

Liana gave a husky laugh. "Hardly. I only like the look of you."

Damien smiled, his fangs punching out. "Do you know that I can see right through this nightgown?" he questioned even though his eyes didn't stray from hers.

"I know," she answered breathlessly. Her hands slid up the column of his throat and pulled him beyond the last bit of space keeping her safe from ruin and kissed him.

She couldn't breathe as she held him, his lips soft against hers. Then he moaned and slid his lips against hers. She gasped for breath, mimicking his movements.

Never before had she been kissed, and she never imagined it could be like this. Never imagined that she'd drown in him. That she'd lose her mind at first touch.

There was nothing beyond his lips on hers. Nothing beyond the feeling of his hands sliding around her back to lift her body into his. His lips were insistent on hers then his tongue teased her lips and she moaned. Damien shifted, climbing onto the chaise with her, his body sinking into her deliciously. Something hit the floor but neither of them paid any attention. Liana thought they'd been close before, now it was as if they were one. His legs tangled with hers as their tongues danced.

He ripped away from her mouth, both of them panting. "Someone is coming," he whispered before he disappeared with vampiric speed. Liana couldn't hear anything, her heart beating like a drum in her ears. She rushed to extinguish her lamp then jumped in bed. Pretending to sleep, she heard her door squeak open. Behind her eyelids, she sensed a lamp lighting the room. It stayed for a few moments before she heard a voice.

"Liana? Everything alright?" Phillipa questioned.

"Fine, Phillipa. Just dropped my book while getting into bed."

"Okay, goodnight." The lamp light disappeared with the soft click of her door.

Long minutes later, she sensed his return. Liana rolled over in bed to find Damien standing over her. He leaned on the bed brushing his fingers through her hair which had been left undone for sleep.

"Temptress," he whispered. She smiled at the nickname. He placed a chaste kiss on her forehead. "Behave while I'm gone."

A devious smirk twitched on her lips. "Never," she declared in a whisper and delighted in the fact that his eyes sparked with amusement and something far darker. She grabbed his shirt before he could escape and pulled him onto her. He fell over catching himself with hands on either side of her head. She kissed him, needing so much more than just his lips.

"Be safe," she said.

"You've got me all twisted up. Am I now to believe that you actually care for me?" he teased.

"Doubtful. I've come to enjoy the idea of being queen. I cannot have you dying before it's official." His body shook the entire bed as he held in his laughter, his face buried in her neck. When his body stilled, his hand brushed away her hair and she arched her neck. Her core heated instantly at the thought of him biting her. In fact, she was on the verge of begging for it. Instead, his lips brushed a gentle kiss to her pounding pulse.

"Dream of me," he whispered so softly she thought she might have imagined it. Then he was gone.

It would be no trouble at all to dream of him.

Chapter Seventeen

L iana spent the next day in worship with the rest of her family which put her behind schedule for the orders that had come in over the week. She and Phillipa went out the following day with Sasha as her ever present guard to gather supplies.

Helen followed through on her end to deliver the orders to everyone a few weeks ago and even took payment from those that could afford it. Which is how she bought the majority of supplies today, in addition to Liana asking her father for a few coins to buy more altar supplies. They gathered the supplies quickly and returned to the house. Liana grabbed a few instruments from her father's study, thanking the gods he was at the council hall for the day so she could use them.

Sequestered in her room with Phillipa while Sasha stood on her balcony to keep guard, Liana began working on all the potions, salves, and objects requested. It took her well into the evening to complete it all, especially when she was required to stop for a few hours to attend supper with her family who hosted Wesley's courtier, Lady Jasmine and her parents, the Baron and Baroness Calva. They were a lovely family with excellent manners and their hands dripped money with their many residences around the kingdom and a town of their own to lord over, but Liana was never one for small-talk or such trivial dinners. Although the family was more powerful than her own, her mind constantly drifted to her work upstairs which Phillipa kept working on.

Even after dinner, Lady Monroe delayed her further by forcing her to join in prayers to the goddesses yet again. They prayed so often to the goddesses for marriage and fertility that, at this rate, Liana knew she was guaranteed a marriage with the king full of children even if their mixed species made it impossible to conceive.

Before anyone could stop her, Liana left early in the morning with Phillipa at her side. A different guard tagged along, one that she usually saw trailing Damien, but she was surprised to find that she was a bit disappointed to not see Sasha. The vampire guard didn't interact with her much. At some point though, Liana became comfortable with Sasha's presence. She kept her word and didn't tell the king about what she did, which surprised her as well. The loyal guard struck her as someone that was unwavering in their values so for Sasha to have done so meant a great deal to Liana.

They stopped at Helen and Bacchus' shop first. Liana knocked on the door which was still locked at this early hour. Helen walked out from the back and opened the door for them to enter. She eyed the new guard then gave Liana a pointed look. As soon as they were inside, Liana erected an opaque shield around them to exclude the vampire.

"The king stopped by the day after you were here last time," Helen informed without wasting any time. Liana summoned the bag of goods and handed it over.

"I am genuinely sorry, Helen. Did he cause too much trouble?"

Her brows lifted. "Not at all, dear. He was quite the gentleman." A smile filled her face as a twinkle of amusement lit her eyes. "Quite the charmer as well."

"What did he want?"

"He bought a dozen pastries, and we had a little chat."

Liana glanced at Phillipa with uncertainty, then back to the shifter. "That was all? Did he mention me?"

"Not at all. He caused a commotion among the other customers though. We've been busier than ever since he came in, the rumors spreading that he likes our pastries best. I'll tell you, Liana, you've got a good one in that male. He walked in all unassuming and waited in line like the others. When they realized who it was, everyone moved aside of course, but he insisted that they not and continued to wait."

"What did you talk about?"

The woman smiled again. "Oh, just this and that. Nothing in particular."

"It is far too much of a coincidence that he came here just a day after Liana," Phillipa pointed out.

"I know, however, I told you, he didn't ask about her."

Liana didn't know what to think of that. Perhaps the man wanted pastries. Or perhaps he supported a business that Liana also supported. She'd have to ask him about it.

"Thank you, Helen. If you could please deliver these items again, I've left a list with names."

"Of course, dear." She turned to leave but halted when Helen grabbed her arm. "He is different, Liana. I sense that he is genuine. I hope he is everything you deserve."

Liana nodded. "Thank you, Helen." When the shield dropped, her guard stood angrily just beyond it, Sasha leaned casually against the entrance.

"She is fine, Owen, now you may leave," Sasha directed toward the angry guard. Scowling, the man stormed off. "At least now I know it wasn't personal. You shield out everyone," the blonde snarked as she approached.

Liana huffed a laugh. "If there weren't so many nosey vampires around, I wouldn't have to shield against anyone."

Sasha smirked. "To the tailor's next?" she asked, already knowing her routine. Reluctantly, Liana nodded and led the way.

Her stop at Claudius's shop was brief. She only stopped by to drop off the bag once more before moving on to Felix's. Led up the stairs by one of the servants, Liana found Felix sitting in a wooden chair among the group of refugees as they sipped on their breakfasts. As one, the group stood.

Sasha moved to stand in front of Liana, sensing possible danger.

"Liana?" Felix asked, his head turned their way as he sniffed.

"Hello, Felix." She eyed the group, sensing no hostility from them. Two stepped forward which had Sasha mimicking them and reaching for the blade at her side. Liana halted the soldier, keeping her hand clasped around Sasha's wrist. The two that came forward were the ones that she'd healed last time. The male sank to his knees before her, quickly followed by the woman. He grabbed her hand in both of his and bowed his head.

"You saved my life, Lady Liana." She refrained from cringing at the man's words. No recognition was needed, actually, she preferred it that way. "I owe you a life-debt," he promised.

"That is kind of you, Sir, but…" Liana cut off as Sasha elbowed her. The soldier widened her eyes and nodded toward the man. Not sure what the woman meant by all that, Liana changed course. "You are welcome, Sir. What is your name?"

"Renatus, my Lady."

"Please, call me Liana."

He kept his head bowed. "Liana, I owe you my life. Your magic and skill saved me."

"Yes, well, as I said, you are welcome." Gently, she detangled her hand from his and looked to the woman who still kneeled but did not bow. "Your name, miss?"

"Adriana, my Lady. And thank you for your kindness and healing. Whatever you need, a favor, I will grant it. Just tell me."

"I appreciate the offer, Adriana. At the moment though, I can think of nothing. Perhaps another time." The woman nodded and finally stood, dragging her friend with her.

"Everyone sit down. Ladies, join us," Felix urged. The group made room for them as Liana summoned three cushions from the hall closet in her home that were often used for picnics. Scones were passed around while they settled in.

"How are you faring after the tragedy?" Liana questioned. There were ten in total, five shifters, two mages and three vampires. All looked a little worse for the wear in the same clothes she'd seen them in last time. Only the shifter that had been gutted wore new clothes. The men all wore long beards without access to a razorblade while everyone's hair looked a knotted mess without a comb. They at least had food and shelter, she thought to herself.

"We are dealing the best we can," a male shifter answered. Liana recognized him vaguely from their previous encounter. "I'm Tavian, and I must thank you for saving my brother and sister as well. We are all family here and their debt is also ours. We owe you for their lives and for sheltering our presence here."

Liana merely nodded. Words seemed inadequate in response. What could she say anyway? You're welcome sounded so pompous, so she kept her lips sealed.

"Is there anything more you've learned of the attack?" Phillipa asked.

Tavian shook his head as he pulled his hand into his lap. It was then that she noticed he held hands with the vampire female beside him. Tall and beautiful as all vampires were, this woman was in a league all her own with rich mocha colored skin and silky, straight black hair. Her face was square and proud with lips that were full while stunning brown eyes held a soft almond shape.

"My mate, Serena, was walking home when she heard the group riding toward our home. She outran them and warned us. It was enough time for us to grab the important documents and get out safely. Well, most of us anyway."

Liana knew there were more important things to discuss but she was caught on that one word, mate. The shifter called this female his mate. She thought only shifters could find their mates in another shifter. If that were the case, maybe the term was used interchangeably with wife in their culture. Still, she had never seen a mixed couple before.

"Did you see any of the attackers? Would you be able to identify any of them?" Phillipa asked while Liana glanced around at the others. She thought she spotted two more couples. A female shifter holding the hand of the female mage, and a female mage sitting in the lap of a male vampire. She should have been more surprised by the females which was strictly taboo among the mage, but her gaze fixated on the vampire and mage, the situation so close to her own. The mage huddled against her vampire while his arms wrapped around her waist.

Liana knew there must have been mixed couples in Triaedian, not that anyone talked of them. They were a kingdom founded on unity among races, of living with one another as neighbors and family. It was only inevitable that they started to love one another romantically. But to have it proven, to see a couple before her was a shock.

It shouldn't have though considering she'd been flirting with the king for weeks now. She'd even accepted his proposal of marriage which would make them the first public couple of mixed species. Panic filled her at the thought of all the responsibility that crashed upon her. She and Damien would be the examples, they would be the ones to pave the way for all those in hiding simply because they chose to love another. Internally panicking, Liana barely heard the others.

"I saw a few of them," Serena answered. "I'd be able to identify them."

"As would I," Renatus said. "I'd especially know the man that gutted me."

"What good does that do us? We cannot go after them. We must stay hidden," Adriana interjected.

"We cannot do nothing," Tavian argued. "They attacked us. We cannot let that go unpunished." Liana sat back as the family debated a topic that they seemed to have talked over quite thoroughly already.

"What will you all do now?" Sasha questioned once they settled on laying low once again. The group wasn't so forthcoming with her, especially since she wore the king's crest.

"We need a new home," the female mage sitting upon the vampire's lap declared. "One far away from here."

"We cannot leave. We will certainly be prosecuted if we try to live together in another kingdom," Adriana said.

Tavian shook his head. "We must stay in this kingdom, but far away from Sancta Valles."

"Yes, somewhere remote and private," Renatus agreed. The group considered where to go but could not decide on a place to settle when Sasha chimed in.

"There is a place to the north," she started. "A place I visited once a long time ago by accident. It's a small fishing village that is not even charted on most maps. Everyone there would support you. The majority of the population consisted of mixed couples."

"Why would we trust your word?" Tavian countered.

"You can trust her," Felix declared without further explanation.

"I have not been there in twenty years, so I cannot say what it is like now, but when I was there, it was a small, peaceful village. It is remote and somewhat difficult to get to which adds protection from being discovered."

Tavian narrowed his eyes on her. "How do you know of this place then?"

Liana glanced at her guard but found nothing to reveal what she felt in the moment. "It is a long and private story. I can write to a contact there to see what things are like now if you'd like."

"I think we should at least try it," Adriana said.

"That is a far way to go, and we have no guarantee it is safe, just her word," Tavian countered.

"It is a better option than any we have," Serena said softly to her mate. "Let her write to this person. If they say it is still a safe place for us, we will go."

"What if it is a trap?"

"What reason would she have to trap us? She has known where we are for almost two weeks now and we are still safe." Tavian stared at his mate, a silent conversation passing between them.

"Does everyone agree on traveling to this place?" he asked, then looked to each of his family who gave nods. Tawny eyes then turned to Sasha. "We will consider your offer. Let us know what your contact writes back." Sasha nodded.

"Is there anything that I can do for you all right now? Spells or healing?" Liana offered. No one spoke up. "Very well. If you all need anything before you leave, just let Felix know and he can contact me. I'd be happy to help in any way that I am able."

"You owe us nothing," Renatus said.

"No, but I still offer my help," she said before turning to Felix. "Are you available for a lesson?"

He smiled broadly. "Why you insist on calling them lessons is beyond me. You haven't needed a lesson in years."

"The lesson is for you, old man. You're getting rusty." Felix chuckled and accepted her hand gratefully as she led him up the stairs.

"And you're getting cocky, child," he teased. She only smiled at the easy banter, the tension in her shoulders from earlier releasing. This is exactly the company she liked to keep. These are the things she enjoyed doing. She hated high society and all the propriety. All she wanted was to be right here with Phillipa and Felix playing the cello or helping those in need. It made her life enjoyable, made it purposeful. And she'd never give that up. Not even for the king.

Chapter Eighteen

This ball already started out differently than the previous. Mainly because Liana was excited for it. She'd never felt so nervous to attend a social function before and she knew exactly why. It all had to do with a certain vampire, unfortunately. Never did she think she'd find someone like him. Someone that was powerful yet kind. Handsome yet humble. Gods, she never thought she'd find a male that valued her in the slightest, yet with him, it felt different. He made her feel valued beyond what she posed as an ornament to his crown. And it left her feeling giddy for the ball ahead when she would finally get that dance she offered him at the start of all this.

Night after night she dreamed of him. He even filled her thoughts during the day. She'd relive that steamy kiss in her bedroom over and over again, unable to stop thinking about it. About him and his devilish charm. Although she told herself it was all a part of the game, she feared that she truly was falling for him. He was intelligent, cunning and seemed to value her opinion. It could all be a farce, but if it weren't… Well then, she was in serious danger of loving the vampire.

Liana behaved and sat still for Phillipa as she braided and pinned her hair into an elegant up-do. It had been a week since she'd seen the king and she found that she did miss the infuriating man. However, it did give her time to catch up with her sister's courtships. She was even forced to attend their functions with her mother since she did not have any prior engagements.

Keeper Olivier seemed to forget about her completely, not that she minded much at all. Charlotte was head over heels for Master Ranville and things looked promising. Hannah had her pick of men, all of them enamored by her soft-spoken manner and youthful innocence, although Lord Dietrich seemed at the top of her list.

A knock sounded on Charlotte's door. "There is a delivery for Lady Liana Monroe," Henry said through the door. Lady Monroe rushed to take it, keeping her girls hidden behind the door.

"Oh, it must be jewelry!" Lady Monroe gushed as she returned with a square, red velvet box. "Here, Liana. Open it!" she urged. Liana took the box and grabbed the letter on top. Hiding it from view, she read quietly.

Dearest Liana,

These emeralds remind me of your eyes although nothing could ever replace the real thing. Nor could these jewels replace the feeling of when you turn that enchanting gaze on me. I look forward to this ball only so that I may look upon you once more.

Damien

Blushing fiercely, Liana ignored her sister's giggles and opened the box. With a gasp, she covered her gaping mouth. Her family rushed around to look upon the most magnificent piece of jewelry. The necklace had one large, teardrop emerald at its center which was lined by small diamonds. Along the rest of the chain were smaller teardrop emeralds, all of it lined with diamonds.

For the first time in Lady Monroe's life, she was speechless. They all were.

"That man is in love," Phillipa commented, making everyone turn to her. "What? A man does not send a woman something like that without having strong feelings. Not even a king," she explained, still fiddling with Liana's hair.

"She's right," Lady Monroe agreed. "The king must favor you."

"I've never seen something so sparkly before," Hannah cooed. Liana snapped the lid shut before she could touch it.

"Girls, we must hurry. We do not want to get stuck in that long line again," Lady Monroe declared. "We must not make the king wait to see your sister."

Lady Monroe got her wish as they rolled up to the castle with little delay. When they entered the ballroom, there were not nearly as many people yet. Luckily for Liana, that meant she was able to sit at a table and stuff her face with as many small bites as she could before things really got started.

"Liana," Charlotte whispered harshly beside her, nudging her as well. "Look who just walked in." Liana glanced up at the balcony. It was Lady Yvonne. The vampire looked stunning with her white-blonde hair curled to perfection and the navy gown she wore sparkling beautifully. "Look at her neck," Charlotte urged in outrage.

It was a diamond necklace, one that rivaled her own. "It doesn't mean anything," Liana whispered to her sister even as her heart plummeted with despair.

"That is an expensive necklace, one only a king could afford," Charlotte said.

"Her family is wealthy. Perhaps it is a family heirloom," Liana said, desperate to believe it. Neither of them did. "Oh, I feel so foolish now. Help me take this off, Charlotte," she demanded, near to tears.

"No," her sister declared sharply. "Do not allow him to win this game. Wear that necklace with pride. Strut about and show off to all these gawkers just how much you deserve that necklace. At the very least, you must show that vampire that she is not alone in this competition."

"I don't want to play games, Charlotte. I don't want to be in a competition, nor do I want everyone's attention."

Charlotte grabbed her sister by the shoulders, forcing her to look her in the eye. "Little sister, I know you abhor all of this. I know you'd much rather be at home reading or painting or tinkering with spells, but this is the world we live in. You must play these games because it is how women survive. We fight for the best husband we can find thereby finding the most stable life to live. We do what we must, Liana. Don't you forget it." Charlotte pulled away and tugged her gloves back up to her wrists. "Now, be confident. Show off those jewels."

Liana sat motionless, stunned by her sister's words. Charlotte always acted so flippant about such matters, speaking only of love and happy endings. She never would have guessed underneath it all lurked a ruthless woman. It made her calm though. Her sister would do just fine in this world.

Liana stayed seated with her parents and younger brothers as the first dance started. Her sisters and Wesley joined on the floor with their partners. She hadn't seen the king yet and started to get antsy.

Liana wanted to see him, but she also wanted to throttle him. She hated that he made her feel so special then turned around and ripped her heart out. She should have known better though. He'd done this before. But then he said he only wanted her, and she fell right back into his charms, his manipulations. She couldn't believe anything he said.

"My dear, stop looking so glum. He will be here," Lady Monroe told her daughter ignorantly. Liana just crossed her arms.

"Come, dance with me, daughter," Lord Monroe demanded, holding his hand out to her. Reluctantly, Liana let him pull her onto the dancefloor. "Why do you seem so sad?" he asked while leading her into the steps.

"I am not sad, Papa. I am merely thinking."

"I'm not sure I'd like to know what you were thinking based on that expression," he teased. She sighed and relaxed.

"Sorry, Papa. Thank you for the dance."

"What is troubling you, daughter?"

"It is nothing. Let us enjoy this dance and forget the world for a moment." And so, they did. They danced for three songs before he bowed out. Liana returned to the buffet table to gather some sweets.

"That is a lovely necklace," a smooth and chilling voice said from beside her. Liana turned to find Lady Yvonne.

"Thank you. Your necklace is beautiful as well." Liana kept her lips pulled into a polite smile.

"Yes, a gift from the king. I assume yours is as well."

Liana nodded, keeping her cool. She wondered where the shifter girl was and what her necklace looked like. "Indeed."

"I do wonder who he will choose. After all these weeks, and all the time I've spent with him, I find that I still cannot puzzle out the king."

Liana did her best to keep her questions off her face. How much time had they spent together? She felt she saw too much of the king herself and that it would have been obvious he favored her, not Yvonne. How did he have time to court Yvonne as well?

The woman probably said it merely to antagonize Liana. She gave the woman a tight-lipped smile. "There is not much to puzzle out. He is the king, and he will choose whichever female will gain him the most."

Yvonne raised a perfectly sculpted blonde brow. "You are so bold and harsh upon our king. That will not gain his favor."

"I do not aim to gain his favor," she declared, keeping the anger out of her voice despite it simmering beneath the surface, her magic sizzling to kindle it higher. "Enjoy the ball," Liana said in dismissal then turned away. She wouldn't play into these games, but she would defend herself and act unaffected. Most of all, she told the truth. She did not want the king's favor. She never had. In fact, she wanted to disappear into the world and be forgotten so that she may live her life in peace with her magic. The gods had other plans though and it seemed as though she would have to play along. For now.

Two women across the table whispered to each other while filling their plates, which of course meant Liana heard every word.

"The king has already made promises to Lady Yvonne. Rumor has it that he plans to propose to her."

The other woman gasped. "What about Lady Monroe and Ms. Stillwater? He gave them each a necklace."

"Just a ploy. He is keeping everyone happy until he can propose to Yvonne. Besides, what would he do with a mage? He needs a vampire that is also immortal."

Despite telling herself it didn't matter, that she didn't care for the king, her heart shattered. Could it possibly be true? Could he have played her so easily?

She scolded herself for being so naïve. Of course, he did. All the while she thought she was playing along so expertly when in fact, he was playing an entirely different game.

He manipulated her from the very beginning, and even when she knew of his duplicitousness, she still fell for his games. She truly believed he was going to marry her for her magic. That he wanted her for that advantage then slowly seduced her over the past few weeks. Now she learned that he proposed to the vampire as well. Did he do the same to the shifter? There was really no telling what the truth was though. Damien was a ruthless, hundred-year-old vampire and certainly not one to trifle with. His motives were clear as mud.

What had she been thinking anyway? She would live another sixty years if she was lucky. The latter half of that time she'd be old and wrinkled, not someone who still looked like Damien would want. Such stupid thinking indeed.

Shaking her head, Liana filled her plate with sweets and pastries. Carlisle and William dug into it as soon as she returned. A servant approached her with a silver tray, holding it out toward Liana. Instead of food there was a letter.

She took it with a polite smile, her name written on the front in his elegant script.

Liana,

I have been regrettably detained on business. I will do my best to make it to the ball tonight. Wait for me.

He didn't sign his name. Nor was it filled with pretty words. Straightforward and to the point, much like the man himself.

"What is it?" her mother asked excitedly. Liana didn't want anyone overhearing so she handed the letter over. "Oh. Very well," she said primly before slipping the paper into the bosom of her dress. Liana was not happy about it. First, he made a fool out of her with the necklace and fake promises, now he expects her to wait. That was enough.

Liana gulped down a glass of wine then found Charlotte. "Suggest to one of your many suitors that I would like a dance."

Charlotte shook her head. "You are with the king, they will not."

"Well, the king is not here, and I want to dance."

"No, Liana. Dance with Father or our brothers."

Liana lowered her voice. "I'm trying to play your game, Charlotte."

"And that is commendable but not this way. Dancing with other men will just make you look uncouth. Find another way." She returned to Master Ranville's arms for a dance.

Liana did the only other thing she could think of, she downed another glass of wine and asked Carlisle to dance. It was an awkward pairing because he was a head shorter than her, but he was a decent dancer despite how much he annoyed her on a daily basis. Little William was next and that was more of her just twirling him around and the little boy stepping all over her feet. Wesley relieved her at some point and gave her a proper dance. Between her father and brothers, they kept her busy and her mind off a certain vampire.

It was getting late, and most people had left. William had taken a nap but was back on the dancefloor doing whatever he pleased since he didn't know the steps. Liana was drunker than she'd ever been and was laughing at his antics.

Charlotte and Ranville sat at the table beside her family along with Hannah and one of the scholars. Charlotte leaned over and nudged Liana to look toward the stairs. Lady Yvonne was leaving. This brought a triumphant smile to Liana's face as she guzzled more wine.

"Really, Liana? Will you stop drinking already?" Lady Monroe complained. She shook her head defiantly then joined William on the dancefloor. They swayed and twirled around the floor, essentially knocking everyone else out. They were still going well after everyone had left.

"Liana, William, let us go now," Lord Monroe called out, gathering his family. Carlisle passed out on a bench nearby while Hannah and Charlotte leaned precariously against one another, their eyes closed.

"But, Father," William complained as the musicians finally ceased their playing. With haste, they left their instruments in the stand and hurried out of the ballroom.

"Let's go, son. It is far too late." Liana dragged her brother toward the table.

"Wait!" someone called. Liana's body froze as she recognized it. King Ashwood sprinted into the ballroom with vampiric speed. "Wait. I am very sorry to have made you all wait so long," he said, fighting for breath. Another vampire followed behind him with two cups. One was a glass of water, the other a copper decorative goblet. He took the water first and gulped it down.

"I know it is late, but please allow me one dance with Lady Liana."

"If you must, Your Highness. My family is very tired though and it is a long ride home," Lord Monroe said in resignation.

"Then you must stay in the castle tonight. There are plenty of rooms."

"Generous, but unnecessary, Your Highness. We will make it home. Take your dance, if you please." He sat back down with an already sleeping William in his arms. That kid could sleep anywhere and instantly should he choose. It really was quite remarkable.

King Ashwood wiped his face then turned his back as he gulped the contents of the goblet. When he turned back around, he held his hand out to Liana.

"There is no music," she said, pouting.

"You know a spell, little mage. Let us dance," he urged.

"I'm sure I don't know a spell," she denied. He blew out a heavy breath and scrubbed his hands through his long damp hair. Another servant appeared with his crown held aloft on a red velvet pillow. Damien grabbed it absently and shoved it upon his sweat-slicked hair, the ornament doing nothing for resolve as it made him all the more handsome and powerful.

"I just ran here on foot for an hour with unrelenting vampiric speed to get to you, Liana. Please, just one dance." One of her family started the instruments and she finally took his hand. She let him lead but the alcohol and her resolve fumbled her steps.

"Will you please guard our conversation?" Damien asked as they danced. She did so because she also wanted to talk. "Are you drunk?" he asked angrily.

She glared up at him with narrowed eyes. "You make me wait all night and have the audacity to ask if I am drunk? Of course, I am. I've been here for hours."

His jaw clenched. "I told you. I had business that I couldn't leave. As soon as I was able, I ran here on foot. Do you know that last time I did that for someone?" he asked seriously. "Never. I've never done that for anyone."

"Don't think to flatter me, Your Highness," she sneered. "You can write your frilly words and spout your nonsense, but I will not fall for it again." They gave up the pretense of dancing and simply stood there.

"What are you talking about?" he asked, planting his hands on his hips.

"The necklace. Your note. The flirtations. It's all just a big game. You make me feel special then rip it all away."

"I meant what I said in that note. I'm sorry I was late. As I've explained twice now," he said through gritted teeth. She slashed her hand through the air cutting him off.

"I'm not talking about that. I'm talking about Lady Yvonne and Ms. Stillwater. You gave them a necklace too. You promised Yvonne marriage as you did me," she accused, her voice rising with her anger too much to control.

He frowned. "I did no such thing. I gave her the necklace to keep her father happy, but I would never propose to her. Where did you hear this?" Liana looked away. Could she believe him? He gripped her chin roughly, forcing her to look at him. "Where, Liana?"

She slapped his hand away, pointing her finger at him as she shook with anger. "Don't you ever touch me in anger, Damien. Ever!" she declared fiercely. He took a step back, planting one hand on his hip and the other rubbed at the back of his neck.

"Everything all right, daughter?" Lord Monroe asked just outside her spell. She lowered it quickly.

"Fine, Papa," she lied, keeping her back to him.

"You may be a king, but she is still my daughter. Do not touch her again," he declared angrily before returning to their table. Liana erected the spell again.

"I'm sorry," he said sincerely. "I promise you, Liana, that I shall never touch you in anger again. And I promise you that I have only proposed to you. You are the only woman I want. Have I not proven that yet? I spend every free moment I have with you. I host your family any chance I get just so I may see you again." His hands fisted then released. "Even when we are apart, I think only of you."

Keeping her side to him, she wiped her tears. "I know you think me duplicitous, that I'm manipulating you. I am not. I swear to the gods that I am not deceiving you, Liana. I've only offered you marriage. You are the only one I want."

She couldn't trust him. What difference did it make though if she believed him or not? There was nothing she could do to rid herself of him. She was stuck in this until the end. Whatever end that may be.

Sensing her defeat, he opened his arms toward her.

"Come here, my little mage. I must hold you. It has been a trying week and the only thing I've looked forward to is having you in my arms."

It was when he said sweet things like that, that Liana found herself melting, her resolve disappearing. She walked into his arms, resting her hands on his shoulders. His hands were high on her waist as he pulled her tighter into his body. She went easily, clasping her hands behind his neck and resting her forehead on his chest.

"Why do you infuriate me so easily?" she wondered aloud, her voice soft.

"The feeling is entirely mutual, my little mage." They swayed gently, not performing any dance. "You look beautiful tonight," he whispered.

"Thank you." She sighed deeply. "And you smell wonderful," she said, breathing him in.

"Glad you think so considering I'm still sweating from my run to get to you."

She leaned her head back, resting her chin on his chest. "I told you I didn't need a knight in shining armor, so you only have yourself to blame for the run."

"And miss you in this dress? Never. Besides, I'm glad I got to see you all glossy-eyed and adorably drunk," he teased with a smirk. She huffed, resting her cheek on his chest. With a big yawn, she closed her eyes. The king buried his nose in her hair and took a deep breath, calming himself with her scent.

"There was something else," she said hesitantly. He sighed.

"Yes, my trying fiancé?"

"What happens when I am gray and old? You won't want me anymore."

He brushed a hand over her hair. "I will always want you. However, there are ways to prolong your life. Drinking my blood is one. It will not keep you alive forever, but far longer than a normal mage."

"Drink blood? I think I need a taste test before I agree to that one," she mumbled, her words hardly intelligible.

"We should call it a night, Liana. Everyone is tired." She hummed and nodded. The spell fell and the music got louder. "Come on, little mage, walk for me." Liana took a few steps away from him before tilting to the side. He kept her tightly against his side as they walked toward her family. "Alright, definitely time to go," he commented. The music cut out. "Very sorry to keep you all so late. My offer still stands to allow you to stay."

Lord Monroe looked concernedly at his daughter nearly passed out against the king. "We shall be fine, Your Highness. Thank you."

After Damien helped Liana out, having to carry her on the many stairs, the family said their farewells. They put all the children in one carriage while their parents sat with Liana as she swiftly passed out on the bench.

"I think he truly loves her," Michael whispered to his wife.

"I think so too. Why do you sound so worried?"

He looked to his peaceful, innocent daughter. "Because he truly loves her which puts her at even more risk from his enemies and his own possessiveness."

Mary didn't have a response to that.

Chapter Nineteen

Liana regretted every drink she had at the ball. It took a full day of recovering before she felt well enough to leave bed. Damien had been thoughtful enough to send a hangover cure in the morning with a letter that read,

Dearest Liana,

Please take this hangover cure. I hear it is the best and I cannot stand the thought of you suffering. If you feel up to it, join me for luncheon tomorrow afternoon. Bring the whole family and your sister's suitors if need be. Your brother's courtier as well.

Damien.

Which is why the entire family was piled into their carriages once again and riding toward the castle. Wesley invited his courtier, Jasmine, who was a lovely girl and seemed to be infatuated by him. Lady Monroe was thrilled about the advantageous match, the girl's family one of the wealthiest in Triaedian. Their family line were keepers of a province in the south, home to the third largest city in Triaedian. They kept a grand mansion in Sancta Valles as well, one that Wesley would inherit along with the council title their own father would pass down to him considering the Baron and Baroness Calva only had one daughter. It would solidify the Monroe's as a vital part in high society which Lady Monroe couldn't stop talking about when she wasn't bragging about the king and Liana's courtship.

Each of her sisters brought their first picks of suitors which meant Master Ranville and Lord Dietrich accompanied them to the castle as well. It was a beautiful summer day when they took their luncheon on the hillside by the lake Damien mentioned he liked to swim in.

"Thank you for hosting everyone," Liana whispered to Damien as soon as they were all settled in their picnic. There were three large blankets spread out for everyone to sit upon. Cushions and stools were also available which Lord and Lady Monroe took advantage of.

"You are welcome. How are you feeling?" he asked, preparing two plates.

"Much better. Is there any chance you would forget all about that night?" she asked, embarrassed. He laughed.

"Never. I will cherish those memories forever." She took the plate from him gratefully.

"I'm sorry I yelled at you."

"Do not apologize, Liana. I deserved it. I should never have grabbed you like that."

"Oh, I wasn't talking about that," she corrected quickly. "You definitely deserved that. I was talking about Yvonne, and my accusations. That was unfair of me."

"Ah, yes. That." He paused, looking out toward the lake. "You listen to a lot of gossip considering how much you shun it."

"I'll admit I jumped to conclusions. And I do not usually pay attention to such idle ramblings. It's just that… Never mind. It is over with."

"No, tell me. Tell me what made you doubt me." His icy eyes were even more white in the bright sun.

"They were saying something very similar to my own truth. That you had proposed to Yvonne but were keeping up appearances with me and the shifter."

He shook his head. "People gossip so much that they very nearly reach the truth," he commented dryly before he sobered, capturing her gaze. "I swear to you, Liana, I am not stringing you along and I have not proposed to Yvonne."

"You don't need to say it again. I believed you." Or at least she convinced herself to believe him because there was no other choice. Even if he did, she would continue the course and seduce him into letting her do as she pleased.

He merely nodded before drinking his wine. "May I ask you some questions?" she queried, her curiosity getting the better of her. He nodded again. "I have tried to learn more about vampires. The books we have do not say much."

He cut her off quickly, "Privacy spell." Chewing on her bottom lip, she glanced toward Master Ranville and the other older mage males. They would surely sense her use of magic, which she told Damien.

"Hence why I've got Master Kinley sitting behind us. No one will suspect it is you." Liana glanced behind them, surprised to find Master Kinley sitting on a chair in the grass sipping on a goblet of wine with his wife beside him. She hadn't even noticed him before because she was too enraptured by the king.

She nodded and said the spell quickly. It would be a shield that still allowed their voices to be heard but the words to be jumbled so no one could understand them. They were all sitting too close for someone to not be able to hear them.

"I've seen the blood cafes, but who do you drink from?"

He popped a few grapes into his mouth and chewed before answering. "We only take from willing subjects. Most of my servants are willing so it makes it quite easy for me and the other vampires in the castle."

"Where do you bite them?" She'd spoken with Felix and Cassia before on such matters, but that was different. This was personal.

He leaned back on his hand which brought his face closer to hers. "Such a curious little mage. Why is that? Do you want me to bite you?" he asked, his voice going lower.

She gulped, looking at his lips. "I think we both know by now that I do." There was no denying it any longer. She dreamed of him biting her every night. Damien's eyes dilated. "Where do you bite?" she asked again. She'd been bitten once before. She was just a young girl at the time, and she offered her wrist to another young vampire girl who starved on the streets. She remembered very little of it, only that it stung a bit.

"It depends on who I drink from. Most often I will drink from the wrist. If they do not prefer it that way, they cut their own wrist into a cup. That is painful though, our bite is not."

Liana waited on bated breath for him to keep talking. "And if you're not with a servant?"

His eyes focused on hers. He deliberately leaned in toward her making her pulse pound even faster and heat pool in her belly. "If I bit you, is that what you want to ask?" he whispered huskily. She chewed on her lip and nodded. "Where do you imagine me biting you?" She lifted a shaky hand to the side of her neck.

He shook his head. "If I were to drink from your body it would be nowhere visible. You'll have to be my wife before I say anything more. It is entirely too improper a place to mention to a lady."

Liana could hardly breathe as she felt something hot and wet between her legs. Damien took a deliberate deep breath. "I smell your arousal," he said with a cocky smirk.

She cleared her throat suddenly and leaned away. "That is not fair," she complained, trying to brush down her skirts and hide whatever he smelled.

"Fair?" He barked out a laugh. "What is not fair, is waiting over one-hundred years for you, Wife."

"We aren't married yet," she retorted but her heart fluttered at the endearment.

He chuckled darkly. "I hear your heart, Liana. I know you like the idea." She crossed her arms and looked away.

"So unfair," she grumbled, which only made him laugh.

"Here, have some chocolate and forget about this unfairness." He teased the chocolate in front of her nose, and she surprised him by snapping her teeth around it, nipping his fingers. She chewed happily while he stared unblinking at her.

"What do you mean you waited a hundred years for me? You are only one-hundred years old," she pointed out and he seemed to break himself out of the trance she'd put him in with her lips on his fingers.

"I simply meant that I waited my entire life to find someone like you." He stuck his fingers in his mouth and sucked them clean. Liana had to look away from the movement. "I thought I was destined to never find my equal, my queen. Until that night at the ball."

Her breath froze in her chest. His equal? Surely, he was playing with her again.

"Why am I so special to have broken your one-hundred-year celibacy?" she teased for her own sanity. His grin was quick and sharp.

"I never said I was celibate, only that I did not find a wife worthy of me."

She rolled her eyes. "And what was it you said earlier about not having an ego around me?" He laughed loudly and unabashedly, which had her joining in.

"You've got me so twisted that I cannot articulate my thoughts clearly anymore," he admitted. She didn't believe him for a second. "Since I was old enough to court a lady, I've only ever found two types of females. Ones too eager to marry a prince, or docile ones that only do as their parents tell them."

"How am I any different from the latter, because I assure you, I am not. If it weren't for my mother, I wouldn't be here right now."

"I doubt that," he countered. "When I saw you in that ballroom, so proud and vulnerable at the same time, yet bold enough to dance with a shifter, I knew you were different. So, I sought you out. I needed to know more. And I was right. You were finally someone I could picture as my queen."

She wasn't sure if she should be flattered or not. He didn't exactly complement her, nor was she any clearer on why he chose her other than he wanted her power, which seemed to be reason enough. "So, you chose me because I was different?"

"Yes. Different from every other sheep in that ballroom. I knew you weren't vying for me simply because of my title. You were intelligent, witty, and unashamedly yourself."

She wouldn't say that. She had been plenty self-conscious as they spoke that first night.

"Enough of your pretty words, King. I like you much better when we are sparring with our wits." In truth, she didn't want him to keep talking and make her weaker. She already enjoyed his company far too much and now he spouted confessions of true admiration. It was too much.

Shaking his head with a smile, he leaned back with his elbows on a pillow to support himself. "Perhaps you'd like it better if we exchanged dreams. I can tell you mine became extremely vivid the longer I spent away from you. Especially after everything I saw through your nightgown."

Her entire face heated as she shoved a cracker with meat and cheese into her mouth. Gods, the man was a menace for her composure.

"Your Highness, do you have any preference?" Lady Monroe asked, and Liana had no idea what she referenced.

"Red wine," he answered smoothly, then smiled at Liana. "Which type of wine do you prefer, Lady Monroe?"

He knew the answer before she spoke it. "White wine, Your Highness." She'd always choose everything opposite him simply out of principle.

"Your vineyard supplies both, does it not, Your Grace?" Master Ranville asked.

"It does."

"And how is the crop this season? We have not had as much rain."

Liana's brows furrowed when she saw Damien's face go blank. He did not want to talk about this subject which had her intrigued to hear the answer as well. "The rain has not been the issue but diseased crops. We had to burn half the crop before the infection could spread to the rest."

"Such a shame. You do have the best wine in the city." Master Ranville took a swig from his goblet. "Did Lord Monroe tell you we have accepted the farmer boy into the school?"

"I have not had the chance, Master Ranville," Lord Monroe interjected.

"That is wonderful news. It is always a delight to hear the people of Triaedian aiding one another." That made her think of Grace and the other homeless. She missed aiding them last night because she had still felt slightly ill. She would have to go to them tonight to make up for it. She also needed to ask Damien if he ever talked to his Keeper of Coin about the funds that were meant to go to the poor because clearly, they were still not receiving it.

"This scholarship got us thinking," Master Ranville continued. "We thought it might be beneficial to open a second mage school associated with the council that would strictly be for soldiers. With the recent attacks, we thought it necessary to start training more mages to defend our people from these rebels. There would be a small fee, but not as extravagant as the normal mage education. They would receive basic combat training."

"If any mage chooses to become a soldier, they may enroll in my ranks free of charge and receive combat training with adequate compensation. Master Kinley oversees training of our mage in the army, and I trust him to continue doing so. No extra school will be necessary, Master Ranville," Damien explained, shutting him down quickly.

"Have there been more attacks, Your Highness?" Lord Dietrich asked, quickly changing the subject although Liana noticed the scowl grace Ranville's face before he wiped it away swiftly. She hadn't much interacted with the man and didn't feel the need to, but he was highly respected in their circles even if she thought him too stringent in his patriarchal ideas.

He shook his head. "No more attacks. We discovered the rebel's hideout and apprehended them all. I believe we are done with the attacks."

Liana's curiosity peaked. She hadn't heard any of this yet. She'd have to get him alone to pry more details out of him.

"I hope so, my King," Master Ranville commented somberly. His face turned into the sun, eyes squinting as he looked toward the lake. "Do you fish on those canoes down there?" Liana followed to where he pointed. Her eyes caught on the many boats tied to the dock and a plan formed.

"I do not fish regularly, but yes, that is what they are used for," Damien replied.

"I fancy a boat ride," she declared, standing and brushing out her skirts. "Would anyone care to join me?"

"Do you even know how to use an oar?" Carlisle teased.

"It cannot be that difficult if you know how," she retorted. Carlisle's face twisted at her insult.

"Allow me to escort you, Lady Monroe. I am a skilled rower," Damien offered. The others followed, only Lord and Lady Monroe staying behind.

Damien and the servants helped everyone into the large canoes. Hannah went with Lord Dietrich, Charlotte with Master Ranville. Wesley took Jasmine which left Carlisle and William to their own devices.

"You two will not go on your own," Damien declared.

Liana needed the king alone, so she urged, "It's fine. Let them go."

"What if they tip the boat and drown?"

"I'd save William," she offered, fond of her youngest brother.

"What about me?" Carlisle exclaimed.

"The fish can have you," she deadpanned.

Damien chuckled. "Mikael, go with them," he ordered the servant. He was a hulking brute of a vampire and nearly tipped the boat as he staggered in. Hearing Carlisle's squeal of terror had her laughing so hard she doubled over.

"Shut up, Liana!" the boy screamed as Mikael shoved away from the dock and started rowing.

"Let's go, troublemaker," Damien called, holding out a hand to her from their boat. She grabbed his hand, still chuckling.

"What happened to, temptress?" she teased.

"Oh, that still stands. You wear many hats, my little mage." She watched raptly as he secured his hair into a tight knot, loving that he pulled it back again. As soon as he started rowing, she put up a privacy spell. "So, what is it that you wanted to ask me so desperately that you forced us all out here?" he asked, all too aware of her schemes. She picked at her nails.

"I'm not sure what you mean. I only wanted a ride around the lake." He raised that damned eyebrow, not believing her at all. "Perhaps I wanted to know what happened while you were away."

"Ah," he said with a chuckle. "There's the truth. Our prisoner gave us the location of the rebel command's hideout. We stalked it for a few days before raiding. Most were killed. A few were taken prisoner." She didn't comment on the brutality of it. He already made his thoughts known about mercy where the rebels were involved.

"And what kept you that you nearly missed the ball?"

"The council in the city caught word of what happened and that I was there. They insisted on a dinner in my honor."

"I'm surprised you are not rotund considering how much people shower you with food."

That cocky grin found its way back on his lips. "Vampires need a lot of fuel. I am also a trained soldier that spars daily. I will not become rotund, as you say." She watched as he pulled on the oars again, his sleeves rolled up to the elbows to show off the corded muscle flexing as he did so. She leaned back on her hands, enjoying the view.

"No, I don't think you will," she said, her voice low and sultry.

"You look rather pleased with your position."

"Most definitely," she purred.

"You could paddle for a moment, give me some rest," he teased. She shook her head.

"I'm perfectly happy where I am. Actually," she said, holding her finger toward him. Slashing down, she tore the V of his blouse down to his belly button with magic. Biting her lip, she admired his rippling muscles. "Much better."

They were far enough away from everyone else that they wouldn't notice his gaping shirt. His vampire guards might but she wasn't worried about them.

"I feel objectified," he complained.

"That was my intention." She gave him a wink before biting her lower lip.

"We could make this a fair fight if you loosen the ties of your bodice, my lovely Fiancé." Liana's hand paused midair to do so when her eyes caught on something over Damien's shoulder. It was a flicker of something, the sun forcing her to squint. "That was a joke, Liana," he said but she didn't hear him, her eyes caught on something in the large oak beside the lake. It was large and moving amongst the branches.

"What is that?" she wondered aloud, her heart dancing in fear. There were many creatures in the forest and the only ones she knew that large were either bears or mountain lions. Seeing as it was in the tree, she was going with a mountain lion. Just as Damien turned to look as well, she saw it. An arrow speeding directly toward Damien's back.

Her magic reacted faster than she could. By the time she gasped, taught strings of golden magic caught the arrow mid-air and halted it. Damien stared at the vile weapon only inches from going through his heart as it vibrated from the angry thrum from her magic. Liana's lungs nearly exploded as she took heaving breaths, her body beginning to shake. That had been too close. Far too close.

She dropped the arrow into the boat and gripped the sides of it, her magic surging inside her, angry and riled like a beast. It did not like Damien being threatened. She did not like him being threatened.

"Liana?" Damien questioned cautiously. She couldn't see him. Only blind fury remained, clouding her vision as she saw that arrow launch toward him over and over again. Damien shouted for his guards just as hell rained down around them. Arrows launched from the forest, a cloud of black against the bright sky.

Damien cursed. "Flip the boats! Get under cover!" he screamed at everyone just before Damien flipped her into the water.

Liana screamed. She still didn't know how to swim.

Chapter Twenty

Liana's scream died in her throat as water filled it. She retched into the water as someone grabbed her. Sputtering she wiped her eyes to find Damien holding her. She clung to him, using his body as a life-raft.

"I can't swim, you idiot!" she yelled right before a hundred thuds echoed under the hollowness of the boat. Liana screamed again ducking into Damien as he grunted under her weight and the blow of arrows as he held onto the boat over them while it acted as a shield. She shook like a leaf, the thunderous noise cutting off just as quickly as it started.

"Although you cannot swim, I thought you'd like it less if you were impaled by a hundred arrows," he retorted, to which she could only nod. "I need you to hold on to the seat. I need to let go so I can swim us back to shore. Do you understand?" he said slowly and clearly. She nodded, her hands shook so badly she was barely able to hold on when he let go. He swam with vampiric speed to the bank where his servants and guards dragged them out of the water. Liana climbed up the muddy bank and sank into the grass, her chest heaving for breath.

"Incoming!" someone shouted. Damien dragged her back to the boat where the team held it aloft to guard from another round of arrows. He wrapped his body around hers as well, giving her extra protection and she clung to him, her face buried into his chest.

"Clear! Master Kinley has a shield a few paces away. Go! Go!" someone ordered. Damien carried her to the shield where he deposited her on the ground, her mother and father falling on her with tears in their eyes.

"What of the others?" Damien asked Master Kinley, searching the lake. There were four boats turned upside down afloat on the lake, all embedded with arrows. One zoomed quickly toward the bank which was likely Mikael with Carlisle and William.

"Still in the water. Reinforcements are on the way," Master Kinley relayed even as Liana saw a line of blurred forms dart from behind, coming from the castle, and going around the lake to attack the archers. They stopped short as shapes exited the cover of the forest. The king's vampires didn't waste time in attacking the rebel vampires. As the two forces clashed together in a frenzy of incomprehensible movements, an army of mage and shifter soldiers rounded the castle. The shifters were in their animal forms while the mage rode hard on horseback around the lake. In response, three lines of mage and shifters walked out of the forest, many of the mages merging their shields together to keep their forces protected from attack.

Master Kinley swore as another volley of arrows soared from the trees. Damien's mages erected shields to cover their people as they continued to charge. Liana's eyes returned to the lake to find one boat reaching the shore. Servants and guards helped them out of the water.

"Take cover!" Damien shouted before he zipped down to the boat. He helped erect it then tucked her brothers into his body, shielding them as he had with her. As soon as the arrows landed, he carried them both into the protective shield. William cried quietly embraced in his mother's arms while Carlisle simply sat shell-shocked with their father. Liana wrapped her arms around herself, her body still shaking. Her magic had calmed to a manageable level but still raged inside her, leaking uncontrollably from her fingertips. While it seethed, she could hardly believe this was happening. Damien had been right that she needed more combat training. And there would be no waiting any longer. Not after today.

Master Kinley let his shield drop as he raced to join his army in battle. Lord Monroe replaced it, keeping his family safe while waiting for the others.

The other boats moved too slowly which is why Damien, Mikael and another vampire dove into the water. They propelled the remaining three boats to shore. Before they could get them out of the water, another cloud of arrows rained down on them.

Across the lake, Damien's forces battled with the rebels. Shields were dropped in favor of one-on-one combat. Whereas Damien's army fought back-to-back with their fellow soldiers, no matter their race, the rebels only fought with their own. It left the vampires and shifters open to attacks by Damien's mage, unable to protect themselves from magic.

As arrows pelted through the armies, there was no distinguishing enemy from ally, all forces that weren't beneath a shield fell prey to the blanket of deadly points. As the last arrows fell, the shields dropped and fighting resumed while on shore, Damien's vampires launched the boats away and everyone sprinted for the cover of the shield.

All except the third boat. She didn't see Damien, Charlotte or Master Ranville so that must have been their boat. Damien finally flung the boat away then walked up the shore. Master Ranville ran toward them now that he was free of the water.

"Damien," she said, her voice cracking as she tried to scream at him to run. Why was he walking? The damn vampire could move faster than any animal alive, yet he walked. Then she saw it, and she knew everyone else did as the group gasped then went still.

Charlotte.

He carried a limp Charlotte in his arms, an arrow protruding from her chest.

Lady Monroe's anguished scream cracked through the air right before the arrows rose from the trees like a cloud of death. There would be no escaping it for Damien.

"Expand the shield!" she demanded.

"I cannot. This is as much as I can do," her father admitted on a sob. Pathetic. Liana could create shields as large as her house whereas this one was only larger enough to fit their group.

She pleaded with her eyes for him to hurry, glancing back and forth between him and the arrows. "Damien, hurry!" she screamed at him.

"I can't move the arrow!" he screamed back, carrying Charlotte so that not a single step jostled her.

He was still too far. He wouldn't make it. Either he risked Charlotte and ran, or he sacrificed himself and they likely both died. Tears poured down Liana's face. Neither of those options would do. They both had to survive.

His guards ran to a boat which they could use to protect them. Relief had her sinking to her knees.

Then she saw it. The person in the tree. She'd forgotten about them.

Everything slowed as she caught sight of it. Another arrow zooming over the lake and far closer than the others. "Damien, the tree!" she screamed. His eyes caught on hers and with his next step, he shifted slightly to his left, still careful not to jostle Charlotte.

His roar of pain tore at her soul as the arrow embedded into his back. He jolted forward with one step but held. Liana looked toward the vampires. They hoisted the boat. As fast as they were, they had moved too late. They weren't going to make it.

Rage was a living thing inside her as her magic surged in her veins. There was nothing left to do except to make those rebels pay for what they did. For hurting Damien, and likely killing Charlotte. Her heart shattered into a million pieces as Damien gave her a look of goodbye and sank to one knee, curling over Charlotte. With his last breath, he was protecting her sister. Her sister, not his own life. The king's life.

Bolting out of the circle, she sprinted toward him as everyone shouted for her. She didn't make it five steps before the magic answered her call. It surged from the depths of her core, filling her body. Her skin glowed a brilliant golden light right before she threw her arms forward and with a roar of vengeance, threw her power out in a rapidly expanding shield of golden light. It exploded faster than the vampires could run, expanding to the size of the lake as it raced across the surface, water surging against the shore as it passed.

The arrows were knocked out of the air to drop uselessly to the ground. Everything in the wake of her power was knocked back, even their own people. They were flung off their feet and collapsed to the ground. It didn't stop as it hit the forest line. Snapping branches mixed with the screams of the rebels as the force hit them.

The golden shield slowed as it peaked over the top of the hill then faded, the world going eerily silent.

Liana stumbled as exhaustion slammed into her. That was too much magic. Too much. Falling to her knees in front of Charlotte and Damien, she panted, her body slick with sweat.

"That was incredible," Damien said before coughing up blood.

"Let me heal you," she mumbled, reaching for him. In the back of her mind, terror screamed at her to flee, to get away from the people that just witnessed her impossible strength of magic. She shoved it away easily, her sister and Damien at the forefront of her concern.

"No. I'll be fine. Take care of your sister."

Liana placed her hand around where the arrow buried itself in Charlotte's chest. "It is too close to her heart. I didn't want to risk pulling it out."

Liana nodded. With what little magic she had left, she forced it into Charlotte, centering around the wound. "When I say, pull it straight out. Quick and clean," she ordered. "Now!" As Damien pulled, her magic knitted flesh back together. A jet of blood hit her face before she could seal everything off, but she didn't falter. Her magic burned brighter until everything healed, leaving her thoroughly depleted and holding onto consciousness by sheer will alone.

Someone yanked the arrow out of Damien's back and let him drink from their wrist to aid in healing. She crawled toward him as he sat in the grass, panting. Climbing into his lap, she forced him to hold her.

"Protect me," she whispered.

His brows furrowed even as he wrapped his arms around her. "You defeated the enemy," he reassured. She glanced at Master Ranville and her father who stared at her with expressions of misbelief.

"From them," she replied. Out of everyone, the last person she expected to trust was Damien. But she knew after that display of power, the male mages would be coming for her.

Darkness claimed Liana as she passed out.

Chapter Twenty-one

Liana woke with a groan. Her entire body ached, and her mouth felt like someone shoved wool socks in her mouth.

"Liana?" Lady Monroe worried. "Liana, can you hear me?"

She groaned again, rolling onto her side. "What happened to me?" she asked, her entire body revolting with each move.

"You've been out for three days after that stunt you pulled by the lake," she scolded then lightened her tone. "You were so brave, sweetie. You saved your sister and the king."

Her eyes snapped open. Yes, the lake. She remembered now.

"How is Charlotte?"

Her mother gave her a watery smile. "Alive because of you. She is resting in the room next door. She's been asking for you whenever you feel ready for visitors." Currently, she wasn't ready for anything with the pain she was in.

"Water," she croaked. Her mother helped her sit upright then handed her a glass of water. She chugged it down then held it out for more.

"Give yourself a few minutes, Liana. You'll bring it all back up if you push it." She fluffed a few pillows behind Liana's back to hold her upright then set about the room to get a bath ready. She handed Liana a bowl and mint paste to clean her teeth. After another glass of water and a few bites of bread, Liana attempted to get out of bed which she immediately regretted as she collapsed to the floor, dragging her mother with her. Lady Monroe called for aid and Sasha appeared. The woman lifted Liana easily off the ground, even such a gentle touch setting her skin aflame it was so tender.

"We were going for a bath," Lady Monroe said. The guard helped her mother undress Liana then placed her in the lukewarm water. Liana sighed as she felt some of the pain recede with feeling weightless in the tub. Her mother scrubbed her then started on her hair.

"Where are we?" she wondered even though she recognized this gray stone and arched walkways.

"The castle. The king insisted we stay here in light of the events. We are far more protected here." Liana didn't have the energy to ask more questions. Between her ministrations and the water, Liana felt herself being lulled back to sleep.

Next thing she knew, she woke in the bed again.

"You are not getting out of this bed again until you are fully recovered," Lady Monroe scolded. "You nearly drowned yourself in the tub." Liana couldn't even shrug her muscles ached so much.

After more water and food, Liana fell asleep again. She woke like this many more times, sometimes requiring Sasha's aid to get to the chamber pot and back, before she finally felt better.

Her muscles were still sore on the third day, but she could at least stand on her own and keep her eyes open for more than a few minutes. All because she depleted her magic so thoroughly. It had been worth it though to save her sister and Damien. To save them all.

She felt well enough to finally take visitors on that third day. Charlotte and Hannah were the first. Hannah jumped on the bed and crushed Liana in a hug. She barely refrained from wincing. Charlotte stood beside the bed with a sad smile on her pretty face.

"We're so happy you're awake, sister. We've been so worried about you."

Liana hugged Hannah, holding the girl against her in the bed. "Thank you, Hannah. I'm glad we are all okay."

"What you did was amazing. It's all the servants can talk about." Liana couldn't hide her cringe this time. The last thing she wanted was for everyone to know of her power, yet they all did. She looked to Charlotte. She had been worth it though. Her sister was worth the threat now hanging over her. Charlotte reached out and squeezed her sister's hand as if she could read her thoughts.

"Hannah, do you know what would really make Liana feel better? Chocolate. Will you run to the kitchens and sneak us some?"

Happy to be of use, Hannah went eagerly to fulfill her task. Charlotte climbed into the bed and lay back, pulling Liana into her side and running her fingers through her hair soothingly. Tears began to fall, and Liana wasn't sure why.

"I was so scared," she admitted. Her sister sniffled but her voice was strong.

"We all were. I saw you stop that arrow and my heart stopped. It could have easily been you that took it. Then I was hit as Michael and I tried to flip the boat. All I could see was this arrow in my chest. I didn't even feel any pain. I thought I was dead."

Liana held her tighter, sobbing into her chest. It had been too much for her to handle. It was why her magic revolted, why it made itself known. Liana had no choice but to release it.

"What are they going to do to me?" she questioned, her body shaking like a leaf.

"What do you mean?" Charlotte wondered, her voice not so steady anymore.

"Master Ranville and Master Kinley. What will they do with me now that they know of my power?"

"Oh sweetie," Charlotte cooed, her own tears falling now as she wrapped her trembling sister in her arms. "Nothing. Papa would never let them touch you. Nor would I," she declared. Liana sobbed in relief, clinging to hope that no repercussions would come her way. Charlotte combed her fingers through Liana's hair until she'd calmed.

"I am also certain that king of yours would tear down this entire kingdom before anyone attempted to hurt you again." She lifted her head, red puffy eyes staring at her sister.

"Is he okay?"

She smirked. "He has been in a rage since the attack. Of the rebels that survived your blast, they are being held prisoner. He's been working with the Masters to pry answers from them in between rallying his army. Sapphire Cove is armed and prepared for battle while the rest of his army has gathered within the castle's grounds."

"Who would've thought I would one day drive a man to incite a war," she teased which had Charlotte laughing.

Then her sister sighed heavily. "Oh, Liana, you have always underestimated yourself."

Liana snorted in response. "That was never my problem." In fact, she was too arrogant for her own good.

"You did, in the ways that mattered most. You've always wanted change but never believed you could do it. Yet here you are, you've brought a king to his knees simply by giving him your heart. The limit to what you can do now is endless."

She'd never thought of herself in that way. Certainly, she knew things needed to change, and she'd gain leverage as queen, but unlimited power? Control over Damien? She thought Charlotte dreamed too big.

"You give me too much credit, sister. I am just happy we are all alive and safe."

Charlotte sighed in disappointment. "I agree, sister. I agree."

Liana woke again not having realized she fell asleep, this time though, she didn't fully wake. It was as if she was just beneath the surface clawing to break through as she heard them talking.

"I apologize for intruding, but they said she was awake," Damien said, his voice muffled.

"She was. She's been drifting in and out for days. Today was the first time she lasted longer than a few minutes," Charlotte explained. Liana kicked and punched trying to break that barrier, to fully wake.

"How was she?" he asked and phantom fingers brushed her cheek.

"Shaken. Scared."

He blew out a heavy breath. "Next time she wakes, tell her she is protected. My army stands at the ready for any attacks."

"That is not what had her shaking in fear. It was the other mage in this castle."

She paused in her attempts to wake, wanting to hear their conversation instead. "Before she fainted by the lake, she asked me to protect her from them. What would they do to her?"

"I am not sure. Her power is unnatural. I did not witness it, but my mother and Hannah tell me it felt different. It didn't feel like normal magic. And power that strong, especially in a female, there is no telling what the Masters will do."

"Did you not just accept Ranville's proposal yesterday, yet you distrust him today?"

"I accepted his proposal, but I do not trust him with my sister. I am not foolish, Your Grace. I understand what greed and power can do to men."

There was a pause that had Liana trying to force her eyes open, but they would not budge.

"I trust Master Kinley. He is not like most. However, I will protect Liana from anyone that tries to harm her."

"I believe that you will. And I also must warn you, Liana is not as strong as she appears. She is fragile and hides behind bravado."

Liana didn't agree with that at all. "You underestimate her."

"I do not, Your Highness. I've known her far longer than you. She is strong, yes, but also fragile. She has the heart of a dreamer which means she will always find the best in you and dream a future based on that. It also means she will never accept this world as it is. She will always dream of something better. You have to give that to her. You have to let her dream and don't you dare break her heart."

His heavy sigh fanned over her face. "I am trying, Charlotte. I am trying to be everything she needs."

Liana drifted back into sleep. When she woke later, she didn't remember a thing.

Chapter Twenty-two

It took another two days before Liana was fully back to herself. And she was just in time for supper. Phillipa came to stay with her in the castle now that she was able to move on her own and helped her dress for the evening. Her sisters and mother joined in her bedroom to get ready together as usual. Despite everything, it gave her some peace to return to routine.

At least, it was routine until the king showed up at her door as they were making their way toward the sitting room.

The ladies curtsied. "Your Highness, what do we owe the pleasure of your visit?" Lady Monroe gushed.

He gave a curt bow of his head in return before clearing his throat. "I came to escort Lady Liana to supper."

Lady Monroe practically shoved Liana at the king, offering her up for whatever the king demanded. "She will gladly accept your offer, Your Highness. We shall meet you down there." She ushered her other daughters down the hall and disappeared around a corner.

Liana looked up, finding Damien already staring down at her. Her heart skipped a beat at seeing him again. Never did she think she could forget his handsome face but seeing him again after nearly a week, after nearly losing him, she drank in the renewed site. The hard lines of his face and those glacial eyes that stared right through to her soul.

"How are you feeling?" he wondered.

"Much better, thank you."

"Are you fully recovered?" His hand reached out as if to take hers, but he pulled back at the last second to fidget with the buttons of his decorative coat.

"I am. How are you faring, my king?" she asked, feeling a bit breathless and uncertain why. There was a tension between them, a force she couldn't place and one that hadn't been there before.

"Well, thank you." His eyes roved over her face then down her body. She would have blushed but there was no heat there, only a detached inspection.

"Is something wrong, Damien?" she asked softly, aware of prying ears. There had to be something wrong. He'd never appeared as worried or unsure before, and he spoke so formally which he shunned every chance he could.

He cleared his throat then tugged on his coat once more before offering his crooked arm. "Nothing at all. Shall we?" Hesitantly, Liana placed her hand on his arm, and he led her toward the formal sitting room. "I am pleased to see you well after being incapacitated for a week, much longer than anyone anticipated."

Liana paused in the hallway just before the stairs, a smirk playing on her lips. "My king, is that worry I heard in your voice?" She had heard a bit of a shakiness in his voice which scared her, so she tried to tease it away.

He cleared his throat again then gestured down the stairs, already leading her forward. "Not at all, Lady Liana. I had every faith in my healers for a full recovery." She raised a questioning brow. They both knew healers didn't help her at all. The only treatment for magical burnout was rest and time. Glancing at him sidelong, she inspected him more closely.

Although he appeared relaxed and at ease, she knew differently. His lips were just a tad too thin, the corners slightly drawn down. Jaw clenching, his nostrils flared repeatedly as if scenting for danger. Shoulders rigid and nearly up to his ears with tension, she couldn't hold back any longer.

Liana pulled him to a stop at the base of the stairs and erected a privacy shield to keep their conversation a secret. "Seriously, Damien, you are so tense and nervous you are making me worry as well."

He blew out a breath and slid clawed fingers through his coiffed black hair, displacing his crown for a moment. "I apologize, Liana, I am feeling a bit tense." She scoffed which earned her a glare. "Fine," he bit out. "I am feeling very tense."

"Tell me why," she demanded. He glanced around the large foyer, only a few purposefully oblivious guards standing nearby.

"You had me worried."

"Me?" she asked incredulously. "Why?"

His eyes narrowed. "Because you erupted with magic then were unconscious for almost a week," he countered angrily.

She crossed her arms defensively. "Do not be angry with me, Damien. I saved us all."

"Perhaps, but at the expense of yourself. My army would have handled it just as well."

Her jaw dropped. "You would have been impaled by hundreds of arrows if I had not acted! To hell with your army, I ended the battle in a matter of seconds."

She hadn't realized she'd moved until his breath hit her face from the vicious growl he loosed. Nose to nose, they squared off with each other.

"You nearly ended your own life in a matter of seconds as well!" he seethed.

"I'm perfectly well, thank you. You should be thanking me."

"Thank you for what? For nearly putting me in an early grave from worry?" He growled again, turning on his heel as he ran his fingers through his hair once more. He paced back to her, his face thunderous, fangs descended, and eyes narrowed on her. The vampire in him was in control and she couldn't help backing away as he stalked her. Damien grabbed her and pulled her tightly into his body, his arms like iron bands around her. He buried his face in her neck and breathed in deeply. She froze, praying that he wouldn't hurt her.

"Damien?" she whispered, voice shaking.

"Liana," he breathed. One hand rubbed up and down her back soothingly. "I was so worried about you. I feared you'd never wake." She melted into his arms at his words and wrapped her own around his waist. There was no danger here, only a traumatized male. Traumatized from worry over her. She squeezed his waist unsure of how to feel about his concern.

"I'm fine," was all she could manage. Throat suddenly thick, she gulped. Did the king truly care for her? Was he genuine in his concern? If so, perhaps Charlotte's words held some merit. Perhaps the king did truly want her, maybe even love her.

He breathed her in again, his hot breath on her neck causing her to shiver. She held him for a few more moments. "Is your temper tantrum over, my king?" she teased. His body shook hers as he chuckled. Pulling back, his hands cupped her face.

"Such a snarky female." Fingers brushed across her cheek to tuck a stray curl behind her ear. "I wouldn't be so upset if you hadn't tried to kill yourself."

She rolled her eyes and pulled away, keeping the shield up while walking toward the hallway that led to the sitting room. "I did not try to kill myself. I saved everyone else. A simple thank you would suffice."

He caught her hand and returned it to the crook of his arm. "Thank you. And should you ever need to use magic like that again, save it. Do not expend yourself to the brink of death."

"You know, a normal man would simply say he cared about me. No need to boss me around," she said with a smirk. He stopped her again. At this rate, they'd never make it to supper.

"Is that what you wish to hear, my little mage?" he asked, his voice soft and gentle, lulling her into him. "Must I say the words that I know we both already feel?" Her brows furrowed.

"What words?"

Damien chuckled, his fingers trailing up the length of her arms before cupping her cheeks. "That I care for you. I thought it obvious by now." His nose brushed against hers, their lips so close as she leaned into him for support, her body failing as her mind focused only on him.

"Not obvious at all," she countered breathlessly.

A clearing of a throat had Damien pulling away slightly. Liana stepped back, her cheeks going red. When she saw who stood in the hallway with them, she dropped into a curtsy, knees nearly touching the floor as panic consumed her. It was the previous king and queen, and she was done for. They'd caught her nearly kissing the king. Her reputation would be ruined. They'd punish her entire family for such sinful behavior.

"Mother, Father," Damien greeted as he dragged Liana to her feet. She kept her head bowed in shame. "This is Lady Liana Monroe, one of the ladies I am courting."

A feminine snort filled the hallway. "If that's what you call courting these days," she chided. Liana's shoulders hunched inward as she tried to disappear.

"Just be happy your son finally picked a bride, my dear," the former king said, his voice deep and smooth like wine.

"Father," Damien scolded on an exhale.

"What? It is the truth. We can both relax now that your mother can fawn over your new wife." Liana didn't think her normal pale complexion would ever return. She'd look like a tomato forever from here on out.

"We have not announced our engagement, Father," Damien informed.

"Ah, but you are engaged," he said cheerfully before taking Liana's sweaty palm. "A pleasure to meet you, Liana." He kissed her knuckles before placing her hand in the crook of his arm. "Allow me to escort you the rest of the way."

Liana's mind blanked as she looked toward Damien. Everything happened so fast. One moment they were about to kiss, the next, his parents were acting as if she were already married to the king.

Damien nodded. "Go. I'll be in shortly."

Liana allowed herself to be led into the sitting room where her family paused to bow for the former king. Resisting the urge to step away to do the same, she kept her eyes on the ground.

"As you were, please," the former king said before the pair were served glasses of wine which she used to her advantage to take a step away. "A pleasure to meet you all. My wife and I only just arrived a few hours ago and are eager to hear of the impressive tale my son promised." He stood there expectantly.

"Father, let us save the stories for supper. I am sure we are all ravenous," Damien said as he entered with his mother on his arm. Liana curtsied again with her family then took a moment to examine Damien's parents without shock clouding her mind.

High Lord Ramone Ashwood was a near replica of Damien. His skin was slightly darker while his eyes matched his black hair. The former queen, Evangeline, had gorgeous blonde curls falling down her back and Liana discovered where Damien got his eyes from as well, seeing his mother's light blue ones.

They were led to the dining room where Damien took his usual seat at the head of the table, his father at the other end with his wife to his left. The men filled in as usual after Damien, followed by the females. Liana was surprised to find Master Ranville in attendance as well. She supposed it was because he was now engaged to her sister.

Over the first course of their supper, Damien gave his parents a brief synopsis of the events by the lake. He mentioned her power but did not overexaggerate, all too aware of the danger it put on her.

"With power like that, I'm surprised the mage school did not snatch you up," High Lord Ashwood exclaimed toward Liana. She nodded her head toward him in answer. "Lord Monroe, why did you not teach your daughter in your school?" he questioned.

"I never knew of her talents, Your Highness. She kept them hidden." Liana loved her father, but she also hated him at that moment. He would have known if he hadn't turned her away at every chance she asked for training.

"How does one keep such power hidden and why?" High Lady Ashwood questioned, her voice low and pointed.

Liana gulped thickly. There were many reasons. Mainly fear as to how the males would react.

"Mother, you know the way of the mage. They do not allow females the proper education to learn their magic. Lady Liana did not have to hide it because she was never given the choice to reveal it." Liana glanced toward Damien from beneath her lashes as she stirred the tasteless soup. She was glad that he stood up for her, but she could also fight her own battles.

"If that is the case, how did she become powerful enough to save you all?" she countered.

Liana cleared her throat as Damien opened his mouth to speak for her again. "I learned as much as I could on my own, Your Majesty," Liana answered.

When the former queen raised one brow, she only saw Damien in her. Now she knew where he developed the habit from. "That seems a bit cruel, does it not, Lord Monroe? To have such a talented daughter so eager for knowledge yet no one to teach it to her."

Lord Monroe gripped his spoon. "It is the way of the mage, Your Grace. Females are taught the magic they need to know."

"And yet here you all sit safely because a female mage knew a spell you all deemed unfit for her to know. Rather ironic," she remarked before sipping her wine. Lord Monroe nodded, his eyes fixed on his bowl, his face flushed with anger. Although Liana finally felt seen, felt acknowledged, she didn't want it at the expense of her father. He had been a wonderful father despite the magic.

"It is unfair to accuse my father alone, Your Highness," Liana countered much to her mother's dismay. "He offered me what he could within the confines of our laws."

The former queen sat unfazed. "He is on the mage council. It is his job to create and change laws for the betterment of his people. Surely you can understand that this is not only about you, Lady Liana. It is about all the female mages that never had an opportunity to learn what is theirs by right of birth."

Liana couldn't believe the boldness of the queen. Nor could she believe the vampire so passionate about mage females. "I agree with you completely, Your Highness. However, female mages have been suppressed for thousands of years. To place all blame upon my father's shoulders is unfair and unjust. There are plenty of mage council members that came before him, some with far more power than his own, yet here we are, still oppressed."

"You absolve your father of any wrongdoing simply because he is not the first?" she accused.

"Not at all but to single him out and persecute him before everyone is not right either."

"Liana!" Lady Monroe scolded, reaching around Charlotte to dig her nails into her forearm. Liana shook her mother off.

"Son, will you not interject?" the High Lord questioned calmly. Liana glanced at Damien who sat reclined in his chair, sipping wine with a smirk on his face.

"No," he replied simply.

High Lady Ashwood paid nobody any mind as she continued. "You are his daughter. You have immense power that should have been cultivated.

If there was anyone in history to have fought for females, it should have been your father." Liana glanced at Lord Monroe who stared at her with regret. She was right but also very wrong. Anger raged in her veins, making magic spark from her fingertips. She hid her fists in her lap as she addressed the woman again.

"I disagree. If there were anyone in history that ought to have fought for mage females it would be the Ashwood line. Your family line has ruled since the inception of Triaedian. You fought to uphold the peace between all breeds. The vampires and shifters made their women equal, yet you left the mage females to suffer. We are all your people. The royal family should have liberated us."

Icy eyes stared back at her. "You know nothing of what has been done. I did fight. There is only so much we can do when the councils have so much control."

"I disagree, Your Highness. You were queen, your husband king. Your word is final. Your word is law despite the Councils."

"It is not that simple. We are vampires. The mage council would rebel against our influence into their sacred culture."

She lifted a brow, mimicking the power move. "Perhaps. However, it would have been far more difficult for one mage to change laws simply because his daughter showed promise. He would have been shunned for nepotism, his good name ruined and females no better off." The former queen stared, Liana feeling as if she made her point.

The High Lady still countered, "To force the councils and the mage to change their culture would incite chaos. It would incite more rebellion and separatist attitudes."

Liana smirked. "It is a good thing I don't mind a little chaos then."

Master Ranville huffed a laugh. "What does that matter? You have no say." Liana leveled the man with her stare. He was a talented mage, a fighter for justice. But not if that justice was equality.

She looked to Damien who looked thoroughly entertained. "It matters because she has the most say in this room. She will be my queen," he declared, followed by gasps. His gaze settled on Liana as he continued. Her heart skipped several beats as she tried to force air into her lungs. She hadn't prepared for this moment. Hadn't readied herself for the finality of what they agreed upon. "I have asked Lady Liana Monroe to be my wife. And she has agreed."

To hear it finally confirmed aloud among other witnesses had her heart beating wildly. It made everything so real. There would be no turning back now. Not that she ever had that chance to begin with. She was fated to marry the king the moment he laid eyes on her. And secretly, she didn't mind that at all.

High Lord Ashwood clapped his hands briefly. "How wonderful, Son. We are pleased to hear. Congratulations to you both." He drew the attention of the head butler. "Bring five bottles from the reserve at once. We must celebrate!"

Charlotte reached over to squeeze Liana's fisted hand and gave her a comforting smile while her mother was near to tears. "Oh my. Thank the gods! Your highness, you are so kind to have chosen my daughter." Liana refrained from scolding her mother after making her sound like a charity case.

"Congratulations, Your Highness. Lady Liana will make a powerful queen," Master Ranville toasted then gulped his wine in one large swig.

Damien reciprocated with a tight-lipped smile as he lifted his own glass. "She will make me a happy king."

After the special wine had been served, Master Ranville spoke up. "Given the discussion tonight, I think it best to offer Lady Liana a place in our school to learn magic. We can find her a private place to study and to meet tutors away from the rest of the males."

It was far too little too late in Liana's mind, but she let Damien respond. "Unnecessary, Master Ranville. My wife shall take control of her own studies and remain in the castle. If she needs a tutor, I'm sure Master Kinley would be honored to oblige."

"I am delighted," High Lord Ashwood interjected. The servants began to remove the first course, replacing it with the main meal. Liana's stomach growled as the scent of the roasted turkey filled the room. "We have been waiting for our son's marriage for many years and are very pleased with his choice of bride." Liana looked to the former queen to see if she agreed. The woman's face remained blank. "How soon is the wedding?"

"I could fetch the officiant now if you are so eager, Father," Damien suggested which had Liana choking on the bite of meat in her mouth. Even as she coughed, her cheeks heated. Although it was far too quick, Liana had to admit that there were some advantages to a quick marriage. Top of the list being Damien's fangs finally sliding into her delicate skin.

The former king laughed. "And deprive the people of such a momentous event? Never."

"Fine. Can a proper wedding be planned in two weeks?"

His mother laughed humorlessly. "One month at minimum."

Damien grinned, looking at Liana. "One month it shall be." Liana gulped. One month. That's all she had left to wait until she finally felt all that he had offered.

Supper discussion turned to wedding details, mainly guests and current feuds among possible attendees. Once they'd retired to the sitting room,

Liana sat beside the former queen while Hannah and Charlotte performed on the piano.

"I must apologize for earlier, Your Highness," Liana started. She had spoken quite frankly to the woman and knew she should remedy that.

She smirked, holding up a hand to stop Liana. "First rule, child, don't ever apologize. You will be queen and must start acting like one."

"Even so, I spoke out of turn…"

"You did exactly as I hoped you would," she interrupted. Liana's brows furrowed.

"You wanted me to argue with you?"

She sipped on her wine. "I wanted to see what kind of woman my son chose to marry."

Liana gaped. The woman had been testing her. "And did I pass your test?"

"Expertly," she said with a grin. "Relax, child. I am pleased you are his choice. There is much I still need to teach you though."

She looked to Damien. He reclined on the sofa, a stronger drink in hand as they watched Lord Monroe and Wesley play chess. He had always been too handsome but knowing now that he would be hers in a short month had her desire for him peeking. As if sensing her eyes, he turned. Catching her staring, he smirked.

"Teach me what?" she asked absently as she imagined the rest of her life with that smirking devil.

"Teach you how to be queen." Liana's mouth went dry. She was really doing this. She would truly become queen.

Chapter Twenty-three

Liana lay awake long after everyone retired for the evening. She couldn't help but worry over what was to come.

She froze in bed when she heard her door open and click closed. Erecting a shield around herself, she changed her vision to adapt to darkness, a spell she learned long ago thanks to her brother's constant teasing, especially late at night.

"Damien," she scolded on a terrified exhale. "You scared me." He sat on the bed beside her, his bare feet hanging over.

"I thought you would be asleep."

She sighed, dropping back onto her pillow. "I can't sleep."

"What troubles you, my little mage?" he asked softly, resting his arm over her legs to lean on the bed.

"I am going to be queen in one month."

He hummed, his hand rising to brush his fingers through her hair. "I will help you. My mother will help you."

"I know. But that is a terrifying amount of responsibility." He chuckled, his fingers still running through her silky strands.

"Trust me, I am well aware of the burden."

"Yes, but you grew up knowing you'd be king one day. I grew up hoping to disappear into the corner of a library and never come out." His laugh was abrupt and loud to which she placed her hand over his mouth to quiet him. "Do you want the whole castle to know you're in my room?"

He gently took her hand and kissed her palm before setting it down. "I would never dishonor you in such a way. You merely caught me off guard. Why I am still surprised by your humor I am not sure."

She frowned. "I was not joking."

He grinned. "I know." She rolled her eyes and lay back.

"Why have you come to my room in the middle of the night? Again?" He fished out something from his pocket then took her right hand again, setting it on his thigh. Her fingers fell around his thick muscle, the warmth of him seeping through the thin trousers. The need to feel more of him had her fingers curling into his muscle. Damien slipped something onto her middle finger, the cool metal raising goose bumps along her arms.

"I wanted to give this to you privately. It's your engagement gift." She lifted her hand, the spell still in place to allow her to see the shining stone. In the center of the ring lay a rectangular emerald held aloft by delicate gold filigree. The gold band formed a braided pattern around her finger. It was simple yet so elegant and completely perfect.

"It is stunning, Damien."

"I'm pleased you like it." Although her night vision altered the tones of the world, she knew this emerald would stun in the daylight. "You are nervous?" he questioned her earlier comments.

"Of course, I am nervous. We are going to marry in one month. That is no time at all." Yet she wished they could have married tonight if only so she could hold him in her arms already and kiss without restraint.

"What are you nervous about?" he asked softly, threading their fingers together and relaxing them on his thigh.

"Everything," she exclaimed. "You wouldn't understand. You were raised to be king."

"Tell me this, my little mage. Are you nervous about marrying me or becoming queen?"

Her lips pursed. "They are one in the same. I cannot have one without the other."

"No, we are separate. I am not the throne. Are you nervous about me or your responsibilities as queen?"

"What does it matter?" She blew out a breath in exasperation.

"It matters to me." He waited.

"Becoming queen, clearly. I already understand you, I know how to handle you," she explained, telling half the truth. She understood and handled him up to a point. Liana knew there were still things she'd yet discover about the vampire, but she understood him to his core, everything else she could adapt to.

That damned brow of his rose. "Handle me?" He shifted, climbing onto the bed on his knees until he hovered over her then slowly pressed his body to hers. "How exactly do you handle me, my queen?"

This close, she couldn't think straight to handle anything but somehow, she managed to not get caught in his lustful snare once more. "It is easy, my king. Sometimes I drag you down and sometimes I build you back up. Sometimes I play nice, and sometimes I defy every word you say." His head drifted closer and closer, their lips nearly touching. "It is a fine balance of giving you what you want and giving you what you need."

"And what do I need?" he whispered. His breath smelled of wine and sugar. She moved before he could, pressing her lips to his. He groaned at the contact, pressing her deeper into the bed. His hands dug into her hair as she clung to his back, tasting him. She ripped her mouth away.

"You need to go get me whatever sweets you were just eating," she demanded breathlessly, licking her lips.

He stared at her for a moment then his brows furrowed. "You jest."

"Most certainly not. Bring me those sweets or I won't allow you in my room until the wedding."

"That is probably a good idea considering how difficult it is to resist you."

"Your choice, my king. Sweets or no more late-night rendezvous." He growled then climbed off the bed while grumbling. Liana giggled and patiently waited for his return.

Rather quickly, he reappeared with a bottle of wine and a plate full of sweets. He climbed into bed beside her, reclined against the headboard. Handing her the plate, he pulled the cork out with his teeth before drinking straight from the bottle.

"Shirking all semblance of propriety I see," she teased before popping a jelly sweet into her mouth. She hummed at the divine taste.

"There was only so much I could carry and still be stealthy while sneaking into your room unnoticed, my queen." He handed her the bottle and took a treat. She took a swig of the tart wine.

"Then I shall thank you for being so nimble as to get this entire plate to me, my king."

He frowned then smirked. "Break me down then build me up," he whispered, mimicking her words from earlier. "You devious, little temptress. You do that quite frequently, don't you?"

"Such an intelligent vampire you are," she gushed. "Although, you probably should have figured it out sooner."

He laughed, stealing the wine back from her. "And here I thought you didn't like me."

She scoffed. "We both know how much I like you. Like the look of you anyway." Leaning in, she kissed his neck. His arm snaked under her and pulled her into the side of his body. One leg fell over his and she didn't move it.

"So cheeky," he grunted. He gulped the wine then handed it to her. "My mother likes you."

Liana nearly choked. "Truly? Even after the dinner?"

"Because of the dinner," he said with a chuckle. "My mother is very vocal about her opinions and beliefs just as you are."

"She did say I passed her test," Liana admitted. "I suppose that will make my transition easier. She is willing to help me." She ate another sweet, this one a soft cookie covered in powdered sugar. She washed it down with wine. When Damien reached for the last one, she blocked him with a shield.

"Not this again." He sighed to which she chuckled. "I did retrieve the tray if you remember."

"Oh, I remember. But you already ate two treats. What payment do you offer for more?"

"The effort of going all the way down to the kitchens and back deserves three at minimum, you stingy mage."

"It would have if you weren't a vampire. It took you a minute to get this. Now, what payment do you offer?"

He frowned. "You don't play fair. I don't have magic to counteract yours."

"You have vampiric strength and speed which I cannot counteract. If I let this shield down, you'd snatch one before I could blink."

He grinned evilly. "Drop it and let's find out."

Her eyes narrowed. "A compromise," she suggested to which he nodded. She picked up the cookie and while keeping eye contact, she placed half the cookie between her lips after saying, "We split it."

Eyes darkening, he leaned forward. Her eyes fell closed as his lips brushed hers. The crunch of the cookie vibrated on her lips before he pulled away. They both washed it down with the wine then he placed the bottle on her bedside table. Wrapping his arms around her, he pulled her closer. "You play a dangerous game, temptress."

"I know," she declared before pulling him into a kiss. Liana moaned into his mouth as he parted her lips, his tongue teasing her own. When he pressed her down onto her back, their legs tangled together. Aside from their clothes, only a thin sheet separated them, and Liana knew it wasn't enough. She could still feel him, feel the hard press of his arousal against her thigh. She couldn't think, couldn't breathe. All she wanted was him.

His teeth nipped at her bottom lip drawing a gasp from her before his lips trailed to her neck. She arched back for him, practically begging him to bite her. His tongue flicked over the spot right before teeth nibbled the skin dragging another moan from her.

"Please, Damien," she begged, the need to feel his teeth sink into her heated skin overwhelming.

He chuckled darkly. "Not yet, temptress." Lips trailing down her neck, he teased her with pinches of teeth as he pulled the top of her sleeping gown open. He bared her to the warm night air, her chest heaving for breath as he cupped her breast.

"So beautiful," he whispered before kissing each mound. A thumb brushed over her peaked nipple making her back arch into his grasp. When his tongue circled one, she clenched her teeth to keep from making any sound.

"Damien," she said in a breathy whisper. More than anything she wanted to let him keep going, but there would be no turning back once she lost her virtue before being married. "I need you," she practically begged. "But…"

"Hush, Liana. I will not defile you." It was already too late for that. His lips claimed hers again, his body resting between her thighs. The delicious friction of him had her moaning, her hips rising to meet his. He growled, a hand clamping on her hip to hold her still. "Gods, you make it impossible to keep my word." Her legs wrapped around his waist and his head fell against her chest with a heavy sigh.

He pulled away, rolling to the side which pulled a whimper from her at the loss of him. His mouth devoured hers, swallowing her cry. Lips pushed at her own, his tongue delving inside to tease and lick while his hand slid down her abdomen.

Liana gripped his shirt trying to force him back on top, but he resisted, pulling away as his hand continued to drift downward over her hip… her thigh… down to her ankle where his fingers connected with skin. She could only stare as those fingers drifted along her calf, past her knee and along the outside of her thigh. When he gripped her hip, she looked into those vibrant blue eyes.

No one had ever touched her so intimately. She had never touched herself so intimately. Looking into those eyes, seeing her own burning lust and desire reflected there, Liana could not bring herself to resist.

He paused, waiting for her to do so. She nodded, biting her lip to keep from begging for more.

Light as a feather, his fingers drifted down her thigh then back up along the inner side. She let her leg fall open just a little more so he could feel the heat of her as he teased too closely.

"Tell me to stop, Liana," he said on panted breaths.

"I cannot," she admitted. She had no will left to refuse him.

He growled. "I will pleasure you, my love, but I will not take your virtue."

Liana's breath hitched. "Did you…" she stuttered as his fingers moved closer to the apex of her thighs. "Did you call me, your love?" she questioned incredulously. He stilled above her. For a moment she couldn't breathe. Would he deny it? Would he say it was a mistake? She didn't think she could withstand the hurt if he denied loving her. Because, gods damn her, she was nearly certain she loved him.

"Perhaps," he admitted, which had a smug smile filling her lips. "What is that look for?"

"You love me," she taunted, not willing to let him see just how much she cherished his admission.

He frowned. "That is not what I said."

"But it is what you implied."

"It was just an endearment."

She chuckled, smoothing her fingers over his furrowed brow. "Do not worry, my king. I shall never reveal to another soul that you have a heart, and one capable of love no less."

"You test my patience, temptress," he growled before punishing her mouth with a kiss. She accepted him eagerly, digging her fingers into his thick hair while he trailed dangerously close to her most intimate place.

He swiped one finger along the seam of her before circling sensitive flesh. She gasped, her head arching back, and his lips fell to her neck. Legs parting wider, she granted him access to continue.

His fingers teased her endlessly but never quite breached where she needed him most. Tongue, teeth and lips drove her wild along her throat, tempting to sink his teeth in as she so desperately wanted. She cupped the back of his neck, keeping him there while her hips writhed under his hand. Magic sparked from her fingers, not that either of them paid it any attention.

"Damien, please." Breathless and on the edge, she did not mind begging for what she wanted. His sinister laugh said he enjoyed it too.

"My mighty temptress brought to her knees," he growled, his finger circling her torturously slow. Biting her lip to keep from screaming at him to go faster, to end this delicious torture he incited, she writhed against his hand. He pulled away on a chuckle.

"Damien," she cried out. Sparks of gold lit his face, magic uncontrollably leaking from her fingers. There was no spell with it, just pure energy that fizzled out as it hit the sheets or Damien harmlessly.

He hushed her with his mouth, his fangs out and painful against her lips. He sucked the bit of blood he drew from them at the same time his fingers found her sensitive core again. Sucking her bottom lip between his teeth, he bit down to draw more blood as he drove her higher and higher. Faster he circled and she felt her core clenching, her entire body tensing with pleasure. It felt as if she might combust from whatever was coming but would not dare move to escape it. She wanted this, wanted whatever Damien wrought from her body.

"Let go, my love," he whispered right before she snapped. Everything went taught then she moaned as her hips bucked against him, her body shaking with pleasure. Light sparked beyond her eyelids not that she bothered to care. He kissed her gently as she gasped for air, her body going limp when he dragged his hand away.

Chest rising and falling quickly, Liana savored the feeling of her blood still singing with pleasure as she slowly came down from the bliss Damien brought her to.

"Your skin is glowing," he whispered as she felt fingers brushing back and forth on her forearm. With great difficulty, she peeled her eyes open to find his face bathed in a soft, golden glow as if a candle were lit. She lifted an arm to her eyes to find that her skin was indeed glowing with some internal light.

"You did this that time by the lake. Your entire body glowed far brighter before you exploded with magic." She could only stare at herself, feeling the magic languidly flowing through her veins as if it were the happiest thing to ever exist. It made her just as happy and relaxed. So much so that she shrugged and dropped her arm, eyes closing again.

"Have I rendered the loquacious Lady Liana Monroe speechless?" he teased on a chuckle while tugging her sleeping gown closed.

Liana rolled her eyes. "If I were not so sated at the moment, I would argue that no one thinks I am loquacious." She rolled onto her side, leaning her head on one hand, and draping the other over his chest.

This time he snorted. "Liar."

"Fine, I speak my mind when needed, otherwise, I keep to myself and keep quiet which is how most people see me."

"Ah, so my little mage shows only her true self to me. How honored I am."

She sighed, looking up into those haunting eyes. "Stop teasing. I want to enjoy this moment." He smiled as he pulled her closer, letting her head fall onto his chest with his arms around her. "Is there a way I could reciprocate?" she asked, uncertain of herself. "To make you feel this way as well?"

"Oh, my temptress, there are many ways, but I must decline them all for if you lay a single finger on me, I will not be held accountable for my actions."

Her brows furrowed. "What do you mean?"

"I mean, that I will have to bribe the officiant to backdate our marriage to this afternoon because I will ravage you should you dare to pleasure me in any way," he declared.

Liana's thighs clenched, her slick heat tender already.

"Can we not have a private ceremony with family tomorrow and the wedding as planned?"

"Gods, I hate the mage's antiquated views on sex and marriage," he complained before rolling her over. He placed a chaste kiss on her lips before sliding out of bed. "I must leave, temptress."

She smiled, pleased with herself. "If you must," she drawled, snuggling beneath the blankets. Truly though, they had already gone too far. She did not regret a single moment, but it was far beyond proper behavior, even if they were engaged.

"Goodnight, my love," he said deliberately slowly so she could feel the impact. He had used the endearment in a moment of passion, but to hear it without the haze of pleasure clouding her mind, it had her heart skipping a beat. And the damned vampire probably knew it. She liked the sound of it, like the idea of being loved by him. And as much as she hated to admit it, Liana loved him back.

"Goodnight, my king," she replied, her skin still glowing. Perhaps she loved him, but she would not play that card just yet. They were still in the middle of their game after all.

A smile plastered to Liana's lips as she readied for the day the next morning. Phillipa bustled around dressing the young woman as she absently stared at the dazzling emerald ring upon her middle finger. All Liana could think about were the king's lips upon her own as he stole her breath with every caress of his fingers upon sensitive flesh.

They had gone too far. He never should have been in her bedroom to begin with, let alone kissing her, making her feel as if she might never move again after the pleasure seared through her veins. It was pleasure she'd never known and wanted more of. She could only imagine what it would be like on their wedding night if that was what he could do without stealing her virtue.

"You seem pleasantly smitten, Lady Liana," Phillipa commented with a smirk of her own. Liana's eyes focused on the maid for the first time, and she dropped her hands to her sides, the weight of the emerald ring a comfort instead of a nuisance as she expected.

"I believe I am, Phillipa," she admitted.

"Why do you speak as if that is an undesirable thing? Are you not happy with the king?"

"That's not it all. I am happy, surprisingly. I believe that is why I am a bit confused. Never did I dream of being happily engaged. I always saw it as a duty, a responsibility I would begrudgingly honor. This is different. The king is different."

Phillipa's smile broadened. "You are in love, my lady."

Liana looked back to her ring to avoid the woman's knowing gaze. If this was not love she was feeling then it most certainly was lust. What did she know of love anyway? All she knew of it came from stories and books. She supposed there were aspects of the king she liked, things she would not want to part with, his handsome face and muscled body certainly part of that list. Those striking blue eyes were her favorite part of him, or perhaps it was his thick hair that felt so soft between her fingers. Or his deep voice that so often carried her into dreams and the sly laughs she pulled from him with quick wit. Maybe it was the way her heart fluttered every time she saw him, or the way she felt safe by his side. Or the way he respected her, allowed her to speak her mind without repercussion and even valued her thoughts. There was also the moment when he nearly sacrificed himself to save Charlotte.

"I suppose I am," she admitted softly, thinking that perhaps this was love. "It feels odd though. It doesn't feel quite real."

"It is quite real. I see it in you both. The king loves you as well," Phillipa said, keeping her voice low, especially in a castle full of vampires. Liana hesitated at her words.

"Do you truly think, Phillipa?"

"Of course. I am surprised you do not see it yourself. That vampire worships the ground you walk on."

At that, Liana snorted. "I doubt he would worship anyone that much aside from himself."

"Do not be so harsh on him. I tell the truth," Phillipa insisted as she secured the last of the ties on Liana's dress. She helped the young woman to the vanity where she started on her silky, black hair to fasten it into an elegant updo.

"What use does a king have with love?" Liana questioned. She may love the vampire, but she couldn't forget her father's words that Damien was king, the throne would always be his first priority, not her.

"Do not think that way. The king loves you because you make him happy."

Uncertain if that were true, she let the topic drop because aside from her teasing him last night about the endearment of, 'my love' she truly did not know if the king loved her. His love was inconsequential anyway. He didn't need to love her. They were set to be married in one month and Liana would make the best of whatever the gods deemed her path in this life.

"Do you have any suggestions on my wedding gown, Phillipa?" she asked the maid as a distraction from her thoughts. She listened to every detail before it was time to join everyone for breakfast.

Her family was already gathered around the table when she arrived. William and Carlisle were missing from the table, not that she was surprised. They were often not where they ought to be.

"There she is, our beautiful bride," Lady Monroe gushed as she hurried around the table to embrace her middle daughter. "We are so proud of you."

"Proud of what?" she asked facetiously while taking her seat at the table. She knew her mother meant capturing the king as her husband.

They treated it like a sport, her and the other ladies of high society, to see who could win the favor of their chosen target.

"For gaining the king's favor of course." Lady Monroe piled food onto Liana's plate although she was quite capable of doing so herself. "We have much to plan for the wedding. The High Lady has already sent an invitation for us to join her this morning to begin planning."

Liana glanced at Charlotte dreading everything her mother said. Charlotte gave her a pitying glance in return then asked their mother, "Do you think Hannah and I could join as well? I would so like to be a part of my little sister's wedding planning."

"Oh yes, she invited all the Monroe women to join. We shall go just as soon as breakfast is over."

"Where are my little brothers?" Liana questioned.

Her father interjected, aiding in changing the subject. "They ran off early this morning with that guard Mikael to help feed the hounds." No sooner did he finish explaining than a blur of movement rushed into the room quickly followed by another. Two vampire males stood where the blurs stopped each with a Monroe clinging to their backs.

"We won!" William screeched before climbing off Damien's back. She did her best not to blush as she recalled their night together, of the things he did to her body. Even now she felt that heat pool in her belly just by looking at him.

Carlisle slid to the ground from Mikael's back with a scowl thrown at the vampire. "That's not fair. He let the king win because he's the king!" Carlisle complained even as everyone stood to attention and offered the king a curtsy or a bow.

"Carlisle!" Lady Monroe scolded on a gasp.

Mikael bowed his head at Carlisle with a smirk. "You are not as intimidating as the king, my young friend." Carlisle pouted all the way to his seat while little William beamed. As he slid into the seat beside Liana, she gave him a pat on the back and a wink.

"Good job," she whispered to her favorite younger brother.

"I saw that!" Carlisle yelled.

"Hush, Carlisle. It was only a game," Lord Monroe reprimanded. "Learn to appreciate loss along with the wins. No one likes a sore loser."

A chair skidded along the floor before Damien squeezed in on her other side between Hannah. "You should really be congratulating me, don't you think?" he challenged with that gods damned cocked brow.

She mimicked it. "Mikael admitted he let you win. What is there to congratulate?"

He smiled before grabbing a plate and filling it.

"It is a pleasure to have you dining with us, Your Highness. Should we wait for your parents as well?" Lady Monroe wondered. The others were nearly done with their meals while Liana had barely started.

"Not to worry, Lady Monroe, it will only be me joining this morning."

"Very well. We were just talking about wedding plans. Your mother has asked that we join her to begin preparations."

Liana shoved a slice of meat into her mouth. The thought of wedding planning did not sound ideal to her. It sounded quite like torture actually.

"You will be in great company then. My mother is the most superb party planner in the kingdom, and it is said that her wedding to my father was the grandest in history."

Liana refrained from groaning at that. All she wanted was a small private ceremony but that would never happen. Damien sensed her disquiet and shot her an amused grin. Seeing those lips, those teeth that nipped and sucked on her skin to drive her over the edge, set her squirming in her chair. They needed to marry immediately then she could drag him back to her bedroom to continue what they started.

Damien's smirk dropped as he scented the change in her. Before another vampire could do the same, she erected a shield to encompass them both but only their scents, they could hear and talk perfectly well. Damien's hand fisted around his fork as he averted his gaze.

"You should join us, Your Highness," Liana taunted with a smile as she discreetly slid her hand onto his thigh. His jaw clenched as he turned toward her again. Beneath her hand lay solid muscle, not an ounce of extra flesh on this vampire. She slid her hand higher and dug her nails into his thigh. If he was going to allow her to be tortured, then she would do the same to him.

"I will be happy with whatever you choose, Fiancé," he said through gritted teeth. "I must head into the city this morning to personally discuss my choice with the two other females I had been courting."

Liana dug her fingers in harder at the mention of the other women then snapped her hand back. She'd forgotten about them for just a moment in the haze of excitement and uncertainty. Although they were never true competition, she still did not like the idea of Damien courting other women. All her attention had been focused on him and she expected the same, as unrealistic as she knew that was.

Lord Monroe nodded his head in approval. "That is the proper thing to do, Your Highness. Their fathers would accept nothing less.

"Oh, how gallant of you, Your Highness," Lady Monroe applauded. "Do let them down gently. It will be such a loss." Liana shoveled fruit into her mouth at her mother's boastful comment. Sometimes she really couldn't stand the woman.

"Your Highness," Charlotte interjected. "May I inquire about the investigation into the attack by the lake? Has there been any progress?"

Flashes of that fateful day assaulted Liana's vision. Flashes of Charlotte collapsed in Damien's arms with an arrow in her chest. Of Damien taking an arrow in the back then laying his life over Charlotte to save her.

She hadn't let herself think about the attack and her dangerous display of power too often since it happened. Particularly because it terrified her. Not only because of how close to death her sister had been but because now they all knew of her power. They avoided speaking about it mostly, but she knew she couldn't avoid it forever. Her power simmered at the mere mention of it, ready to protect her at all costs.

"We have many prisoners. However, there are not any higher-ranking individuals that have valuable information. We will keep searching though."

Charlotte nodded, shoving food around on her plate. Liana should check on her later. She should see how her sister is dealing with her near-death experience. So wrapped up in her own life, she'd not been paying much attention to her family's lives.

"Wesley, when will you be marrying your lovely bride?" she asked, plastering on a smile.

"Not for a while yet. We will wait until your dust settles, little sister," he added on with a grin.

"Do not hold back on my account. In fact, have it now. Give us something to celebrate."

"Your wedding is going to be the only thing this kingdom talks about for the next month. We shall wait."

Liana slumped back in her chair. "You make me feel guilty, Wesley. I did not mean to overshadow you." She looked at Charlotte then Hannah. "Any of you."

"No need to feel guilty, Liana. We are all happy for you and the king," Charlotte commented.

"Yes. There is no rush. Do not think on it any longer. We will marry when the gods deem it time," Wesley said, settling the matter.

Liana sipped at her water, looking to Damien out of the corner of her eyes and mumbled, "I can think of one good reason to rush." He had the unfortunate luck to also be drinking at that moment and spit it back in surprise.

"Excuse me," he apologized before giving her a glare as he patted himself dry.

She smirked until William blurted. "What reason?" Her face blanched as she prayed to the gods that he kept quiet. She should have been quieter.

"Nothing," she said quickly.

Carlisle snickered glaring at his older sister. "She meant sex," he said loud enough for the whole castle to hear. Lady Monroe gasped while Hannah giggled.

"Carlisle!" Lord Monroe yelled while Liana's face blushed down to her neck.

"I meant no such thing," she denied, lying through her teeth.

"You did. That's why he laughed," he accused, pointing toward Damien.

"I did not!"

"Then why are you blushing?"

Liana fumed. "Insufferable child! I'm going to strangle you," she declared. She shoved William's chair back as she launched at Carlisle. The boy yelped and sprinted away. He ran behind Mikael who stood guard by the door laughing at them as well. "Don't hide behind him," she yelled, reaching around the vampire to grab him. Carlisle dodged and ran back toward the table, racing around to the other side. They stood facing off with each other while their parents tried to wrangle them.

"Behave, children!" Lady Monroe screamed.

"Carlisle, Liana, sit down this instant!" Lord Monroe demanded.

Liana gestured to Carlisle's chair which was closest to her. With a simple thought, her magic transformed the red velvet cushion into ruby spikes. "After you, little brother," she suggested in an overly sweet tone.

"Father! Look what she did to my seat!"

All except their parents laughed. Lord Monroe pinched the bridge of his nose and sighed. "Liana, do not spike your brother to his chair. Return the cushion to normal." Reluctantly, she let the spikes morph into the padded seat. "Carlisle, sit down and stop instigating trouble."

Cautiously, they stepped past each other to reclaim their seats.

"You are to be queen, Liana. Honestly, can you not control yourself?" Lady Monroe scolded. "Chasing your brother around as if you are children." She clucked her tongue in disapproval.

"Can we not have one calm, family meal?" Lord Monroe complained.

Nobody answered.

William's innocent voice broke the silence. "Is sex like mating? Do vampires mate under full moons like werewolves?"

Damien let out a roar of laughter that had everyone following except their parents of course.

"A delight as always, Monroe family," Damien conceded. "As much as I would enjoy continuing this, I must go. I shall see you all for supper." As he stood, he placed a chaste kiss to the back of Liana's hand. They all stood to bow in farewell, but he halted them. "Please, as you were. We are family now. Such formalities are not needed."

"Appreciated, however, some formalities still remain," Lord Monroe countered with a pointed look between the two of them. Damien nodded.

"Agreed. Some formalities remain." Liana fumed at the men discussing her virtue like it was theirs to own, and in front of everyone no less.

As Damien walked out, he flicked Carlisle on the ear.

"Ow!" Carlisle complained while Liana chuckled evilly. Damien gave her a wink before disappearing.

As embarrassed as she was, she couldn't help thinking that maybe she didn't need to know if the king truly loved her. Maybe she didn't need his love. If this is what their marriage would be, full of teasing and laughter… full of desire and companionship, she could be happy.

"We should go to the High Lady before you two start fighting again," Lady Monroe suggested to which Liana groaned. This would be torture.

Chapter Twenty-five

The family stayed one more night at the castle while Liana, her mother and sisters, and the former queen decided on all the details needed for the wedding. Mostly, Liana sat back and let the two mothers battle it out on what would be best. She entertained herself and Hannah with a deck of cards she summoned from home and eventually a duet on the piano. It was two days of torture in her mind because she didn't care what kind of flowers lined the aisle or filled her bouquet.

After the attack at the lake, everyone discovered her power which put her on edge, so was her magic. It felt good to be home and safe in a familiar space.

She couldn't take her mind off Damien either which didn't help her nerves. She couldn't forget his lips on her skin or his fingers inciting a pleasure she'd never known before. He was sin incarnate, a dangerous temptation she couldn't get enough of. Liana could only pray to the gods to give her strength until the wedding.

A gentle breeze wafted in from the open balcony doors, the night air far cooler than the day. Liana sat cross-legged on the floor of her bedroom with a cauldron and cutting board before her. Phillipa sat upon a stool beside her grinding herbs with a mortar and pestle. Even with the fresh air, the room filled with the scent of mint as she made a spelled mouth rinse to keep tooth rot and bad breath at bay. It was a rather popular item among everyone, no matter their gender or race.

She knew a guard lurked on her balcony, likely behind the open doors. Which is why she kept a silencing shield around their conversation.

"Have you heard from Felix yet?" Liana asked, finally remembering the refugees at Felix's home. It had been a busy week since she'd seen them last… a taxing week, in fact.

"I have not heard from Felix. Although, I did ask Sasha before we left the castle. She said the group left about four days ago for the northern village. Her contact said it was safe and they'd be welcomed."

Liana's hopes lifted for them. "I do hope it works in their favor. They deserve a home to feel safe."

"Agreed."

Phillipa handed the mortar of mint paste to Liana, then she added it to the boiling liquid in the cauldron which heated without flame thanks to Liana's magic. She stirred until the paste dissolved then let the solution rest as they prepared the bottles for filling.

In light of her own happiness, Liana eyed her maid with a smile thinking about Felix. "Phillipa, may I ask about Felix?"

The woman avoided her eyes. "What do you mean?"

"Are you together?"

The woman blushed. "That is none of your business."

"Phillipa, please. You know everything about me, everything from my fears and desires to what I wear to bed every night. Can you not let me in on your life for once?"

She eyed her skeptically. "Felix and I are not in a relationship."

"Why not? You two clearly have feelings for each other."

Phillipa passed a bottle to be filled with the funnel. "He is an ageless vampire, Liana, and I am not as young as I once was." Liana paused while pouring with the ladle. Damien was an ageless vampire, and she would age just as Phillipa. But Damien said if she drank his blood, she would not age. Perhaps that was too much for her maid to consider.

"He adores you, Phillipa. Have you ever told him how you feel?"

"Don't be a fool, Liana. The man is a decorated warrior with a successful business. He has no feelings for me."

Liana glared at the woman that was more of a mother to her than Lady Monroe ever was. "Do not put yourself down like that. You deserve everything your heart desires, you only have to be brave enough to go after it."

She huffed out a disbelieving breath. "Not everyone is as brave or as privileged as you, Liana." That gave her pause.

There was no doubt in her mind that she was privileged. That she had everything she could ever need and more. It allowed her to learn as much magic as she had when other females were stuck with the bare minimum. That did not dispel the need for the freedom to make her own choices though.

"Besides, I have no time for a man when I am so busy trying to keep up with you."

"You make me feel like a burden," Liana commented.

"Not a burden, just far younger and quicker on your feet," Phillipa teased with a smile. "Like I said, I'm not as young as I once was."

"Fine. Indulge me for a moment then. If you were not my maid, would you pursue Felix?"

"If I were not your maid, I would never have met Felix. And women do not pursue the men," Phillipa countered.

Liana groaned in annoyance. "Venus, give me strength," she muttered. "Just tell me if you like the man."

Before she could respond, a piece of parchment magically appeared in Liana's hand. Cautiously, she opened the letter. All the blood drained from her face when she read it.

"What is it? What's wrong?" Phillipa worried. Liana sprang to her feet, handing the letter to her maid.

"It is from Felix. Cassia is struggling with the labor. We must go at once." She dropped the shield and grabbed her cloak from the wardrobe to cover her sleeping robe and dress. Her thin slippers would not make running easy, so she pulled on a pair of boots.

"I will meet you in the foyer. I need my cloak," Phillipa said.

Liana ran down the stairs to her father's study where she filled a satchel with various healing potions just in case.

"Where are you going?" a male asked from the doorway. Liana spared him a glance as she also threw in a few scrap cloths. She recognized him as a guard that typically followed Damien around.

"To a friend. They are in trouble." She shoved past the male.

"I cannot let you go somewhere that is not safe."

"It is safe," she argued. Phillipa already waited by the front door, the rest of the house dark and silent at this late hour. Liana rushed out the door, only for the vampire to block her path.

"Get out of my way," she seethed.

The male matched Damien in size and intimidation factor. They even had similar features and dark hair, but she would not cower beneath him. "Tell me where you are going first."

"A friend is in labor and having difficulty. Now, move before I make you," she threatened while raising her hand, magic sparking from her fingertips. He still did not step aside.

"Tell me where, I will get you there faster," he offered. Liana didn't hesitate to tell him if he would help, then she wrapped her arm around his neck as he picked her up. They were across the city in seconds, standing in front of Marc and Cassia's home.

They lived in one of the newer, cleaner neighborhoods where there were only townhomes. Liana raced up the few stairs to the brick building and barged through the door. She ran up the narrow stairs to the second floor and into the bedroom where she found Marc and Felix on either side of Cassia in bed with a female vampire kneeled between her legs.

Her guard stayed in the doorway as Liana rushed to Cassia's side where Felix sat. She grabbed over the man's hands that held his daughter's hand. Drenched in sweat, Cassia panted heavily, her skin a shiny red while her pretty blonde curls matted to her head.

"What's happened?"

The midwife answered for them. "She's been laboring for too long. It's been over a day, and the babe's heart rate is declining. It needs to come out now, but she is too weak."

Liana summoned a cloth from the bag and wiped at Cassia's drenched forehead.

"Please, Liana," Cassia cried. "Save my baby, please. Don't let her die."

"Hush, Cassia. You're doing great. She's going to be fine." She handed the rag to Felix then hurried over to the chaise lounge. Ripping off her cloak, she shoved it down then emptied the contents of the satchel onto it.

"Liana, get your guard out of here," Marc growled as his wife whimpered in pain. Liana grabbed two potion bottles then turned to the male.

"I am safe here. You should not be in here anyway. Go get my maid and bring her here." The vampire hesitated. "You could have already been there and back by now and, I will not tell you again, soldier. Bring my maid and stay out of this room." She slammed the door in his face then rushed back to Cassia. "Take these. One is to relieve some of the pain, the other to bolster your strength."

Cassia downed them gratefully. Standing beside Felix, she looked from Cassia's haggard face to Marc's terror-filled eyes. Phillipa entered the room, shutting the guard out once more but Liana could not tear her eyes away from Marc's fear. Cassia grunted and pushed once more with the midwife coaching her through it.

"Save her. You have to save Cassia too," Marc said between them. Liana didn't know what to do. She knew only a few spells to aid in birthing, the rest she'd never bothered to learn. Regret ate away at her now as she searched for any ideas or spells.

"It's okay. I'm okay. I feel better now, stronger," Cassia said through her quick breaths. "I can do this." Phillipa handed Liana a few cool wet cloths to damp at Cassia's face and neck. They helped her for too many more pushes before she slumped back against the pillows once more.

The vampire pulled Liana with her to the wash basin as they dunked the rags. The women nudged her and mouthed for her to erect a spell. Reluctantly, Liana did so. "She will not make it through this. She is bleeding too much, and the babe's head is not even in the birth canal yet. I fear neither will make it," the midwife whispered even though her words were protected.

"What else can we do? We have to save them." Liana rang out the cloth and dunked it simply to keep her hands moving.

"We may be able to save the babe. I could cut it out of her." Liana gaped at the woman.

"How in the gods do you do that?" She couldn't fathom cutting a child from their mother, nor could she allow that for her friend.

In her veins, her magic was quiet which surprised her most of all because it responded to her emotions. And when her emotions were riled, so was her magic. If only there was something she could do. This wasn't a cracked skull like Henry though, Liana couldn't heal whatever was going on.

"Cassia!" Marc shouted. They spun in time to see Cassia's eyes roll back, her body going lax. Marc shook her shoulders screaming her name. Felix stood, his hands clasped around hers.

The midwife rushed back to see if the babe made any advancement. "Her heart still beats, and she still breathes. Marc, you must make the choice now. Save the baby while your wife still lives or let them both die," the midwife declared. Liana's vision blurred as she stumbled back to the bed.

"No!" Marc shouted. "We save them both!"

"You hear her heart, son," Felix said, his voice quiet and defeated. "She will not make it much longer."

Marc shouted into the night. "I can't. I can't lose her." He sobbed, dropping his head onto her chest. "Please. There must be something we can do."

"There is not. Every second we waste is another second the baby loses for a chance at life. I will get the babe out of her," the midwife declared, already grabbing the box of tools from the floor.

Marc roared, sending the box flying. Liana gasped as something came at her. She barely flinched out of the way in time as it sliced along her scalp instead of her eye.

"Liana!" Phillipa called, rushing to her side.

Before she knew what happened, she leaned over the bed nose to nose with Marc. He held her by the neck with an unrelenting grip, his face transformed into sharpened features, fangs on full display. The vampire guard burst through the door directly toward her. He growled at Marc, a blade appearing at Marc's neck.

"Release the lady," her guard threatened. Liana couldn't breathe, couldn't think. Everything was happening too fast. Her head burned where the cut was while she felt the sticky heat of blood running down her neck and chest.

"You have to do something. You have to save Cassia," Marc demanded.

"I don't know any spells…" she cut off when his hand tightened around her throat. Phillipa screamed, grabbing at Marc's arm. The guard pushed the dagger hard enough to draw blood.

"Release the girl or I will slit your throat over your dying wife."

"Marc, stop this!" Felix screamed at him. Marc's grip loosened the barest bit. Enough so that the guard made his move. With vampiric speed, he wrenched the hand safely away from Liana's neck and tackled him to the ground. It was a quick fight which ended with her guard restraining Marc.

"Please! Please, just save her!" he cried, his head falling to his chest.

Liana slumped on the bed, her own hand at her neck as she tried to remember how to breathe. Phillipa rubbed circles into her back whispering nonsense into her ear. She heard none of it. All she could think was how unfair it was that she could help so many with her extraordinary magic, but she could not help a dear friend when they most needed it. There had to be something. She didn't need spells all the time. She didn't need one to heal Henry. She didn't need one now.

"Goddesses guide me. Goddesses protect Cassia. I pray to you all to help me save her," Liana whispered then shut her eyes and laid her hands upon Cassia's belly. Her magic lit within her veins as she called to it. "Goddess Hekate, please, show me how to help. Guide me with this magic you've blessed upon me. Help me save them both." Liana urged her magic into the woman not performing anything yet.

As soon as it touched the vampire's blood, Liana knew everything about Cassia's condition. She understood what was wrong, understood what needed to happen, but still didn't know how. "Please, help me," she prayed through gritted teeth. Her magic needed no guidance when it healed Henry, so she wondered why it did nothing now. She begged her magic to do something, begged for it to save her friend.

Nothing happened.

Tears poured out of her eyes mingling with the blood to create a red river down her neck. This couldn't be. She wouldn't let it. Her magic was special. It was different. She could do this. Liana surged her magic, fanning the flames until it felt like she was an inferno of power.

Still, with all that power, nothing happened.

"Please!" she screamed into the room and into the universe. She needed help. She needed guidance, but there was no one there to aid her. There never had been. No one to help her with this overwhelming power.

Liana wasn't aware anything had changed until she noticed the deafening sound of silence engulfing her. Slowly, her eyelids opened, a bright light forcing them to squint. It was a golden shimmering light full of life and movement. Even as she watched, it seemed to breathe and pulse. She searched the foreign light only to realize that it came from her. It lit her body from within, her skin a brilliant gold like the night of the attack on her balcony and in bed with Damien.

It was her magic, come to life.

It surrounded Cassia and herself. The others stunned into immobility as they watched. A separate force, a welcoming and warm force urged her to direct the magic. It directed her on what to do first. Then, step by step, the gentle guiding hand helped Liana save two souls.

Her magic stopped the bleeding. It allowed the baby into the birth canal and forced Cassia's womb to contract. The midwife stirred out of her stupor to catch the baby.

Liana imagined the piercing cries of a healthy baby filled the room beyond her silent sphere of magic. She watched as the baby writhed and wailed while the midwife cleaned it. Her heart nearly burst with joy when she was presented to her father who was still restrained by Liana's guard. Reluctantly, he let the father go to hold his new daughter. Liana smiled at the new baby then turned her focus back to Cassia. The woman was exhausted and depleted of blood. Liana healed the woman from the birthing process and cleaned her of the sweat and blood. She even replaced the sheet and her gown.

That invisible guiding hand radiated with pride before it drifted away. Liana let her magic fizzle out, sound rushing back in. Feeling surged into her body which brought with it pain and terror. Terror for what it meant for her to have performed such magic in front of all these people.

She stumbled backward, dizzy and panicked.

"That was amazing," Phillipa said, trying to support Liana.

The guard approached while Marc climbed onto the bed with Cassia who was waking up. "You'll need a healer for that wound. It's still bleeding."

Liana ignored the man. "She will need blood to refill what has been lost," she said in a hurry before sprinting out of there. She didn't know where she would go, didn't know what would happen. All she knew was that she needed to get away from this city as fast as possible.

Chapter Twenty-six

P anic blinded her as she ran. Magic surged around her, lashing out at whoever gave chase. It urged her forward, told her to keep running. It would protect her. No one else would ever harm them again.

Liana cried from the sheer terror in her veins, at the confusion that swamped her memories. Something happened a long time ago. Something happened to make her feel this way, she just couldn't remember what.

Her boots thudded against stone until it turned to dirt, then she was running over sticks and branches. Magic lit the way through the depthless forest as she fled. There was no destination in mind, only that she got to safety. She ran until her legs gave out. Ran until her heart nearly exploded with exhaustion. Even then, her magic bolstered her energy to keep her walking.

Thankful for the boots instead of slippers that adorned her feet, Liana climbed the mountain, her throat dry and calves burning. Her head had cleared somewhat of the terror and panic, but now clouded with exhaustion. She couldn't fathom how she made it to this point at all. One moment she saved Cassia and the baby, the next she was fleeing for her life. She'd felt this way before, practically all her life, but this was the first time she acted so desperately.

Perhaps it was because of the sheer amount of power she exhibited in front of the others. But she'd done this just a week ago by the lake. That had been even more extraordinary and in front of far more people. Then again, she didn't have a chance to escape because she'd been unconscious for three days afterward. She'd been scared though, even when she woke, she feared what would be done to her.

She didn't know where this inherent fear stemmed from. It had always been a part of her. Had always been a guiding beacon of caution to keep her power hidden as much as possible. If it weren't for Damien, she would have succeeded. The moment he came into her life, more and more people discovered the true extent of her magic. She'd been helping everyone since she was a little girl, but they just thought her an ambitious child, not powerful. Even when she did boast of her power to the king, she didn't reveal all and this terror didn't consume her.

It made no sense. None of it did. Not her extraordinary power, the things she could do with it, or the fear.

Without much energy to keep going, her magic finally fizzled out. As the first rays of the sun began to light the sky, Liana sank against the base of a tree and tried to lay down. As she rested her head on her arm, she hissed in pain, forgetting about the cut she suffered from Marc's rage. She rolled onto her back and stared up at the canopy of trees.

Out of everything that happened this evening, she was at least happy that Cassia and the baby survived. Liana remembered the look on Marc's face when he held his daughter for the first time, the utter joy and love he held for her. They would be whole; they'd be a family thanks to her. She saved them yet this fear of how others would react to her magic would keep her away from her own.

She couldn't return to Sancta Valles. She couldn't return to a place full of people that would use her for their own gain, or worse. Panic threatened to pull her under again, but her magic was too depleted to react. She needed to get somewhere safe before she passed out because the last time she felt this depleted, she was out for three days and could hardly walk for the remaining week.

Tears spilled over her lids as she faced the reality that she would be stuck in the forest unconscious for days while she recovered. She couldn't even muster enough magic to send a message to anyone. Not that it would be helpful considering she had no idea where she was. They could always do a locator spell to find her, but there was no telling who would find her. She could only hope it would be her family.

Unable to resist the exhaustion any longer, Liana let her eyes fall closed.

Crinkling of leaves had her eyes flying back open a second before she felt the metal against her throat. Her body froze as a man stood above her. Panting and dripping sweat, he held the dagger to her throat looking as if he had been following her since the city.

"You're going to stand up slowly and do exactly as I say," the man demanded. He whispered a spell rapidly which had her wrists flying together and locking with magical cuffs. If she had any magic left, she would have mourned its loss due to the spell.

Liana had no energy left for this man as she clumsily climbed to her feet. He backed off a little to let her rise then returned the blade to her throat. Now upright, Liana's gaze sharpened on the familiar man's face.

Surprise struck her as she recognized him as the one from her balcony that stabbed her.

"I told you, you'd pay for what you did to me," he seethed.

Legs shaking from exhaustion and likely fear, Liana kept her voice as strong as possible when she asked, "What do you want?"

"I want you to pay, and I want my life back. Because of you, I lost everything."

"I did nothing…"

He cut her off, stepping closer so that his rancid breath fanned over her face. "You cost me my life. We were there for the councilman, but you got in the way. Then I thought I found something special, someone powerful when you erupted on that balcony and perhaps, I'd be redeemed."

Liana swayed as he continued his monolog, leaning back into the tree behind her.

"I told them of your power. I told them what you were capable of, but it didn't matter. They only punished me for failing the job and letting the other two be captured alive."

"And what do you plan on doing with me now? Are you going to bring me to them?" She wasn't sure who 'they' were, but she had a good guess it was the rebels.

He smiled, all his vile teeth showing. "They'd pay me handsomely for you. Do you want to know the bounty the rebels put on your head?"

Liana gulped. This is exactly what she feared for so long. The moment someone discovered her, they would start coming for her. Now she had a bounty to her name. "The rebels have been defeated. I destroyed their forces," she retorted, her voice wavering.

The man merely chuckled, the blade tickling her throat. "You have no idea how wrong you are."

"Liana!" a voice screamed, and the man jerked, his smile replaced with fear.

Her heart lifted because she'd recognize that voice forever. Damien had come for her.

"Liana!" he screamed again; this time closer.

The man pulled Liana around as a human shield, keeping the tree at his back while he erected his own magical shield as well. Just as Damien ran into view, the dagger appeared at her neck once more.

Damien halted immediately, two other vampires coming to a stop just behind him. She recognized her guard from earlier. Damien growled, his features sharper and darkened with rage as glacial eyes fixed on the dagger touching her skin.

"Back off, vampire, or I'll slit her throat!" the man yelled, jostling her weakened body. Knees shaking, she stared back at Damien, her eyes watery and defeated. The mercenary wrapped an arm around her waist, hoisting her up as she nearly collapsed.

"You let me walk away or she dies," he threatened, yanking her around the edge of the tree. Boots dragging, she did nothing to help him make his escape. If only she wasn't burned out, she could blast him and get away. If only she didn't have this pit of fear lurking deep inside her that brought her here in the first place.

Damien growled once more, the sound purely animalistic. It was the sound of death coming to claim its target. "You will let her go unharmed," he declared.

The mercenary dragged her a few more steps. "We are going to walk away, and you are not going to follow. I'll leave her safely at the harbor once I'm sailing away."

Damien took cautious steps with them. "I'm not letting her out of my sight, and you will not see one more sunrise."

Liana whimpered as the knife cut into her skin, cuffed hands clawing at the man's solid, unmoving arm. Damien froze, his eyes darkening as he focused on the fresh blood amidst the crusted blood from earlier. "I live, or she dies."

A slow, rumbling growl came from her fiancé, his lips peeled back like a feral dog to show off lethal fangs.

The shield around them suddenly dropped and in a brief second of shouts and blackness, Liana found herself face down in the dirt panting heavily. Screams of terror and pain filled her ears. She lifted her head to find Master Kinley and High Lord Ashwood forcing the mercenary to kneel as Damien gripped his head and tore it right from his shoulders.

Red filled her shocked gaze.

Master Kinley erected a shield to protect himself and the High Lord from the mess as blood spurted into the air and poured like a sheet of rain out of the man's neck. Damien tossed it aside with little care, the thick, fleshy sound of it hitting the earth was the last straw that turned her stomach.

The acrid scent of vomit burned her nose as she coughed and sputtered for air. The violence. The blood. The flesh and sinew dangling from his neck flashed through her mind over and over, and she collapsed into a heap. Someone grabbed her and lifted her into their arms before she could roll into the vomit. She was surprised to find her guard once more held her while Damien stood a few paces away, his back toward them.

The High Lord had a firm grip on his shoulder as he spoke quietly but sternly to his son. The tense lines of his shoulders and fisted hands were enough that she didn't question them. Master Kinley approached, blocking her view.

"Let me heal your wounds, Your Grace," Master Kinley said. Liana didn't have the energy to balk at the new title. She certainly wasn't queen yet but when his healing light touched her face, she forgot about the title. He finished her neck just as Damien appeared.

"Are you alright, Liana?"

She could only stare up at him. Gone was the fierce mask of death but all she could see was that man's head ripping away from the rest of his body.

"Liana?" he questioned; brows furrowed as his hand reached to caress her face. She flinched from the blood still fresh on his hands which had him tensing and pulling away. It wasn't that she was scared he would hurt her, but she wouldn't be forgetting that image any time soon, of how he did that with his bare hands. Through gritted teeth, he told the others, "Let's get back to the castle."

***

Liana had been soaking in the tub for a while, sequestered in one of the guest rooms in the castle, when Sasha entered. The guard didn't bother to acknowledge Liana's state of undress, nor did Liana as she simply looked away from Sasha.

"How are you, my Lady?"

Liana stared at the ornate stone table beside the tub which held her soaps and cloths for bathing. "Why are you here, Sasha?" she asked instead of answering.

"I heard what happened. I wanted to check on you."

She sighed. "You can tell the king, I am fine." He knocked on her door earlier to check on her, but she didn't answer. She wasn't ready to face him yet. To face anyone yet. She rolled onto her side, giving the guard her back as a clear indication of what she thought of their hovering.

"Very well. Do you need anything else?"

The servants already left spare clothes and a tray of food. Liana shook her head, and the only sound of the silent guard leaving was the closing of the door.

She didn't want to see anyone right now because she didn't want to have to face their questions. His questions in particular. She knew he would ask why she ran, why she lost control of herself in a fit of terror and left the safety of her guard.

Sinking beneath the water, she tried to drown out her thoughts. Tried to make the lingering fear drift away. It was no use though. She had been scared all her life, always with this pit deep inside her that was a hairpin trigger away from setting her magic off. Brief flashes of pain were all she recalled from whatever happened to her so long ago.

Lungs burning for air, Liana stayed under for just a few moments more. Before she could rise on her own, someone grabbed beneath her arms and dragged her to the surface.

"Liana?" Phillipa questioned in a panic while the girl swiped water out of her eyes. "Oh child, you frightened me!" she scolded, grabbing a drying cloth. "Now, get out. You are more wrinkled than I am." She held the cloth aloft and Liana reluctantly stood and stepped out of the tub, into Phillipa's waiting arms. Her maid wrapped the long cloth around her body and pulled Liana into a tight embrace. "I was so worried," she whispered.

Liana lay her head on the shorter woman's shoulder and soaked up her warmth. "Me too," she croaked, the tears starting again.

Phillipa fussed over her, getting her ready for bed and drying her hair with magic that Liana had very little of left after tonight. As it neared dawn, she finally climbed into bed, Phillipa tucking her in.

"The king is pacing a hole in the floor outside your door. Can I send him in?"

Liana's eyes fell closed with a grimace. "Not now, Phillipa. I am too tired." She wanted nothing more than to feel his comforting warmth wrapped around her, but she didn't want to face him after everything. Didn't want him to know how much she was still just a scared little girl parading around as a confident, powerful woman.

Phillipa's mouth pursed as she nodded. When the woman left, she heard Damien ask, "How is she?" before the door was fully closed. She rolled over and willed sleep to claim her.

Chapter Twenty-seven

Sleep would have claimed her easily if Damien didn't barge into her room despite Phillipa's warning.

She sighed, opening her eyes once more and sat up against the pillows. Damien bent one leg and sat beside her.

Brows furrowed with worry, he asked, "How are you feeling?"

"I am fine, Damien. You don't need to be concerned."

His frown told her all she needed to know about how much he appreciated her suggestion. "You were covered in blood and had a dagger held to your throat when I finally found you. I don't consider that to be *fine.*"

Sinking into the pillows, she pulled the blanket up to her chin. "The cut on my head was an accident. If my magic would have cooperated sooner, it wouldn't have happened." If only she had control of her magic, or if she had known the proper birthing spells like the real mage healers then all the drama could have been avoided. Instead, she resorted to begging the goddesses for help and forcing her magic to do something.

He pulled on her chin to look at him then loosened his grip. "Don't you dare blame yourself, Liana."

"But if I'd only known the proper spells…"

Damien interrupted to ask, "How did you save them if you didn't know the spells?"

Liana looked away again and tried to roll onto her side. Damien moved quickly, trapping her with arms on either side of her, hovering over with his face so close to her own.

"You didn't require any spells, did you?" he asked, and Liana's heart rate sped up as fear threatened to take her again. "You often cast magic without saying a spell. I thought you might be saying the spells in your head, but Master Kinley said that was impossible, all mages have to say spells." He paused, eyes full of wonder. "But you don't have to, do you?"

She thought she'd been so secretive, so discreet. Clearly, she'd been nothing of the sort. Blind terror gripped her once more. She shoved at Damien in an attempt to dislodge him, but the bastard was made of stone and didn't even budge.

"Get off! Let me go! I'm nothing."

"Hush, Liana. I'm not going to hurt you. And your magic is nothing to be terrified of. Your magic is special, it's one of a kind."

Liana thrashed beneath him. "No! I'm not special. I'm nothing. Let me go!" Her magic tried to rise. There was only a spark left, but nothing of use.

"Liana! Stop. I'm not going to hurt you." He let go and she rolled right out of bed, sprinting toward the door. He followed, his speed far too fast for her and stood in her path. "Liana, calm yourself. I will never hurt you."

A memory surged forth and it was as if she weren't in control of her body any longer. Her mouth moved but she had no control of the words that left her. "Please, I'm nothing. I am not the savior. I am not a child of the gods." She fell to her knees, sobbing into her hands.

Damien kneeled before her in an instant. "Where did you hear that?" Liana scrambled away from him. "Liana, where did you hear those words?" His voice finally penetrated through the terror. She halted her tears.

"I… I don't know." Her mind ached when she tried to recall the origin of what she said.

Tenderly, he took her hands into his own. "Liana, the day we had tea in the garden, during the rainstorm, you didn't faint. I made mention of your magic and you reacted similarly."

Her brows furrowed. "I don't recall that."

He nodded, his lips pursed. "I believe your maid took away your memory of the event."

Liana gaped at Damien. "Phillipa would never do such a thing. She is more of a mother to me than Lady Monroe."

"It is difficult to hear, but I witnessed it. One moment you were panicking, the next, you couldn't remember what happened." Liana didn't believe him. Phillipa would never do something like that. To steal someone's memories was punishable by death. "You said something at the tea. You said, 'don't hurt me,' and asked what I would do with you." Glacial eyes warred with indecision and pain as he struggled to say his next words. "I think you suffered a great trauma in your past. I think your maid knows and took the memory of it from you."

She pulled out of Damien's grip. "How dare you accuse Phillipa of such a heinous act. She loves me. She would do anything to protect me."

"Exactly," he interjected. "She would do anything to protect you, even protect you from yourself." That gave her pause. "How long have you felt terrified about people knowing of your magic?"

Liana didn't want to answer. She didn't want any of this to be true. Not about Phillipa, and not about whatever happened to her. She shook her head while standing to get away from him.

"I'm trying to help, Liana. Just answer me." She shook her head, her legs hitting the bed and she sank down.

"Nothing happened."

"Nothing you can remember," he implored.

Phillipa. Her sweet and loving maid would never take away her memories. That was advanced magic anyway. She wouldn't have been capable of that. Her eyes narrowed on Damien.

"Why are you pushing this? I am telling you that Phillipa didn't do anything, she can't even perform that level of magic."

"Perhaps it wasn't Phillipa. Perhaps someone else took your memories of the event, but your maid knows something. She knew exactly how to calm you, exactly how to take your memory at the tea." Liana shook her head disbelievingly. "There is no denying that something happened to you, Liana. You are terrified the moment someone mentions your magic. You flee in fear if someone witnesses your true power, yet you can talk about it freely without fear. It doesn't make sense."

"Why is this so important to you? I am fine." The lie tasted like ash on her tongue.

"You clearly are not fine," he countered. "You were lost to us all night until your magic finally depleted enough for Master Kinley to track you with a spell. What happens the next time someone witnesses your magic? Will you run again? Look what happened tonight. You had no magic to defend yourself from that mercenary."

She flinched away from his anger and stood sneering over her shoulder, "I can take care of myself, Your Highness."

He scoffed. "You think you can. When it comes down to it though, you put yourself in danger without even realizing it. All those times you snuck off to the slums alone, the way you brazenly walk into a blood bar."

If she had any magic left, she would have set him on fire with the glare she directed toward him.

"I didn't realize I was such a burden of worry to you, Your Highness. If you have such issues with me, I will gladly take my leave of you and this farce of an engagement." She stormed toward the door fully intending to make a dramatic exit. Damien foiled her plan as he grabbed her around the waist and flung her onto the bed. Hands shackled her wrists to the bed while his body weighed hers down.

"Why must you always twist my words?" he exclaimed.

"I do nothing of the sort. You are too insensitive to realize the impact of your words."

She pulled against his hands, but they were like iron. "Why can't you see that I am only trying to help?"

"A manipulative bastard like yourself would never help me out of the kindness of your heart. What's your angle on this? Are you trying to tear me apart from my maid so that when we are married it'll be easier to keep me under your control?"

He growled, his fangs plunging out. "You insult me greatly. I have told you time and again that I only seek you as my wife. I have no nefarious plans."

"Liar," she snarled. "All powerful men, especially kings, use those that are weaker for gain. I am no different. You said from the start that you wanted me for my magic."

His head tilted to the side. "How can you talk about your magic now without fear?"

"Because I am enraged, and I won't let you get the better of me."

His hands softened around her wrists as his fangs retracted.

"What happened to you to make you so distrustful and scared?" His voice came out soft and defeated. Damien let her go and took a few steps away from the bed. "I am not planning anything in which you are a pawn. I was merely trying to help you because I care for you." A hand grabbed at the back of his neck to knead at the muscles there. "I want you for my wife for no other reason than I want you. I merely told you I wanted your power because of how angry and distrustful you became of me after that first night. I knew you wouldn't believe me if I told you the truth, but I hoped in time that you would come to trust me, perhaps even love me."

Liana crossed her arms, glaring at the male. "Love? You expect me so pathetic as to fall for talk of love? You truly are a manipulative bastard."

Before she could blink, Damien stood nose to nose with her, growling. "You are so entrenched in your own denial and biases you cannot even see the truth when I lay it at your feet."

Tears pricked at her eyes, but she refused to let them fall.

"We both know something happened to you. We both know Phillipa knows something, but you refuse to acknowledge it. And not all men are greedy assholes. You'd rather deny it all than face the truth. You call me a manipulative bastard, and perhaps that is true with others, but I'd never do that with you. If you'd stop being such a coward, you'd realize I'm the only one that's helping you discover the truth."

She couldn't help it when a single tear spilled over. Then more. Damien watched her tears fall before storming out.

Liana fell onto the bed, emotionally and physically exhausted. She couldn't think anymore. Couldn't decide what was truth, and what was a lie. She knew part of what Damien said was the truth, knew something terrible happened in her past that she couldn't remember. But for Phillipa to have known, to hide it from her. She felt betrayed simply thinking about it.

She lay there a long while, her tears finally lulling her into sleep.

Chapter Twenty-eight

Terror followed her into sleep.

Darkness swallowed her dreams. A black so dark that she couldn't see anything filled her vision as she forced her eyes wide open. She only heard a voice. A garbled voice screaming at her followed by pain. There was a flash of iron bars slamming shut in her face right before she jolted awake.

Feeling that inherent need to flee once more, Liana scrambled out of bed and sprinted for the door. So blinded by fear, she ran out the door, tripping over the body that lay in front of her door. Barely able to keep herself from face planting, her hands caught her fall onto the plush carpet, her body landing with a dull thud.

"Liana?" Damien asked groggily. She looked at him, taking in the dark circles beneath his eyes, the lines of worry etched above his brow and his wrinkled clothes from sleeping on the ground. Even after their fight, after her cruel words and obvious denial, he stayed. He slept on the floor outside her door because he cared, because he wasn't like the males she hated. Damien far outshined those males. She didn't deserve him. She didn't deserve his kindness or his devotion. She didn't deserve his love.

She was just a broken female with uncontrollable magic, and a fool to think she could ever enter into this high-stakes world of power and espionage. Burying her face in her hands, she hid from his gentle, worried gaze. She opened the gates to her emotions and sobbed.

Wordlessly, Damien picked her off the ground and returned to her room, kicking the door closed behind them. Reclining on the bed, he kept her wrapped in his arms and just held her. Liana clung to him, clung to his warmth and safety, the feeling of her fear melting away in his arms. They simply lay there, his hand rubbing gently up and down her back until her sobbing stopped and her tears dried out. Still not ready to talk about her denial, she settled on gathering more information about the terrible evening.

"How did you find me?" she asked, her voice hoarse and nasally from all the crying.

"A tracking spell. It wouldn't work for a while which we assumed was because of your magic. It's why I also couldn't track you by scent."

Staring at the exposed skin of his chest she absently drew circles into it to avoid those piercing eyes. "That man," she started, then had to stop, her mouth suddenly dry. "He was the one that stabbed me on the balcony."

His arms tightened around her as his entire body stiffened. "What did he want?"

"He wanted revenge. He was supposed to kill my father on behalf of the rebels, but I got in the way. And when he told them…" Her words died in her throat as what little magic had returned threatened to lash out once more at the mere thought of someone coming after her.

"Hey, it's okay. You're safe. No one is ever going to harm you again," Damien promised, his voice gentle yet unyielding.

"He told the rebels of my power. At first they didn't care, but now… Now there is a bounty on my head because of my magic."

"The rebels were taken care of. You made sure of that," he reassured.

Liana shook her head. "The mercenary didn't seem to think so."

"The rebels will never be truly defeated, but their numbers were decimated that day by the lake. They will need time to regroup and rebuild, years even. And I will continue to hunt them each and every day so they may never build a force against us." He kissed her forehead, lingering for a few seconds. "I promise you, Liana. I will protect you from any threat until my dying breath."

A sniffle escaped her while she worked to keep from crying once again. "You are too good to me, Damien. I don't deserve you."

He rolled so that she stared up at him, his solid weight a welcomed presence above her. Finally, she looked into those stunning blue eyes. "Don't you ever think that. You deserve anything your heart desires." Gentle fingers brushed her hair off her face.

She tried to turn her face away, but he wouldn't let her. "I'm not strong enough for this, Damien. I am scared all the time and I don't even know why." Tears pooled in her eyes as she once again felt that pit of terror deep inside. "Last night, I don't know what happened. I just… I couldn't stop. I had to run. I had to hide."

His eyes closed as he pressed his forehead to hers. "Liana," he whispered, his voice full of anguish. "What terrifies you so much?"

"I don't know. I know something happened but I can't remember. I get these flashes of pain and a cell," she admitted, her body beginning to shake. He tightened his arms around her. "I'm so lost, Damien."

"I know, my love. I know."

"What do I do? How do I move past this?"

"We will figure it out together."

Liana truly didn't deserve this man. She always thought no man deserved her, but she was so wrong. Damien deserved someone far stronger and courageous. Someone who didn't let their magic control them. But she was selfish. She wanted everything he gave so freely. She wanted his love, his comfort and safety. She wanted the freedom he offered.

"I don't deserve you," she whispered. "I'm not strong like a vampire."

A growl vibrated against her chest. "I told you not to say that. You are strong, Liana, stronger than any vampire I know. And I'll never let anyone hurt you. I don't care what you are capable of with your magic, if anyone tries to take you or harm you, my face will be the last thing they ever see. Not even the gods will save them." He kissed her brow then each cheek slowly before settling on her lips. "You are strong enough, my love. You've always been strong, no matter what happened in the past. We will figure out what happened, and when we do, we'll deal with it, together. Even if I weren't here, I have every faith that you'd do it all on your own and be even more marvelous because of it."

Her lower lip wobbled even as she nodded. Liana tucked her face into his chest and heaved a deep sigh. She let it all go. Let the fear and terror melt away. Let the pain and loneliness fade. Let the burden of her magic lift.

Never before did she think a man would be her salvation. She always thought they'd be her damnation. They would marry her off and control her life, even stifle her magic. Yet here Damien kneeled for her. He made her feel valued, made her feel wanted. Most of all, he made her feel safe.

She looked up at him. He stared back with so much love and warmth that her own hardened heart cracked. Liana pulled him into a heated kiss, consequences be damned because she finally realized that she could have everything she wanted even with a male at her side.

Pulling back, she stared into those glacial eyes, the eyes that, in one short month, she'd wake to every morning for the rest of her life. "I love you, Damien."

Pupils dilating, eating up the beautiful blue, he smiled. "I love you, Liana. I've loved you since you threw a cream tart at my face."

A surprised laugh escaped her even as she blushed. "That was the first night we met," she declared incredulously.

A wicked smile tilted his lips. "Exactly," he crooned.

Even as her heart thumped joyously, she returned his wicked grin. "My handsome and powerful king, how sweet you are. I must confess I did not love you until this moment."

He frowned before he caught on. Laughing, he shook his head. "One of these days you're going to have to stop doing that." He nipped at her lips.

"I'm not sure what you mean," she replied innocently.

"You may think your little game of stroking my ego and tearing it back down is cute, but my poor heart can't take it. It beats only for you, my love and I will surely die if you don't love me as much as I love you."

Liana mocked him with a raised brow. "So sappy, my king." She shoved him off so that she could straddle his waist instead. Large, calloused hands gripped her hips through the thin sleeping gown, his eyes roving over the diaphanous material. "Who knew a little female mage would bring the mighty Damien Ashwood, King of all Triaedian, to his knees." Her smirk faded as he sat up quickly, one arm banding around her back, the other digging into her hair as he tugged it lightly. Breathing became difficult, his eyes alight with fierce love.

"For you, Liana. My little mage. My temptress. My love. For you, I would burn this kingdom to the ground to keep you safe."

Her heart stuttered in her chest. Damien had not been teasing. He was deadly serious.

She cupped his stubbled face in her hands. "And I would help you build it back up, better than it was before, my king." Her thumb brushed over his bottom lip.

It had been difficult getting to this point, difficult to realize that she could be happy and be married. That may not have been true though if it weren't Damien becoming her husband. It was because of him that she could now see a joyful future where she became a wife and still studied her magic freely. Because of him that she wouldn't be hidden away by some lord used only to produce heirs and host dinner parties. With Damien, she would get the life she truly wanted and would marry for love, not money or power.

"For you, Damien, my love, I would show the world my power if it meant staying by your side."

His eyes fell closed in silent relief and a tinge of regret. "I'm sorry I've put you in such danger." She cut him off with a kiss.

"You've done nothing except set me free and I will always love you, Damien." His mouth was hot against hers and she pressed herself into his body, laying atop him as his lips claimed hers.

He pulled away on a growl when her hips ground against his. "The first thing we do as King and Queen is get rid of this damned virgin until marriage shit for the mage."

Liana couldn't help it as she laughed. Despite the seriousness of their conversation, despite the heat pooling between her legs, she had to laugh.

She slid to his side, keeping one leg over his hips.

"Be strong, my vicious vampire. We only have one month left then you can ravage me all you want."

He sighed, holding her close. "One month until you're my wife, until you're mine."

Liana mimicked his sigh and closed her eyes as she rested her head on his chest and declared, "You're already mine."

Afterword

Liana and Damien's story comes to a close in, *Improper Queen*.

Thank you all for reading my debut novel. Although I've written plenty of stories, this one is very dear to my heart. This is the first story I've completed in its entirety and edited for distribution. Also, it is the first story I've ever considered letting others read so, it will always be special to me. Liana and Damien's story has been a long time coming and I am so happy to finally share it with the world.

If you like their story as well, consider leaving a review!

Acknowledgments

Thank you to my family and friends for always supporting me, no matter if my obsession with reading and writing has left me a hermit on more than a few occasions.

A special thank you to my mom and sisters for being exactly who I need them to be. For always being the kind of women that inspire me with their vast and variable talents. For being strong and independent and showing me that love comes in many forms.

To Katie, thank you for being the most supportive and loyal best friend as I took her on this journey with me to construct my first novel. You'll always be my sounding board.

To Tina, thank you for also being a steadfast best friend and being there with me through it all, and always ready to go on our next adventure no matter how far away it takes us.

To Lance... no words needed really. We're friends for life. I guess I could say I appreciate you trying to force socialization on me even if I gripe about it. I've written too many club scenes based on the shit we've seen together. I still prefer a simple night of too much Thai food though.

Thanks guys, and now back to my cave to finish another story.